WANTED

I0712214

Other Books by Amy Kulp

Stand-Alone Novels:
- Innocent*

Poster Series
1. Missing
2. **Wanted**

*Read the first chapter in the back

WANTED

Amy Kulp

This book is a work of fiction. Any references to historical events, real people, or real places are used fictionally. Other names, characters, places, and events are products of the author's imagination, and any resemblance to actual events or places or person, living or dead, is entirely coincidental.

Copyright © 2024 by Amy Kulp

All right reserved. No part of this book may be reproduced or used in any manner without the written permission of the copyright owner except for the use of quotations in a book review.

First paperback edition January 2024.

Paperback ISBN 979-8-9859309-2-4
Ebook ISBN 979-8-2150194-1-2

Published by Amy Kulp
Edited by Jason Letts
Cover design by MadliArt
Marketing by Rodney Hatfield

For business inquiries, contact
amy.kulp1@gmail.com
For more information, visit the author's webpage at
http://amykulp.weebly.com

*To all of the people (my mom) telling me
to write a sequel, thank you* 😊

-Chapter 1

The van ride back is always quiet. It has been that way ever since I could remember. However, as soon as our driver parked the van and we unloaded what was in it, we waved goodbye. The proper measures needed to be taken to remove all evidence of blood, hair, and other forensics. After all traces of DNA were out of the van, it was to be shampooed and sanitized again to ensure that it looked brand new. The keys were placed on the ring with the same license plate and as we all made it to the back of the garage, we had to wait patiently for the elevator to come up to the ground floor. While the wait only took about two minutes, it felt like years to me. I made sure there was enough room for everyone, and we all waved again to our driver as he started the preparations to clean out the van. I was just glad it wasn't me who had to do that anymore.

The elevator had four floors in total. The first one was on the ground level and was hidden away from the public eye. Obviously, people would be curious about an elevator that goes underground. The first level underground was to be welcomed back. We were debriefed to ensure that we didn't make any mistakes, scanned to make sure that we didn't have any bugs on us, and medically reviewed to make sure we didn't have too many injuries. Otherwise, we would just be useless. The second floor underground was our home. I, personally, liked to call this my base. The third was where we met with our teams. Only higher-ups got to go to the fourth floor though.

As my team and I split up to go into different lines, I made sure to take everything out of my pockets and place them in the gray bin. I always held up the line when I had to get my gun from my thigh and had to get my pepper spray from my back pocket. The pants I was wearing were too tight today.

"Y'know, with how much you fight, I'm surprised you struggle to get those out of your butt pocket," one of my team members shouted. I looked over at him and saw that he was already getting wanded to see if he had anything medal on him. He smirked at me, and I just rolled my eyes.

This smart-ass was Carlos. He was a little piece of shit who liked to question authority, crack jokes, and demand respect. With how draining this place is on the mental psyche, I never would have thought someone could light up the joint as much as he did. He was good-looking too — his pitch-black hair was cut into a military style, and his muscles were beautifully sculpted underneath his t-shirt, which always hugged him. While I often didn't work with the same people, I worked with Carlos the most. Over the past ten years that we have known each other, we have worked together about nine times. He has watched me grow from a newbie to a leader in no time. However, I knew my husband didn't like him too much. He probably felt threatened.

"I think you should watch where your eyes wander," Santiago warned. I looked behind me and gave a smile of thanks as I watched him start to put his belongings in the gray bin. He looked over at me and smiled.

Santiago was the brains of the group, but he also had a lot of muscle. Although he never talks about his past, I'm pretty sure that Santiago is an ex-soldier. I wasn't there to invade people's backgrounds, so I never brought it up. Should I even ask? We have worked together only twice, but the way he watches out for everyone showed that he cared about the team he was with. That was a rare quality to see in this place. He may care about his team, but he didn't seem to trust anyone. There was always that edge of mystery about him.

"I think you should ice your face," I replied as I spread my legs out for my pat-down. I watched as Carlos's face reacted to my comment. He was already sitting on the bed for his physical examination, and I couldn't help but laugh as the doctor or nurse gave him an ice pack. "I remember that she kicked you pretty hard."

As soon as I was done being patted down, I joined Carlos at the physical examination beds. I sat across from him, and we were instructed to do the same stretches and exercises. Santiago joined us about halfway through, and when we were released we all walked toward our last examination.

This one took the most mental strength: the debriefing. All three of us were separated as we went into stark white rooms. I always dreaded these because someone always got tortured and beaten for how they reacted during the mission. They took all of what was said and determined who was the weak link of the team and then decided they needed to be retrained. By now, I learned not to be emotional during a mission, but I knew for the newer recruits it was hard to listen to someone screaming for their life.

I was desensitized to it though.

After about ten years of doing this job, you get used to the demands and orders. Some things that our new recruits find insulting and surprising, I think of as just another day on the job. Do I get paid to do this? Partially, but I am provided with food, entertainment, and a safe place to live. Our pay depends on how much each girl goes up for auction. Obviously, it depends on their looks and worth. So, a girl in high school with a future ahead of her is worth a lot more than a homeless person. However, you must work yourself up to those good assignments—they're never just given to a newbie.

I liked to think I was one of the best here. Not only have I been here for a long time, but I had adjusted rather quickly to the major changes of this place. Our organization started off with everyone being split into their own groups. This stayed that way for two years. However, things started changing, and the groups were constantly moving when members were being killed and some were moving up the ranks—the only two ways out of here. Originally, I had hoped that my husband would be in the same group as me. It became clear that wasn't the case. He was destined for great things, and he began moving up the ranks faster than anybody else had. He became the leader of the organization and the major reason everything changed.

Instead of always being in the same group, we were now like an underground academy. Every single person in this organization was under the same roof. There were assignments given to different team members. It was made this way so there couldn't be any leaks or undercover agents. If you were constantly switching roles and teams, who could you learn to trust? Nobody.

That's why, as I sat in this debriefing room, I felt myself growing anxious. What if I was the one who everyone thought screwed up today? What if I was too emotional while getting the subject transported to her safe house? That didn't mean I had to be emotional at all, but if I was the weak link of the team I would get tortured and shown how to do everything again. However, out of the four hundred successful kidnappings I have done, I only had to be tortured once.

That was when I was new.

"Welcome back, Y," Dr. Dowell said as he sat down in the chair across the table from me. I nodded to pay my respects but didn't show any emotion. "We're going to get you hooked up to the lie detector test before we begin our usual line of questioning."

I nodded again. I knew the drill by now. Dr. Dowell got the equipment out and quickly attached the wires to various parts of my body. I already felt my nervousness multiply but tried to calm down my breathing. The key was not to get caught lying.

"Are you ready to start?" Dr. Dowell asked. I nodded yes and waited for the first question. It was always the same questions in the same order. "Who was the weakest link of your team excluding you?"

"Howie," I answered.

Howie was our driver. He remained silent and distant from the entire group. He stayed in his seat the entire time and didn't help when our subject was getting a bit too rowdy. Right now, he was responsible for cleaning our van.

"Who was the weakest link including you?"

"Howie."

"Who was the leader of the group excluding you?"

"Santiago."

"Who was the leader of the group including you?"

"Santiago."

I winced when I felt something heavy bang against my knuckles. I watched as Dr. Dowell picked up his metal stapler and placed it back on his desk. Immediately on my skin a blue and purple bruise began to form. I stretched out my fingers to make sure they weren't broken and scrunched them so he would have less to hit.

"You're lying," he stated. "Who was the leader of the group including you?"

"Me," I replied dryly.

"Did your mission go exactly as planned?"

"No."

"What went wrong?"

"Our subject was more interested in Santiago than Carlos," I answered. I watched as Dr. Dowell kept reading my graph as I talked. I had to pause to make sure I wouldn't be slapped with the stapler again. At least he didn't try to staple my fingers. "So, when Carlos suggested that they go back to his place, she rejected him."

"And how did Carlos react?"

"Carlos left like he was supposed to. However, it was Santiago's turn to try to get her to go outside. I don't believe it would have taken much because she was so willing. I think she liked the nerdy type, or maybe Santiago seemed less threatening to her." I shrugged and watched as Dr. Dowell played with the stapler for a second. In an instant flash, he slammed it against my fingers again. I resisted groaning out in pain and clenched my fingers harder. I wanted to slam my head on the table and cry out but knew that could have too many consequences.

"Now tell the truth."

"Okay," I whispered. I cleared my throat before speaking. It would, at least, buy me a bit of time. "She didn't seem interested in either of them. However, she seemed more comfortable around Santiago."

"Why?"

"He wasn't flirting with her."

"Then what happened?"

"Santiago brought her out, and she was dazed. I think he managed to slip a roofie in her drink. However, she didn't drink all of it because she was coherent. She willingly got into the van, but when she saw Carlos she started freaking out and kicked him in the face. She fled the van, and Santiago chased her. That's where I came out from watching them and acted like a random bystander. She trusted me—they always do. You learn from a young age that if you're in trouble, find another female. Carlos and I dragged her back, and Santiago prepared the drug. She fell asleep on Santiago after that." I paused. "Everything else was smooth sailing from there."

"So why do you think Howie was the weak link?" Dr. Dowell asked.

"Because Carlos and I had to drag her back. He could've made it easier and driven after us." I shrugged. "I've worked with Carlos plenty of times. He had to face the dejection or could risk getting the cops called on him."

"Are you sure that you are not projecting feelings onto Carlos? You have worked together multiple times."

"What are you suggesting, Dr. Dowell? I am happily married to the love of my life. Carlos and I are just coworkers." I gritted my teeth and moved my knuckles down to my pants. There, I squeezed the fabric as I let a bit of uneasiness and anger slip through. I hated that he suggested that I would be unfaithful to my husband. He shook his head and wrote something in his notes. "Am I done, or do you have any other questions for me? I'd like to leave."

"You may collect your things and wait for your team to finish with their debriefings."

"Thank you."

I hurriedly snapped all the wires off of me and waited for the buzz for the door to be let open. When it did, I made sure to slam the door behind me. I was met in a little oval hallway space where all the other doors came together. There was only one way to go from here and that was forward. When I met up in the waiting room, I saw Santiago, Carlos, and Howie all waiting for me. My debriefing usually never took the longest, so I was shocked to see that I was the last one.

"Welcome back, Chief," Carlos said. He smiled brightly at me, and I found myself scowling at him. He had lost the icepack somewhere in the debriefing room but as I glanced at his hands I didn't see any additional marks. I glanced over at Santiago and saw a little red bruise forming on his wrist. I wonder what he lied about. The last person I looked at was Howie, who was also looking at me. I annoyingly showed him my fingers without humiliation, and he stared wide-eyed at me. His reaction was how I felt for him being down here. He cleaned the car, came to his debriefing, and finished before me. The debriefings didn't even take that long. "Alright, get ready to stand on the line," he instructed everyone.

I nodded my head and stood in between Carlos and Howie. We waited patiently until the screen that was mounted on the wall was lit up blue. It caught all of our attention at the same time, and we all stood a little quieter with our backs a little straighter. When I looked to the sides of me, I could see everyone else's gaze was trained on the screen. Exactly where mine should be too.

"Congratulations on another job well done," the voice on the screen said. The voice sounded familiar, but I couldn't pinpoint who it used to belong to. Did I work with them? "Listed in order are your most valuable teammates to your least valuable teammates. Once all names are called, everybody but your least valuable teammate will grab your gear and head to the elevators to rest until your next assignment. You can take that time to improve your strategies, physical strength, brainpower, and training techniques. Your most valuable teammate is..."

The screen flickered to a slide with Santiago's name on it. I could see his body relax in line as he read his name. A chorus of claps followed, and I could see a small smile form on his face. Although, he had to of known not to show too much emotion. He might get hurt if he did.

When the screen flickered to another slide, it showed my name. I instantly slouched over and listened to the claps from everyone else. I was safe now. I didn't need to worry about being beaten, tortured, and having my brain picked through for why I did things. I didn't need to worry about having to survive another day or wonder when they would feed me. I didn't have to worry about whether the man coming into the room had intentions of killing me or just using me for my body. I didn't have to worry about anything except getting a good night's sleep.

When the screen flickered again, my eyes immediately read the name on the board. I felt myself sigh and felt the person next to me forget

                    AMY KULP

about his posture. Carlos was safe. I knew he was going to be, but I don't remember there being a time when his name was so low on the charts. Granted, we usually had more people on each team. This team was small. Usually, there were five or six of us.

"You may grab your items and step through to the elevators."

I was the one who took the first step. Howie stayed behind as we three grabbed our gear. I made sure to have my gun ready. I watched as the boys took out some money and their wallets as well. After all, we all had fake IDs in case we ever needed them. Nobody was allowed to know our real names except those we worked with. Still, maybe Carlos's name wasn't Carlos. I would only find out if he told me.

But why would he trust me?

When I finally grabbed all my equipment, I stepped inside the elevator. I watched as the doors began to inch close in front of us and watched in horror as Howie was tackled to the ground by the torturers. I could see a bat being thrown at him, and I saw some fists in the air. Without thinking, I closed my eyes and frowned. I wasn't supposed to show emotion though.

How could someone not show emotion for one of their own being beaten like that? They did it on purpose too. Right before the elevator doors closed, they sent the guys who tortured people out. They would beat him up until he was unconscious. They deprived him of food, clothes, water, and safety. They tortured him until he was close to death. Then they rehabilitated him. They talked to him about how to improve. They made sure he got new training and was better before. If he were a girl, he would get so much worse.

"Don't worry, he'll come back better," Carlos reassured. He placed a hand on my shoulder, and I flinched away from him. "You know that it's how we become better."

I nodded because I knew that. He was only going to get better through the torture. He would only come back stronger. It didn't feel right though. It crushed your spirits until you couldn't fight back. It crushed your spirits so much that after a while you just let whatever happen. Sometimes, it just felt like something to prey on the weak.

Then again, we were sex traffickers. We shouldn't have any remorse for anybody.

When the elevator doors dinged open, so much relief slipped through my body. We all walked forward into the lobby of where our rooms could be, and I stopped when I saw what station the TV was on. It was always playing the national news coverage because we needed to know if anyone was onto us.

"Damn, Y, is that you?" Santiago asked as they all watched the TV screen too.

"Our girl made national news," Carlos said as he pretended to wipe away a tear.

"Keep a look-out for this girl you see on your screen. She is known to those as Y and is part of a sex trafficking ring. With over four hundred abducted girls in the past ten years, she is known as one of the most ruthless criminals on our list. She is number three on the FBI's Most Wanted. We believe that—"

"Four hundred cases?"

"Technically four-hundred and one," I corrected. I shrugged. "I do about forty a year."

"About three or four a month," Santiago stated. I nodded and his mouth dropped open. "I never would have guessed you have been doing this for so long." He shook his head and excused himself to his room, but I continued to stare at the TV screen, trying to hear what they were saying about me.

"How do you do it?" Carlos asked.

"I don't get to know the girls," I said finally. "Most of the time when I'm on a mission, I'm leading it and am there to give the girl false hope. Girls—"

"Trust other girls," he said over me. I nodded and looked at him. "You are ruthless. You deserve that number three spot but let's hope you don't get too famous."

"You know them, they'll probably have me locked in here for a while, at least until the news coverages stop."

"Yeah, good luck," he said. "I want more money, so I hope I get another job immediately."

"So you can buy hookers?" I asked. I looked over at him and noticed the door he was going into. I didn't realize his bedroom was so close to the lobby area. He smirked at me as he waved goodbye, and I just smiled back.

Guarantee that they won't have Carlos and me together for a very long time. Especially with how Dr. Dowell was questioning me. How could he think that I would cheat on my husband?

Carlos was like too many of the people here. He used to be homeless, and he saw a flyer at his homeless shelter saying he could make quick cash. Once he passed most of the tests, he was trained to be one of us. This job was his opportunity. This job was his saving grace. Like so many other people.

The only other people who came here willingly were ex-soldiers who were dishonorably discharged. They needed an outlet for their anger, so they had a nice fit here. Most of the anger management soldiers were our torturers here. Who else would be a better fit? I'm not sure how they got recruited, but I wasn't sure I wanted to know.

Finally drawing my eyes away from the TV screen, I walked down the silent hallways until I came up to my door. I quickly unlocked the door and jammed the door closed. While our bedrooms were small, I didn't have to sleep here all the time. Whenever my husband comes around, I always sleep in his room. He has the largest room I have ever seen. It could probably fit five king-size beds in it. You would still have room for the dresser and other decorations. However, my room had a twin-size bed, a dresser, and a small bathroom hooked up to the side.

I quickly changed out of my uniform and found myself some comfortable shorts and a t-shirt to lie in. I was planning to skip dinner and just go right to sleep. As soon as my head hit my pillow and I closed my eyes, I was startled awake by a bell

                              AMY KULP

going off in my room. With a huge groan, I got out of bed and put my uniform back on.

That bell meant that I was being assigned another mission.

I am Y. I'm happily married, have been a part of this operation for ten years with four-hundred and one successful missions, and the FBI's third-most- wanted criminal. I am usually a team lead in missions or a last-minute distraction. I was usually the reason the girls got caught. I was the reason they never escaped. While I can't remember my past, I am proud of the job I do because it is important.

--Chapter 2

As I walked down the never-ending hallway, I felt each footstep cover less and less ground. My body ached, I was exhausted, and I hadn't eaten yet. Physically, I probably wasn't capable of being the best on this mission. Mentally, my brain lagged, and I felt that I wouldn't be able to outsmart those around me. Why couldn't they just let me nap for a few seconds?

The TV from the hallway was still blaring. Right now, the weather was on with a forecast of rain. As I yawned to make myself walk forward, I traced my fingers along the walls, so I knew when the individual bedrooms stopped and I was close to going to the conference room. Everything here looked the same on the outside and the inside of each bedroom. The only things we really had control over were our hair and makeup. Our clothes were picked out for us, and we had all the same supplies. We were as uniform as we could get here.

I opened my eyes and picked up the pace when I heard footsteps come from behind me. When I tried to glance back to look, I could only see a shadow of the person who was following me. They must also be someone who was called to be in the next group with me. While I wanted to slow down, I knew not everyone was thrilled to work with a female.

Most preferred not to.

The men here didn't have respect for females. It was understandable considering we sex-trafficked only females. The men here usually hated us. Some sort of mommy issues or girlfriend issues were brought to light. A lot of the girls were abused, tortured, and killed at the hands of the men here. A lot of the girls never returned from their missions because they "vanished". After all, we are a group of misfits, criminals, and ex-military. Most of them had bad tempers or wanted a power struggle.

I was lucky that I was married. Any wrong look at me and I would immediately tattle to my husband. I also had the legacy here. People knew who I was. People knew that I have been doing this for ten years. People knew that I could kick ass. However, nobody knows of my origin.

I don't even remember my origin. I have tried asking my husband about it, but he never tells me. Sometimes I will get weird parts of flashbacks or dreams about another life, but it all seemed foreign, like it was a completely different person. Maybe it was what could have been of my life. However, I don't want that life. I like being told what to do. I like being chosen for missions. I like being in charge. I like seeing the shock on men's faces when they realize I will be telling them what to do. I like it here.

This place is my home.

"Please place your identification card on the slot and wait for the scanner to let you in the room." As I approached the final door before the elevator, I did exactly that. It only took three seconds for the scanner to beep at me to collect my badge and wait for the elevator doors to open. Once inside, I heard the person behind me being told the same exact thing. "Congratulations on being selected for a mission. You will be transferred down another level to the conference room. Please go to conference room number five."

The ride down was short, but as the elevator jolted to a stop I rolled my eyes and braced myself. I keep forgetting to tell my husband about that. Of course, how would he know? He rarely ever comes to the third floor below ground level. His stop is usually the fourth floor—something barely anybody gets to see. I'm not even sure what is level four. However, level three also includes master bedrooms for all the leaders here. I believe there are four or five. I know of my husband and the leader of this organization.

Mr. Barnett.

I don't like the guy. He gives me the creeps. Whenever I see him, I clutch onto anybody else in the room. I scoot further away from his gaze. Whenever he says my name, he drawls out the only letter he has to say. I never make eye contact, but I have no idea why. Something in my gut tells me something is weird about him. Did he try to torture me at one point? There are so many little details that I forget about this place. I can't even remember my first mission!

"Welcome to conference room number five. Please stand still as we do a body scan to allow you into the room," the automated voice called. I took a step back from the door and peered into the camera.

The stiller I was, the faster this process would be. As soon as I heard a lock, I turned the handle and pushed the door forward.

I didn't say anything as I took a seat where my nametag was. I didn't dare look across the group and waited patiently as two more people came in. When all the seats were occupied, I prepared my body to hear a high-pitched siren noise. After it went off for a few seconds, I relaxed and started to look at the name tags and girls around the room.

First up was me. My name was shown to those around me, and underneath was the position. I would be taking control as a leader. I sighed in relief as I read it and found comfort in my usual role. I oversaw the whole group in its entirety. Whether our group was successful or a failure, I would be the ultimate reason we were a failure but only a slim part if it was successful. After all, I usually didn't allow myself to be involved too much with the mission, as I liked to stay in the van and be on surveillance duty. I was safe there.

When I turned my head, the person to my right had a card that read that she was a driver. Above that, I could see that her name was Mattie. She seemed skittish to me, her scrawny body shivering under others' stares. Every time she sensed movement from the corner of her eye, she flinched, which made the dark coils of her hair bounce up and down. When she realized a physical attack never came, she would go back to shivering like a small dog, which was fitting since she seemed to be the smallest of the group. Her gaze was trained to a place on the table, and she refused to look around. As I studied her body and her face, I could see a part of her scalp that indicated a chunk of missing hair. It seemed to bruise in that spot, and I could see scabs healing. From the looks of it, I would say that Mattie was new. Maybe she wouldn't comply, so they tortured her for obedience. It would make sense as to why she was the driver of the group—they usually stuck newer people in that role.

Next to Mattie was the smarts of the group: Sloane. Despite wearing the same thing I was, she looked like she was being swallowed in her uniform. Bone-thin arms poked out from her sleeves, and her face seemed aged despite knowing she couldn't have been older than me. Her hair was pulled back into a thick bun and as she surveyed the room, I could see her thinking. She whispered unintelligibly every so often, and when her gaze got to me her lips turned into a straight line. She nodded at me, and I did the same. Her lips began to move again as if she was speaking a foreign language that only she knew. She quickly analyzed Mattie, and when her gaze went to the same spot that Mattie was staring at I knew that she was thinking the same thing I had been. She looked back over at me with wide eyes, and I only nodded in agreement. Hopefully, she would be smart enough to know I would talk to her later.

Directly across from me, I could see the muscles poking out of the tank top. Sitting down, I could see that she sat a foot taller than everyone, and before I looked at the name card I knew that this girl was going to be our strength. My eyes twitched over her name quickly, and when I looked up at Briley, I could see that she was trying to intimidate some of the other girls. She sat with her back so straight that she appeared even taller than I knew she would. She was flexing her arms but was trying to make it seem as if she was in a relaxed posture. This girl was all about the looks, so I wasn't sure if I could count on her to be strong. Would she be able to lift a body?

The last girl I looked over at was the lure of the group. She was the first person to make contact with our subject. She had to make fast friends with them and earn their trust. This could take months if not done properly. Jaycie had one of the most important jobs. However, her smile radiated through everyone, and I could tell that she was a people pleaser. She seemed to be perfect for the role.

"I want to get this meeting started," I announced. I stood up and felt all eyes on me. I looked at each girl and was surprised to see how different everyone reacted: Jaycie smiled up at me as if we were old friends, Sloane looked at me like I was someone new that she had to study, Briley had a smug smirk on her face knowing that she could beat me up if she wanted to, and Mattie looked at me like she was scared. My eyes had to do a double take to make sure I could see her failing to keep eye contact with me. Every time she looked at her favorite spot on the table, she sunk down further and further in her seat. That was strange. "I'm sure by now that you noticed something very peculiar about our group." I paused as everyone looked at each other. "We are all girls." The realization hit all of them at the same time, and I watched as their faces dropped. "Most groups only have one girl. We are the first in history to ever be made up of all girls."

"Which means we really can't screw this up," Briley interjected. She had the same smirk on her face as when I looked at her before. I could tell that she already had a cocky but humorous personality. I couldn't tell if I liked her or hated her. I guess it depended on how cocky she was or if she had a right to be that way. "I'm Briley," she announced. She flexed a muscle and then slowly brought her arms down under the table. "The only person I know who can read is Sloane since she's the brainiac of the group. So, if you can't read, don't worry about it because I'm the strength of the group. You need a heavy-lifter? I'm your girl."

I misjudged her. I nodded at her as I listened to another girl start talking. When my eyes pinpointed on Sloane, I knew that Briley had given her the best introduction she could get. I wonder if they have worked together before. Or are their personalities just matching well?

"As Briley said, I'm Sloane." She shyly put her hand up and waved to everyone else. I only nodded back but didn't look around in time to see what everyone else did. So far, this group seemed to be picked perfectly for their roles. "It's not that I'm brain smart. I think I'm more computer savvy. I can look things up in a blink of an eye, and I have my own method of organization. So maybe if something is said you might hear me tapping on the computer keys so that I remember it later."

　　　　　　　　　　　　　　　　　　　AMY KULP

"Computer savvy is still smart," Jaycie interrupted. "My typing is so slow that it's almost like an actual chicken could get more than me." She pantomimed how she typed with one finger on the keyboard, and Sloan instantly groaned.

"Not the chicken peck!"

"Yes, the chicken peck." Jaycie smiled brightly at her and darted her eyes toward me nervously. I instantly stopped smiling in reaction and watched as she cleared her throat and shifted in her seat. "I'm Jaycie. I'm assigned to be the lure. I think I just have a secret talent for connecting with people." She shrugged. "I try to break everyone out of their shells but can also just talk to myself for hours." Her eyes darted toward Mattie, and we all waited patiently.

She continued staring at her favorite spot on the table. When she realized that we were all staring at her, she made eye contact with me before darting her eyes back. Almost instantly, I watched as her entire body began to shake, and she shook her head no. However, she didn't stop staring at her favorite spot. That was odd. Why wasn't she talking at all? She could at least just say her name.

"And I'm your leader. My name is Y," I finally said. I stood up from my chair and immediately commanded attention. "Whether you like it or not, you answer to me. If I give you an order, you take it. It might not seem reasonable at one moment, but I am dedicated to all our missions. We will get every girl we are told to capture. I have not lost one yet, and I'm not going to start now. My ass is on the line much more than yours are. If we fail, I fail. I get credit for all the lows but none of the highs. We need to work as a team, and that means I need to trust every single one of you." I turned to look at every one of them. The only person I was having a hard time trusting right now was Mattie. "I have the envelope that tells us our mission." I scooted the brown envelope closer to all of them to see but put it back down. "However, for the first day, I believe it is important we get to know each other. When we go back, you will find three bedrooms—two with two beds, one with only one. Those bedrooms are yours to bond with each other. I will have my own as I read over the mission and prepare us for tomorrow. Use your time wisely."

I nodded at each of the girls and listened to the doors behind them automatically open. I carefully let my eyes wander toward each girl and watched as Mattie was the first one out of there. She evaded everyone's chit-chat, and I immediately crossed my arms.

"Jaycie, Sloane, stay back for a minute." They acknowledged my command with a shake of the head, and I waited until Briley had also made it out. This wouldn't concern her for right now. "Jaycie, I need you to make Mattie feel more comfortable. Right now, she looks afraid of everyone. I can only assume that she is newer to the program here and is afraid to make mistakes."

"Okay, I'll room with her," Jaycie said. I nodded my head and watched as she skipped out of the room. When she was completely out of eyesight, I waited five more seconds before turning to Sloane.

                                          AMY KULP

"I need you to find out how new Mattie is. I don't care if you hack the servers to find her stats or what. Just don't get caught." I paused. "Something is off about her, but I can't tell what."

"Do you want a theory?" Sloane asked. I nodded as she pushed up her glasses. "Her swallowing patterns are weird, and I doubt she would have made it out of the training regimen without being able to talk to people." She looked up at me and sighed. "Is it possible that Mattie was originally trafficked and tortured until she became part of this group?" Sloane asked. I immediately shook my head.

"No girl has ever been trafficked and picked to be here," I replied.

I am Y. I am happily married, have been a part of this operation for ten years with four-hundred and one successful missions, and am the FBI's third-most-wanted criminal. I am usually a team lead in missions or a last-minute distraction. I was usually the reason the girls got caught. I was the reason they never escaped. While I can't remember my past, I am proud of the job I do.

----*Chapter 3*

As soon as I heard a light knock on my door, I picked my head up and felt a piece of paper stick to it. It freaked me out at first until I realized that it was just the plan I was writing out. I detached it from my cheek and looked at the crumbled-up notes and scribbles all over the paper. There had to be dozens of them all over the desk, near the trash can, and all over the floor. Did I end up figuring out what our plan was? Or did I fall asleep first? I looked around to try and see if I circled anything, but my attention was diverted back to the door.

Oh yeah, someone was there. I immediately got up from the chair and listened to my back crack in multiple places. From that sound alone, I knew that I would be stiff for the rest of the day. Maybe our plan would take so long that I would have an extra day to work through the kinks that I was struggling with, although the entire mission seemed to be full of them.

I haven't complained about an assignment I have gotten since I found out the consequences if you did complain. Torture. Not having worked with any of these girls before, I wasn't too sure if I could trust any of them to complain to either. I wasn't immune to any of the disciplinary actions they had just because my husband was one of the leaders. They weren't exempt from it either. There were loads of checks and balances here.

They wanted to make sure that nobody could overthrow the current leader, although I wasn't exactly sure who the current leader was. I am proud to say that my husband was the one to come up with the idea that nobody had a consistent team. After all, we would start trusting each other more than our leader. If I could trust this team, I would hope to escape. However, my family was here, and nobody ever left here alive.

"Yes?" I asked when I opened the door. My hazy vision cleared up as I saw the tight bun wrapped on the top of the head of the girl in front of me. Not a single hair was out of place. She pushed her glasses up the bridge of her nose, and I couldn't help but stare at the stack of papers in her arms. She seemed wide awake for how early in the morning it was, and it filled my gut with regret. It probably looked bad that I wasn't prepared for the morning. "I'm assuming this is what I asked for?" I questioned.

Sloane nodded, and she moved back enough that I could peer out of my room to see if anyone was watching. When the coast was clear, I allowed her in and watched as she plopped her stack on my already-messy desk. Some papers flew around the desk as the pressure increased on them. I could already see that some of them creased awkwardly with the new stack on top. I hated clutter and mess, but you wouldn't be able to tell from how it looked right now.

"I'm assuming that's our assignment?" Sloane questioned. She peered down at the papers and looked like she wanted to snoop. Instead of looking longer, she turned around and smiled politely at me. "I'm curious, but I can wait until the whole group learns about it."

"Yes, you can," I stated.

I could see the hope deflate in her; her back slumped, her eyes darted back toward the papers, and the twinkle in her eyes disappeared. It's almost like I knocked the breath out of her. Maybe I would've shared the plan with her, but as of right now I didn't know what the plan was yet. I didn't want her to think that I was incapable of doing my job. After all, any weakness and she would probably say I was the least valuable member.

"What did you find out about Mattie?" I asked. "I won't ask how you found out any of this information."

"I'm smart enough not to tell," Sloane mentioned. I nodded, and she twisted around to grab the top sheet of paper from her stack. "I couldn't find much besides the notes on her observations from when she was being trained." She whisked through the first page, and I watched as her cheeks began to blush.

She just accidentally admitted to me that she went through the database to find sensitive information. I didn't want to get her in trouble, but the next time I talked to Emmanuel I would have to let him know that it was able to be breached. Or they could raise Sloane's pay and level. They were probably underestimating her because she was a girl.

"Pretty much, she is easily manipulated, and she is afraid of everyone." Sloane shrugged and put

                                    AMY KULP

the paper down. "Everyone is when it's their very first mission."

As soon as Sloane said that, I felt dread flow through my body until I let out an audible groan. If this was her very first mission, this meant I had to babysit her. She didn't know how we did things here. The more missions you work, the easier it is to adjust to the situation around you. Since this was her very first mission, she couldn't do any of that. She might even be a flight risk. Now I had to keep my eyes on her.

"Did you find out anything about her torture sessions?" I wondered. I didn't want to say it, and I was hoping that she wouldn't make me ask the question that was hanging between us. I know that Sloane had noticed Mattie wouldn't talk. I know that others realized she wasn't talking either. Could she not talk?

"I don't like to read those," Sloane admitted. She looked uneasy for a second, averting her eyes from making direct eye contact. After a hard swallow, she looked back up and nodded. "They mutilated her mouth." Sloane opened one of the folders she had in her stack and tossed it toward me. When it landed on my lap, I looked down and read the header on the top: **Detailed Training Session #10: Passed - Mattie Kenlin**. "You can read about it in this case file. I only skimmed it." Sloane stood up urgently and looked down at me. "I know that I can get in trouble for this and can be valued as the lowest member on the team, but I feel as our leader you need to know." I instantly tore my eyes away from the file and looked up at Sloane. "I am not a torturer." She seemed to survey my reaction, but I made sure not to give her one. She should know that I know how to survive here. I don't talk about my feelings, and I don't talk about anything I do in these missions. Once they're over, they're over. It's how I protect myself. "I can sense you aren't either."

I didn't object to her assumption about me. If I trusted her more, I would agree with her. However, right now, I needed to know more about my team which included Mattie. Even if I didn't want a newcomer on our team, I couldn't change our course of events. I was not in charge of putting these teams together, and I wasn't going to be the one to tell anyone they made a mistake. I knew my place and it wasn't to correct those above me. However, as I flipped through Mattie's file to skim her first, second, third, fourth, fifth, sixth, seventh, eighth, and ninth training sessions, I knew that I had underestimated this girl.

I was afraid to flip to the tenth page. This girl has endured so much torture. I couldn't imagine why she would want to go through so much trauma. No payment seemed worth it. I flipped back to the front of her file before I could muster enough courage to flip to that last page. I had to know what brought her here. Yes, we get paid well, but was it worth what she went through to get here? My eyes skimmed the page briefly before I had to look away.

I have never seen such an in-depth report about somebody's life before. I wasn't supposed to be reading this either. However, the only reason I had so much detail on her was that these were reports from her record in juvie. It seemed that ever

                                          AMY KULP

since a young age, she was in trouble. Mattie was a constant runaway teen who needed money. Now that she was older, she must have seen a sign somewhere and joined us. She must have been desperate, but she would slowly gain rank here. Or she would die trying.

I knew that I wouldn't be able to avoid that tenth report forever, so I took my finger and flipped to that final investigation. When I flipped to see how long it lasted, it seemed to be five pages, which was four pages longer than the other ones. After all, it had to be the one where they finally broke her. Where she finally became part of the team. Where she would get her first case. A historic case that was full of all female agents.

Detailed Training Session #10: Passed - Mattie Kenlin

Written by: *Craig Moore*
Trainer(s):   *Reggie Beers*
                 Warren Clapper
                 Tristan Wilcox

On the tenth (and final) day of Mattie Kenlin's training, she was given multiple tasks to perform to the satisfaction of the trainers. Each task either tested strength, mental capacity, loyalty, planning skills, or implementation. When asked to perform certain tasks, Mattie would beg for them to release her, claiming she would "never tell anyone about this place!". Each outburst would be met with physical punishment from Warren Clapper.

<u>Strength</u>: Mattie did not display abnormal strength unless she felt threatened. She could not lift a 100 lb. weight, but when Reggie (235 lbs) got on top of her, she was able to move him off her. **Passed**.

<u>Mental Capacity:</u> While Mattie displayed normal skills, she did not pass a fifth-grade test. She seemed to be more street smart than book smart. **Passed**.

<u>Loyalty</u>: Mattie appears to struggle with loyalty to those around her. When the door was left open, she tried to escape. **Failed**.*

<u>Planning Skills:</u> Mattie was able to add thoughtful insight into a plan while working with those around her. Did not take rejection well. **Passed**.

<u>Implementation</u>: Mattie was able to implement the plan that was discussed prior. However, when others around her deviated from the plan, she was not able to carry through with her part. **Passed**.

***Loyalty**: When Mattie was soon caught, she screamed about wanting to leave. She kept yelling and insisting she should leave to help her baby niece get food. She just wanted money for her niece. She promised that she would not tell anyone about this place. Upset and annoyed with her screaming, Tristan hit her in the face. Upon the sudden quiet

                                    AMY KULP

*environment, the trainers decided it would be best to reduce how much she could talk. Forcing her mouth open, Warren pulled multiple teeth from her mouth. Hearing her scream more, Tristan placed a knife in her mouth until she became quiet to avoid having her tongue touch the blade. After ten minutes, he attempted to remove the blade. Accidental movement from Reggie ended with her tongue being sliced off. She passed out immediately and was woken up with bruises on the back of her throat and Reggie sitting next to her. Grabbing her hair, he pulled her closer to him and was able to recite her niece's name. He then mentioned that Warren and Tristan were on their way to traffic her if she didn't comply. When Mattie attempted to talk, she found out she was unable to produce words—only sounds. After several minutes of crying, an agreement was made that Mattie would work here for the rest of her life as a team member and Warren, Tristan, and Reggie's personal assistant. **Passed**.*

<u>Results</u>: Unbeknownst to Mattie is that her niece and sister were already kidnapped and trafficked at this point.

Her older sister was eighteen with a darker complexion. Hair was bleached and curled to be brown. Standing at 5'2" and weighing only 126 lbs, she was easy to capture. The sister was sold for $560,000.

Her niece has brown eyes, a dark complexion, and dark curly hair. Her niece was sold for $90,000,000.

A meeting will be held about selling female juveniles, as they seem to make more money.

<u>Meeting Results:</u> In the best interests of everyone, Mattie will not know of the outcome of her sister and niece. She will continue to work here and be the personal assistant of Reggie, Warren, and Tristan.

In the best interest of the company, they will continue to specialize in young adults 18-21 with specific cases specializing in children. While this would produce more money, it would be much riskier to kidnap children, as they tend to have more security and protection around them. While they hold an interest in a select few of our clients, most of our clients are not interested, as babies cannot fight back.

<u>Conclusion</u>: Mattie passed all her tests and will be loyal if she does not know the results of her sister and niece. She is afraid of confrontation and leaders but will do as they say if she fears them. She cannot talk. Let Reggie, Warren, and Tristan know if she is not doing as she should.

I flipped the page one more time to see just how horribly she was treated. There were four pictures taped to the last page and four more taped to the back cover. Two of them were of when she

　　　　　　　　　　　　　　AMY KULP

was getting her teeth pulled. The blood filled her mouth and dripped down her chin. I could hear her screams in the picture as Reggie held onto her throat. I could see how much pain she was in from how much they had to restrain her. I could see the sweat from the guards. One of the pictures was when she was passed out on the floor, and you can see inside her mouth and the other was of her tongue in one of their hands. I felt myself beginning to get squeamish and had to look at the last four pictures that were on the back cover.

I immediately felt my face crumble as I realized what these next pictures were. One was a picture of a girl who looked vaguely like Mattie. Despite how pretty they had her appear, she still had bruises on her eyes and a cut going around her neck. The next picture of her was where she was standing with some old Asian couple. While she had a frown on her face, they had smiles. I knew instantly that they had bought her. The next two pictures were of the little girl. She seemed fussy, but she was untouched. Holding her was an old white man.

I tore the picture off the folder and closed the papers. Running my thumb along the edges of this picture, I let my intrusive thoughts win. I folded the picture and placed it in my bra. Nobody would check me there. They would be too afraid to do that.

I threw the folder onto the ground and into the closet that this small place had when I heard something come from the lobby area. I looked back at my desk and knew that I should be working on details about our assignment, but I found that my nose wanted to go out there. I sniffed the air again and listened to what the commotion was that I had originally heard. I couldn't hear it, but my nose smelled breakfast in the morning. Maybe bacon. I didn't know that we had bacon here.

I peeked out the door and saw a light in the kitchen was on. They were not trying to be subtle that they were making food. I wondered if I could barter some food from them. When I walked into the kitchen, I was surprised to see Jaycie was cooking food with a smile on her face. When I entered, she looked up at me and offered an empty plate to me. My mouth seemed to water out of reaction.

"Come on in, boss," she said playfully. She smiled at me and then nodded toward the table. "I'll have more eggs ready in a second. I figured that I would make breakfast for everyone since this will most likely be our first and last day together."

"Thank you," I said. I skeptically took the plate and sat down next to Briley. She had already started scarfing down whatever was on her plate. "Why are you up so early?"

"I smelled bacon," she stated simply. "I also get up early to start training with the weights." She flexed her arm muscle before going back to grab a piece of bacon. She stuffed it in her mouth and smiled as she chewed. I knew my mood would improve as soon as I popped a piece of food in my mouth too. "While it was lovely chatting with both of you, I am already half an hour behind my schedule." I was shocked to hear that. I hated waking up early. "And that's why I have muscles," she said. She got up and immediately put the plate

 AMY KULP

in the sink. She waved goodbye, and I only turned toward Jaycie when eggs were landing on my plate.

"How'd it go last night?" I wondered. I dug my fork into the steaming yellow yolks and waited patiently for Jaycie to talk. For how bubbly she seemed, I was a little taken aback by how reserved she was right now. She probably learned to think before she talked. It was a good quality to have.

"She's tough," Jaycie replied. Her back was now turned as she finished cooking the rest of the bacon and eggs for Sloane and Mattie. I wasn't sure if she was talking about Mattie herself or if she was tough to crack. Could Mattie learn to trust Jaycie in just a day? If anyone could do it, it would probably be Jaycie.

I continued to watch Jaycie as she cooked, but I knew she was acting different. Her posture was too straight now. She was worried about something, but I wasn't exactly sure what. It had to be something about Mattie, but I knew everything about her. This would just reveal to me how much I could trust Jaycie to tell me what is happening. If she doesn't, it would show me that I can trust her to keep a secret.

"Sloane probably won't eat until later," I finally said. "She was up doing what I asked her to do."

"Okay," Jaycie answered. She spun around as she put the last of the bacon and eggs on the last plate. There was a heaping bunch, and I was confused about who was going to eat it all—Sloane was a tiny girl and I wasn't sure how enjoyable eating was to Mattie. "Wow, great timing," Jaycie exclaimed as Mattie made her appearance. She wore a shirt that was out of regulation, the sleeves extending beyond her hands. She gripped them tightly and scooted into the room. Her expression changed as soon as she saw me.

While she was still timid around Jaycie, she was relaxed. She was afraid of making a wrong move with her, but whatever happened last night added a little spark of trust. Her eyes found the floor, and she stared at it as she went over to the food. Okay, so she could still eat. I watched as she spooned some of the food on the plate but could see her hands fidgeting with nerves.

I wonder what they didn't put in the report to make her that afraid.

She sat down in the farther chair from me and kept her gaze on the table. Jaycie took a seat in the middle of us and added some pepper to her eggs. I probably needed some too. As soon as Jaycie let the seasoning go, I reached over to grab it and saw from the corner of my eye how Mattie reacted. She flinched and covered her face with her hair. I could see her entire body shivering now. When I slowly pulled my arm back to my plate, she peeked out from her hair and resumed cutting her food into small portions.

I forgot how careful I must be around new agents.

"I am a very fast eater," Jaycie said as she put her fork on her plate. At the sound of the clang of the silverware, Mattie froze. She seemed to freeze anytime someone talked too. I moved my

                                    AMY KULP

gaze away from her and back to Jaycie to see her beginning to wash the dishes.

"Mattie and I will get those," I announced. Jaycie turned around instantly and nodded. She knew how to read social cues. She smiled at me as she left the room, which suddenly became too quiet.

Mattie didn't move and just stared at the food on her plate. After a moment, I realized that I wasn't eating either and tried my best effort to keep it going. I was trying not to focus on what she was doing, but I did manage to see her body relax a bit. That was a start. After I finished my food, I put my fork down gently and watched as Mattie continued not to touch hers.

"Are you going to eat the rest of that?" I asked. Mattie shook her head in what looked like a fidget at first. I brought my body around her and grabbed the plate that was next to her. "I think you should eat more. I only saw you put a couple spoonfuls in your mouth." I paused and watched as she shakily grabbed the utensil she was using. She placed it in her mouth and got away from the chair. She showed me the clean spoon and dropped it in the sink. I guess I was too close for too long. "Does it still hurt?" I asked. Mattie ran the water to try and avoid the question. She began washing the dishes at super speed, probably to avoid any conversation with me. "I know what they did to you." Her speed started to slow. "If it hurts, I can get you medicine." She continued to wash, and when she finished she turned the water off. "We are a team. I want you to trust me. I am not going to hurt you." Mattie wiped her hands on her pants and hid behind her hair as she turned toward me. Her eyes were back on the floor, and as she walked out I knew that I had to get her to trust me.

I could start that by getting her something to help with the pain. I'm not exactly sure how long ago her tongue was cut off, but it still had to hurt. I went back into my room and instantly wrote myself a note. I had to get her a pain reliever somehow, but first I needed to figure out our plan for our new target.

Was it wrong if I didn't think we could do it? I have never been so stumped before on what to do. I have never been so discouraged about if we could successfully complete the mission. If I didn't have confidence, how could my crew have confidence? I was starting to get this nagging feeling that we were specifically given this assignment because they didn't think we would be successful.

That alone was enough to encourage me to figure out what I wanted us to do. We might be successful, but it all depended on how we were as a team.

Coming out of my room after four hours of working, I rang the bell that told the crew I was ready for them. The first to come into the interrogation room was Sloane. She had some eggs in her mouth and quickly swallowed what was left. She didn't want to miss any of the opportunities to talk and show off her intelligence. Next, Jaycie made her way in. She smiled proudly at me before taking her spot in the seat she was assigned yesterday. Briley came in with Mattie trailing behind her. Briley must have been taking a shower because her hair was wet and dripping down her back.

"Okay," I announced. I put my hands on my hips and looked over everyone once again. I felt more intimidated by this group of girls than if I were with a group of boys. However, I knew it was just because I would feel personally responsible for anything that happened to them. "We were tasked with a very special assignment. This might be the highlight of our lives but will be our most difficult. Be prepared for a challenge. Each of you—all of us—will have to work as a team better than any group before. We need to be prepared to go off-book in the blink of an eye. We need to be flexible in our jobs, so Sloane shouldn't be the only one on the computer. Sloane, I should see you helping when you can. Simply put, if you just stick to what your title is, then we will fail as a team. If we fail as a team, we all go back to get retrained." I attempted to make eye contact with Mattie, but her gaze was on the floor. I could see that her face hardened at the mention of that. "That's not the important part. The important part is figuring out who our subject is. Before I can tell you who it is, I want to ask you something. How long have you guys been working here?"

"Six months," Jaycie started.

"One year," Sloane bragged.

"Three years," Briley whispered.

I knew my question wasn't going to be answered by Mattie, so I saved her the trouble. I turned back around and began writing a name on the board: Trinity Barone. When I turned around to study facial expressions, none of the girls seemed impressed. Underneath her name, I wrote another name: Roman Barone. When I turned around this time, I saw two faces change.

"If you don't know who Trinity Barone is, you most definitely know who her father is. Roman Barone is a known comedic actor. He is best known for being the lead voice actor on *Bartholomew the 87th*."

"And our assignment is to kidnap his daughter?" Briley asked. I nodded. "I like being challenged, but have they ever kidnapped someone who was so high-risk? I'm sure he has lots of security guards and cameras."

"Is he always with her though?" Jaycie asked.

"I'm assuming that if he is acting he won't be able to be with her all of the time," Briley answered. "Besides, who wants to spend all of their time with their dad anyway?" Mattie instantly hit the table out of deviance, and Briley looked startled. I turned to watch her reaction, but she only made eye contact with her for a second before going back to her silent ways.

"Some of us have families outside of this place," Jaycie intervened. "We took this job for money with the promise that it would fix our messed-up home lives. Not all of us willingly walked in here. A lot of us are forced to stay here. We can't go home to our families."

"You knew what you were signing up for," Briley sneered. "Maybe if you were more loyal to

 AMY KULP

the program you would be able to go home between missions."

"They let people do that?" Sloane asked. She turned to me, and suddenly everyone was also staring at me.

"Some people are allowed to go home. There are criteria you have to follow: you have to be here longer than a year, you have to be in the top three most valuable teammates for the past three months, and you have to be willing to put your family up as collateral."

"What does that mean?" Jaycie asked. She looked over at Mattie for a brief second, and I was glad I was looking, because if not I would not have seen the glance. I'm not sure what Jaycie had told Mattie to get her to trust her, but it was growing too fast.

"If you do anything to hurt the integrity of the organization, your entire family is endangered of being auctioned off, killed, or made to be part of this group," I stated. I watched as Briley sat up with more agitation than before. She tried not to make it seem like she was insulted, but with Jaycie's verbal pestering I wondered what exactly brought her here. I only knew of Mattie's background. "But I think Briley makes a fair point. If her dad is smothering her in any time of way or maybe hasn't let her make friends, she would be desperate for a friend. Someone who isn't interested in her fame or money."

"Noted," Jaycie said.

"First thing we all need to do is our research on this girl," I reminded. "We need to find out her dislikes and likes. Someone needs to figure out where she hangs out. We need to brainstorm a way to get Jaycie infiltrated into her life."

"I'm assuming she freshly turned eighteen?" Sloane questioned.

"She will be eighteen the day we kidnap her."

"Oh, so this is a timed mission?" Jaycie wondered. "I've never been on one before."

"I've only ever heard of them happening once before," Sloane spoke up. She eyed me for a second before looking back down at her notes. "Well, she has to go to school, correct? I feel like that would be the easiest option. I could hack the school's system to give Jaycie all of the same classes as her."

"You would have to give me two without her, otherwise that would be too suspicious," Jaycie mentioned.

"Good point."

"Aren't most famous parents' kids homeschooled?" Briley asked.

"I can look it up in two seconds if you find me a computer," Sloane mentioned.

"There are computers built into the table," I said. I tapped the table in three different spots before a computer appeared out of the table. I watched to see what the others would do and was pleasantly surprised to see Sloane pick up on it so fast. It was then followed by Briley, Jaycie, and Mattie. Once on, they all began typing.

"She is homeschooled," Sloane said after two seconds.

"But it looks like she's training in classical music," Jaycie mentioned. I walked over to her computer but only saw her social media up. When I looked over at Mattie's screen, she had her article about her life. On it, there was a picture of her playing the saxophone. I gave her a small smile before moving back to the center of the room. On the board, I wrote about her love for classical music.

"I'll work on finding out where exactly she goes," Sloane said as she typed.

"Jaycie, do you know how to play an instrument?"

"I can play the recorder," she admitted. "I was more of the drawer in school."

"I guess it's time for you to learn a new instrument. We all can handle the research while you learn how to play an instrument. Nothing too fancy as this is probably a school for kids who want to get better."

"Right," she said. "I'll look up videos on the saxophone."

I nodded but was immediately torn to pay attention to what Briley was telling me. It felt like hours before we came up with a solid plan for everyone to follow. At one point, Briley was solid enough on the information that she was relieved to begin weight training for this girl's body weight. After all, she would be slinging her around and making sure she could hold her down even if she was fighting. When Sloane's computer eventually died, I allowed her to escape for a good night's sleep as well. She promised she would do more research in the morning, but I wasn't too worried.

"Hey, Mattie, I think it's time to pack up," I said as I yawned. She immediately shut the computer screen down and hopped out to go to the door. "I have something for you." I instantly reached into my pocket. When she realized I was handing her pills, she looked up with wide, untrusting eyes. "It's to help with the pain. I found them when I went back to my room earlier today." I smiled weakly at her and was surprised to see her accept the pills and nod at me. However, I knew not to press my luck. That would probably be the end of this interaction.

As I stumbled back to my bedroom, I laid my head down and immediately tried to sleep. However, my head was full of nagging thoughts and doubts about self-confidence. I was worried. I have never been worried about a mission before. How were we supposed to get this high-end girl away from all these people? There were going to be paparazzi. There were going to be security guards everywhere. There were security cameras. These people were rich enough to make their own rules and get away with the crime.

However, I couldn't forget who I was. I started out as the lowest on the team and now was the highest ranked. I couldn't let one girl get the better of me. One girl wasn't going to ruin my reputation. One family wasn't going to make me a failure. This was going to be success story four hundred and two. She would not mess this up for me.

                         AMY KULP

I am Y. I am happily married and have been a part of this operation for ten years with four hundred and one successful missions and am the FBI's-third most-wanted criminal. I am usually a team lead in missions or a last-minute distraction. I was usually the reason the girls got caught. I was the reason they never escaped.

-----*Chapter 4*

"What can you see?" I asked as I looked over Sloane's shoulder at the computer she had on her lap. She was busy watching surveillance cameras inside the rehearsal hall. She tilted the computer screen toward me so that I can see it, but we were only able to see bare hallways.

Sloane was fast with finding the information on where Trinity practiced her classical training. With a little luck, she was able to apply with a fake resume of Jaycie's achievements and wired money to an account for her to attend the lessons she was about to take. I knew that I would eventually have to ask her about that and figure it out myself. If I could produce fake money, I would be buying my team fast food all the time. Not much else I could really spend it on unless I wanted to share it. I also knew that I was going to let my superiors know as well. If Sloane could do that, she should be making more and doing more tech than fieldwork.

Thankfully, since Sloane was able to do her job so fast, we were able to get Jaycie implemented into Trinity's life quickly. However, it seems that while Trinity did play the saxophone, that instrument was not considered to be in the classical music genre. We had to spend way too long getting Jaycie to learn the trumpet now. Even then, it seemed that Trinity knew how to play that instrument but wasn't, because for this concert she was playing the clarinet. Not wanting to make her learn another instrument, Jaycie knew the importance of interacting with Trinity as much as possible.

She was always wearing a wire so that we could hear everything that was going on. Although Briley hated classical music, so we often muted it whenever they were practicing. She also had a camera on her instrument so that we could see exactly what was going on. Sloane hooked everything up to display on our van's monitors. Jaycie also managed to put some hidden cameras in some of the hallways. Unfortunately, nobody was allowed in the practice rooms by themselves, so she never had the opportunity to put them in there.

"Did you hear her squeak?" Jaycie asked as she walked out of the practice room. I immediately shushed everyone in the van and watched the monitors. Just like I assumed, she was glued to Trinity's hip.

This girl was a tough cookie to crack. While working hard, Jaycie knew that she couldn't show any interest in her. She couldn't know who she was either. She was tired of people using her for her dad. She was tired of people pretending to be her friend. If Jaycie kept the act up, I could assume that they were going to be friends. Although, Trinity wouldn't know the truth until it was too late.

"How could I not?" Trinity asked. "I was sitting right next to her! Someone needs a new reed." She rolled her eyes as she got to their normal water fountain spot. It was always the same spot every day. This girl liked patterns and routines. If she didn't always have so much security on her, she would be an easy target.

"Hey, there's a man just staring at you over there," Jaycie said. She bumped her hip into the wall and nodded toward one of the security guards. Of course, Jaycie knew who they were, but Trinity was putting up the false pretense that she was just a normal girl. "Kind of creepy. Do you think we should tell someone?" She looked around the room for another adult until she locked eyes with someone up front. When she went to walk toward them, Trinity grabbed her arm.

"No, it's alright," she mentioned. She shrugged. "It's probably someone's dad picking them up." She rolled her eyes at the thought. She was such a bad liar. "You can have a drink now. I'm done."

Jaycie looked unsure for a second but leaned down anyway. When Jaycie was down, Trinity sent a nasty look toward the security officer, and he seemed to vanish. I had to assume he sat down where our cameras were not pointed.

"He's probably checking you out because we're the only older kids here," Jaycie mentioned. "Still gross though."

"Hey, I'll be eighteen soon," Trinity objected.

"Ooh, what do you plan on doing? A big, extravagant party." I swear I could see the twinkle in Jaycie's eyes as she said it. She probably didn't have anything like that growing up. Despite how excited Jaycie was, I could see Trinity tense up next to her.

          AMY KULP

"No, why would you say that?"

"Oh shit," I whispered under my breath. I lunged toward the microphone and turned it on without a second thought. "She thinks you know. Say something else." I clutched onto the metal in my hands and closed my eyes. What was she going to say? Would it deflate Trinity's suspicion? I looked over at Sloane, but she was too busy typing something up.

"I always dreamed of having an extravagant party with thousands of guests and so much food. All I have is a homemade cake with family around." Jaycie shrugged. "Don't tell anyone, but I'm on scholarship here."

"Really?" she asked. Trinity stepped closer to Jaycie and seemed to study her for a quick second. Turning her back to the camera, I couldn't see anything of what she was doing. "I didn't know we had a scholarship program." Jaycie just nodded. She was perfectly portraying someone embarrassed to talk about their upbringing. "I won't tell anyone."

"Promise?"

"Promise." There was a moment between them before Trinity looked over to the practice doors. "We should probably get going in there, but I want you to come to my birthday party."

"I don't think—"

"You don't need to bring anything. Come on, I'll tell you more when we're back in there." She grabbed Jaycie's wrist and led her back to the practice room.

There was a moment of silence in the van, and once again we heard the different sounds of musical instruments warming up. Some squeaked, some sounded amazing, and to the untrained ear they were all in tune. Once again, I swiftly turned the racket off and stared at the empty hallways.

"She's good," Sloane mentioned. I just nodded. There wasn't much to say. We had to stay focused and continue to watch the cameras. "Our meter is almost up," Sloane reminded. I watched her move the computer and wires off to the side. She jiggled the coins in her pocket before waiting at the back door for Mattie to unlock them.

When the sound was heard, Sloane quickly slipped out and Mattie relocked the doors. While she could have been helping us with the cameras, I allowed her to stay up in the front seats. She was to look out for Briley or very suspicious people. If it was Briley, she oversaw unlocking and locking the doors.

I wormed my way from the back up to the front. Mattie didn't flinch when I came up, which was progress from when we first met. However, she kept her eyes on me. I watched the streets, and after a while her gaze went back to the road too. Stakeouts were some of the hardest and most boring parts of the mission. However, it was the most important to obtaining our victim.

"I read your file," I whispered as I stared at a random man as he crossed the street. I listened to Sloane pull at the back door and do our knock on the door. "Don't let her in just yet." I could hear her try again, but Mattie didn't press the button to unlock the doors. "I don't care what you do, but I am not reporting any behaviors to Reggie." I

                                    AMY KULP

watched as Mattie looked at the floor at the sound of his name. "If you do something wrong that jeopardizes this mission, you answer to me. Am I understood?" Mattie barely nodded before she unlocked the doors.

I stared at her while Sloane got in the back, but she refused to meet my gaze. She was already disobeying orders. I knew it was a risk when I told her I wouldn't report to Reggie. He was vile, creepy, and repulsive. However, he put fear into her. He made her listen. She thought since I was female that I would take it easier on her. While I had a soft spot growing in me, we could not risk the mission because of her.

"Don't forget who you're trying to protect by being here," I whispered before moving to the back. I was willing to play dirty if it meant she listened. This could be a secret that I held with me. Nobody else knew that her sister and niece were already sold. Nobody had to know except me. I could see the terror in her eyes, but it wasn't the conversation we were supposed to discuss right now. Not in the presence of Sloane.

And Briley.

"I didn't see you come back," I mentioned.

"I took a short detour to check out the building of the music hall," Briley mentioned. She popped a fry in her mouth and handed the greasy bag to me.

"So, you disobeyed orders?" I asked. Briley immediately opened her mouth, but I shook my head. "Does no one here know how to follow orders?" I asked the entire crew. I looked toward

Mattie, but her head was flat against the seat, and she was still staring at the windshield.

I felt my anger build up inside of me and knew my skin was getting red. I huffed and immediately threw the bag of food at Briley. She flinched but was able to catch most of the things that flew out. If I wanted a physical fight, she would be able to take me, so I had to think on my toes. I opened my mouth to yell but was interrupted by Sloane.

"They're done!" she yelled.

I stared at Briley for a second longer before grabbing the food and bag from her hands and sitting down. I peered over Sloane's shoulder to see what exactly we were witnessing but hadn't yet seen Jaycie or Trinity come out. I leaned over to the speaker to put the volume back up.

As we listened to their conversation about mundane things, I passed Mattie and Sloane their food. I made sure to eye Briley and get out my own food. After a moment has passed, I handed Mattie extra fries and Sloane an extra burger. When the realization hit Briley that she would not be getting any food, she sat down next to Sloane and watched the monitors in the van. I hated to do it, but I needed her to know that she needed to follow directions. They weren't optional. Her doing her own thing could jeopardize us and the mission.

I was not going to take the fall for stupid people.

"I will see you tomorrow at practice," Trinity said.

                                    AMY KULP

I found my way back to the monitors and could see that Jaycie was holding something with a bright smile on her face. With no other interaction between the two, we heard our knock on the door. Without a second thought, Mattie unlocked the door and Jaycie popped inside. Without thinking, I gave her the bag of food, and she happily showed us the gold, shimmery envelope in her hand.

"I got the birthday invitation!"

****
****

"Wow, these almost look exactly the same," I said as I peered over the three gold envelopes. "I can't tell which one was the original." I scanned the three again before marveling at the scripted handwriting, the exact same envelope size and pouch, and the perfect replication of the signature. "Excellent job, Sloane and Mattie."

"Finding the exact envelope, pouch, and font used was the easy part. I could pull that up immediately. It was the signature that was the tricky part," Sloane mentioned. "You did well with choosing Mattie, because she is excellent at forgery." I looked over at her, and she just shrugged. Of course, she was going to be modest about it. She didn't want to reveal any additional information about her.

"I'll have to let them know in your file," I mentioned.

"But for right now," Jaycie said as soon as she came out of her room. "We need to get you and

Briley ready for the celebration. I can help with makeup."

"I can do accessories," Sloane piped up. "Mattie can do hair." Mattie immediately looked over to everybody in shock. "We see the little braids you keep in your hair."

"And you did mine one night before bed," Jaycie offered.

"Then it's settled," I said. "Briley and I will get ready, and when we're done changing we'll come out to you three to doll us up." I nodded my head and hovered near her door. She was still mad at me for not feeding her some of the fast food that she had to get. But that was a week ago, and now we're ready to move on with our plan. I knocked on her door and waited patiently. Although I'm sure I could just get Sloane to get her to come out. When she answered, sweat was glistening on her body, and I could feel the heat radiating from her room. It felt like a sauna in here. "We need to find our dresses."

"Does it have to be a dress?" she asked.

"Yes, it's black tie."

"Jaycie's dress isn't black-tie," Briley noted.

I looked back at what Jaycie was wearing and nodded. She had a basic sweater dress on. It was warm enough for the dress to be shorter but cold enough that the thick wool wouldn't suffocate her. It was not black-tie. It was something you would wear to school if you didn't have a dress code.

"Jaycie is supposed to be poor. We need to follow up on the lies she told Trinity. Otherwise, something might catch her off guard."

Briley just nodded in satisfaction. With that nod, I didn't feel like she was trying to just do whatever she wanted. It seemed that she was more concerned about following through with the plan. If we didn't have Jaycie at the party, then our plan wouldn't go as we wanted it to. We probably would not be able to get Trinity either. She was always surrounded by guards.

I led Briley out of our small apartment suite and into a barren hallway. I stepped in front of the scanner and waited patiently as my body was scanned and configured into the system. It printed out a small piece of paper with a list of my possible sizes. Briley was up next and remained still as it continued to scan her repeatedly. It probably wasn't used to a female with muscles. After a long minute, it printed out a long piece of paper. She stared at it for a second before shaking her head and stepping into our unit's wardrobe department.

With how many scenarios we go through, they found it was easier to have a communal closet for girls and boys. That way, we could still stay in uniform but only purchase a type of outfit once. Inside, it was separated by size and then by occasion. It looked like a storefront with how wide it was going to go.

"Can you help me?" Briley asked.

I cocked an eyebrow for a minute before nodding yes. This would probably be the only time I received a request for help from her. I had to show her that I wouldn't judge her when asked either. Even if finding an outfit for the event seemed like a simple task. I could tell that Briley would be out of her element. She cared more about her body than what she wore on it.

She led the way with her size, and the further we traveled there seemed to be fewer options for her. Still, we walked and walked until we got to her size. There were barely any clothes here. We searched through them anyway and when we were left with no clothes suitable for her we stood there awkwardly. I could sense that Briley was uncomfortable next to me, and I did not want to upset her by saying something insensitive.

"Well, you're tall," I began. I paused and looked her up and down. "We can go into the smaller sections and look for a floor-length dress. It won't be floor-length on you and if anything we can make sure that Sloane pairs you with flats." I marched forward to the center of the dress piles again and started searching for dresses I felt would suit Briley. "Do you just want plain black?" I asked. Briley didn't answer out loud, but I could see her nodding. As soon as I found a gown in black, I pulled it from the rack and felt envious.

This looked like it would perfectly fit her. Briley immediately stripped in front of me and tried it on. It had strappy sleeves, and for an instant I thought it would fit. When I took a step back to examine it, I could see that it was cutting off circulation in her arms. I immediately sighed but wasn't going to give up. With a slit in the thigh, it would give her enough room to kick if she needed

     AMY KULP

to. I wasn't going to give this up because of the sleeves.

"When we get back, I'll cut the sleeves off, and we'll use fashion tape to keep it lifted up. Go back and get your hair, makeup, and accessories done," I instructed. Briley nodded and quickly left.

Now it was my turn to find the perfect dress for the occasion. I scoured the racks, and for a moment I felt normal. I felt like this was what I would have done if my last ten years were not robbed from me. If I had a life where I could have gone shopping or just enjoyed the clothes on the rack.

Did I ever have the chance to do that?

I quickly shook my head and scolded myself for the thoughts. I was here to be the perfect wife and perfect leader. I was here to take girls who were suffering in their home lives to give to people who wanted them. I was here to humble those who already had a perfect life. This job saved me. Who knows what would have happened if I wasn't here? I could have been killed or homeless. This job was a blessing because I would never have met my husband.

Still. As I pawed through the rest of the dresses, I stopped on one that was a bit inappropriate for the occasion. This sparkly blue dress would have been more appropriate for prom. Did I get to go to a prom? I couldn't remember. Why couldn't I remember?

It's been haunting me for years now. Sometimes I ask my husband what my outside life was like, but he never answers. He gets mad at me and accuses me of wanting to leave. He tells me how much is at risk and that I was being stupid for wondering. He always threatened to find someone younger who would love to be in my shoes. He threatened to tell the higher-ups about my thoughts and that I must have a brain injury to be wondering those things. Maybe I do. Why else wouldn't I be able to remember them?

Against better judgment, I grabbed the sparkly blue dress and tried it on. It dragged in the back, but with a pair of heels it would barely touch the ground. I could still run in heels. I could still fight in heels. I could still hide my gun and my knife up my thigh in the dress. If anything, I had more leverage because of the low-cut neckline. Men would get distracted.

Without a second thought, I grabbed the dress and flew out of the room.

****

****

"Do you have eyes on the building?" I asked through my earpiece. I touched my ear hoping to hear the other end better but found it incredibly hard to hear anything. They had live classical music here, and although it was peaceful to hear it was too loud. People were shouting at the partners they were having conversations with, but they sounded like whispers. "I repeat, do you have eyes on the building?"

"I'm hacking the security footage now. They have a tough firewall system," Sloane said.

     AMY KULP

I looked around the elegant hall. This place was huge. While most people could only afford one room in this place, it seems that Trinity's dad rented out the entire building. It made our scheme easier, but we would have to find a room without people in it.

"Let's talk about the plan," I said as I accepted a champagne glass from a waiter. How did he know I was over twenty-one? Did I really look that old? "What cigarette is the tainted one?"

"Any from the first row," Briley answered.

I looked around the hall and caught her eye. I watched as she began talking with someone. It seemed that no one here was Trinity's age. Not even the friend she had invited. I moved on and sipped the champagne as I moved around the hall. I bounced my head to the music and put my fingers back up to my ear.

"What are we doing before Trinity tries the cigarette?" I asked.

"Trying to get her as drunk as possible," Jaycie answered innocently. I smiled as she recited our plan exactly. "If none of that works, you have an extra pill in case."

"I'm in! I can see everything," Sloane said on the microphone.

"Alright, Jaycie, you can enter. Keep your earpiece on and cover it with your hair."

I stared around the room and found myself sneaking back toward the entrance. Briley and I had the fake invitations, and while they received a mild inspection we were passed along rather quickly. I didn't like that there were paparazzi outside, but nobody was interested in taking pictures of me or Briley. Just the celebrities they knew about.

"How do you know the birthday girl?"

"Oh, we practice music together," Jaycie replied. I grimaced at her enthusiasm. She probably didn't realize they were having difficulty believing that Trinity would be friends with someone who wasn't dressed properly.

"And did you not read the invite? You are supposed to be dressed in black-tie attire," he nastily said. "We have been getting a lot of fakes today."

"She told me to just wear a dress," Jaycie replied. I could hear the waver in her voice. She was starting to realize what was going on. Hopefully, this wasn't just a trick being played on her.

"We're going to have to deny you entry on the grounds that—"

"Phillip!" Trinity yelled from somewhere in the crowd. I tried to nonchalantly look for her but couldn't pinpoint where the voice came from. "This is the friend I told you about." I watched from the corner of my eye to see her yank on Jaycie's wrist to come through. "Don't worry about him. I don't know half of these people."

"How could you afford this place?" Jaycie wondered as she looked up at the ceiling. There was one giant chandelier hanging down in this room. There seemed to be thousands and thousands of layers to it though. As you moved up the floors, it was still going. I wondered if this was Jaycie acting or if this was her genuine reaction. "It must cost millions of dollars."

"Not when you have a rich father," Trinity said. She rolled her eyes and just shook her head. "Let's just focus on the party!"

"It doesn't seem like a party," Jaycie said. "Where are the balloons? The cake? Presents?" As they moved toward the center of the room, I could easily see how much Jaycie didn't fit in there. She was severely underdressed, as was planned, but her excitement radiated from her. Everybody else was sophisticated and boring. "How about music we actually like?"

"I like classical music."

"You like to play classical music," Jaycie corrected. She smiled at her. "Is this party for you? Or did your parents plan it for them?" she wondered. Trinity stopped to stare at her for a second before nodding. "I don't see your parents here—"

"My dad is here somewhere."

"But you don't know where?" Jaycie asked as she adjusted her earpiece. I heard the soft rustles of her moving it and winced slightly. "Have you ever had fun in your life?" she wondered. I felt my eyes go wide and knew that Jaycie was pushing her fast toward our goal. However, I had to keep my faith in her. She knew when to push her and when not to. She's the one who spent every rehearsal with her and every bathroom break with her. I watched as Jaycie looked around and grabbed two champagne glasses from the tray. The servers didn't even blink an eye. "It's time to celebrate you turning eighteen."

"But we're underage," Trinity whispered. Jaycie ushered her toward the side and handed the glass to her. I could see Trinity's uncertainty. "I don't want to get in trouble."

"Have you ever gotten in trouble?" Jaycie asked. She slurped down the champagne without a second thought. "It's your birthday. Your dad isn't going to yell at you on your birthday." Trinity nodded. "At least not in public, right?" Trinity grinned.

"What does it taste like?" she wondered. I weaved through the crowd to step closer to the duo. I couldn't see them from my spot. When I sat down at the nearest bench closest to them, I could see Trinity inspect the liquid.

"Fruity and bubbly," Jaycie answered as she hiccuped.

"Stop pushing her," I whispered in my earpiece. I could see that she was getting uncomfortable. Her body language gave it away. "We have other methods to get her out of here."

"If you just have one, you won't even feel it," Jaycie reassured. I looked around the room for Briley, and it took me a little longer to see her chatting with a friendly guy on the second floor. She was looking down at the floor below and gave me a slight nod. I had to trust Jaycie.

"Okay," Trinity finally spoke. Without a second thought, she closed her eyes and flung the drink to the back of her throat. She swallowed it, and when she opened her eyes she gave a smile. "That wasn't bad."

"I told you," Jaycie responded. "Don't drink too much though. You can get drunk way faster with champagne."

                    AMY KULP

"How would you know?" Trinity asked. "Aren't we the same age?"

I couldn't tell if Jaycie was messing up on purpose or if it was because she was a lightweight and couldn't think. Either way, she was messing up now. She needed to cover up more than she has in the past weeks. Was it possible that she didn't want to kidnap Trinity? Was there a possibility that she considered them friends? I shook my head at the thought. There was no way Jaycie would risk jeopardizing all of us.

"Not anymore," Jaycie remarked. "You're an old woman now." They both smiled at each other, which turned into a batch of giggles.

I walked away from the two as they fought the urge to control themselves and made eye contact with Briley before going to the bathroom. She knew what she had to do, and I knew what I had to do. Now was the time to do it. I could see Briley saying goodbye to the acquaintance she was chatting with before I got inside.

Even the bathroom looked like a million dollars.

I scooted into an empty stall and listened as Briley talked to herself. I shut off Jaycie's microphone for a second and listened to Briley breathing. I could hear the music growing fainter and fainter the more she moved.

"I think I found an escape route. It leads to the alleyway."

"Does it lead to the street?" Sloane asked.

"I think so, but I can't be certain. The door locks from the outside, so I don't want to risk it."

"We'll drive around," Sloane informed. I could hear the van starting up as I pressed my earpiece further in my ear to drown out flushing toilets. "Do you see us?"

"I do," Briley answered.

"Alright, Briley, start smoking. We'll get Jaycie and Trinity out there shortly."

I immediately set Jaycie's microphone back on and flushed the toilet. Going out, I rinsed my hands briefly and shook my hands off. I didn't actually go to the bathroom, so I didn't need to wash them.

"I'm sorry, maybe it's just that I'm not used to being in this formal setting." I could see Jaycie shrug as she sat down on one of the benches. "But I think I need some air."

"Go to your right, and it's the first door on your right," Briley relayed.

"Let's sneak out for a minute?" she asked. "I might be sick." She faked like she was about to throw up and held her stomach in. "Please."

"We can't get out the front," Trinity mentioned. "Um..." She looked around as Jaycie began running toward the exit Briley had told her about. "Ooh, there's one down here!" She pushed Jaycie out the doors, and when the door slammed shut I couldn't help but smile.

I could hear Jaycie puking on the ground. At first, I thought it was her faking it, but when I heard liquid hit the sidewalk I wondered if she was able to force it or if she actually had to puke. Regardless, it worked in our favor. I waited patiently on a random

　　　　　　　　　　　　　　　　　　AMY KULP

bench I found and stared at the ceiling. It truly was gorgeous.

"You okay?" Briley asked. I heard a scream from Trinity and a panicked voice.

"Oh, I didn't realize anyone else was outside with us." Trinity patted on Jaycie's back and as I listened I tried to decide if I should go outside yet. "I think she's fine. Maybe anxiety."

"Want to smoke?" Briley asked. She blew out a breath of smoke, and I felt my nose crinkle up. I hoped she didn't get addicted to nicotine now. "It helps relieve anxiety."

"Um," Jaycie said, unsure. "Will it get the taste of vomit out of my mouth?"

"Possibly," Briley said. "What about you? Do you want one? I have a whole pack."

"Uh, no thanks," Trinity said. Her voice dropped in the next instant. "I don't think you should have one. Smoking isn't good for you."

"Neither is champagne, and we had that for the first time today," Jaycie replied. I winced again when I heard her intake and then cough a bunch of times. "Okay, I don't think I like smoking." A few more coughs came out.

"Try it again. It'll get easier the more you do it." Briley sucked some more in before blowing out. I hated this. I wished they didn't have to do it.

"I think she's good," Trinity answered. "We're just going to go back to the party."

"Suit yourself," Briley said while shrugging. "Although, I think she's starting to get the nicotine in her body. That's the part that helps relieve the stress. I think you need some too. You seem awfully high-strung."

"I said I'm good."

I took the earpiece out of my ear and grabbed two more champagne glasses from a waiter. I thanked him, and when I was near the door I put the pill in the drink. Busting through, I felt the door slam into something and when I looked around I saw Trinity on the floor. Well, that wasn't supposed to happen.

"Are you okay?" I asked as I knelt to her. She held onto her head as she nodded. "Here, drinking this will help."

"No," she groaned. I forced the glass into her mouth and watched as it spilled down the sides. She swallowed some of it, but I doubted it would be enough. "I don't feel good." I nodded as I got up. Jaycie knelt next to her and helped her up. She stumbled closer to the door and when they tried to open it, she was surprised it was locked. I could see that the drugs were beginning to get into her, and she looked from Jaycie to me and then to Briley. She already seemed dazed and confused. When she turned back to Briley, she already had her arms around her and was pushing her toward the van.

Mattie immediately started it up, and Trinity immediately shook her head no. Shouting words of protest, she grabbed at her wrist, and for a moment I watched her fingers on her bracelet for a second too long. Immediately hearing commotion inside, Briley picked up the pace, and Trinity began dragging more. Soon, she would have to fully carry

                                    AMY KULP

her. Without any warning, I could see the van pull away.

"Wait, what?" I asked. I jabbed a finger in my ear but was horrified to find that I didn't have an earpiece anymore. As I stared down the alleyway longer, I could see people running. "They're her bodyguards," I whispered. "Hurry, find another door."

"Hey!" one of them yelled. "What are you doing? We're looking for Trinity!"

"In here!" Jaycie whispered to us. It was another door. Thankfully, it wasn't locked, and within a second we were all back at the party. "Now what?" she asked.

"Split up," I whispered. "Act natural. Briley, keep Trinity as normal as you can." I looked over at her and saw her head beginning to hang. She was getting loopy. "Good luck."

I separated from all of them but there was no way that Briley could get Trinity to act natural. There was no way nobody would notice a loopy girl in her arms. Briley was an eyesight to begin with. People drank up her height and her muscles. Now that she had an accessory on her arms, people were going to notice. I had to do something.

I don't think Jaycie was going to do something. She did her part. She got the girl where we needed her. How did the security guards know where to find her? How did the security guards know to come to get her then? They didn't search for her all night. What happened? Did we set something off? Did that exit have an alarm attached to it? I didn't hear an alarm.

Briley couldn't create a distraction. She was too busy slipping through crowds and trying to blend in. I don't think she's ever blended in. She is the muscles. She wasn't used to being part of the main team. She was used to protecting us and fighting her way through situations. This wasn't an event where you could just fight. Briley had other things to do.

Mattie was driving the van. I had no idea where they were. I had no idea where they were driving off to. I had no idea if she was planning to come back. But she could definitely not be the distraction. I wasn't sure if she would think of it either. This is her first assignment. Why would she purposefully disobey me?

Sloane was out of the question too. She was in the van with Mattie. Besides, if she were to get caught, our team would get screwed. Her smarts and computer-savvy were the reason we were constantly on top of things. We were able to get into the party because of her research skills on different envelopes, materials, and where to buy them. She was able to wire us enough money to get us food every day too. She was probably one of the most valuable people on our team.

This left me. I had to be the one to make the distraction. I immediately lifted my dress and let my hands travel up my thighs until I felt the holster. I slid my gun out of it and looked around me. There were a lot of people around, so I had to act quickly. I backed up against the wall and pointed my gun up. Before I could shoot, I already heard the screaming. However, I still shot at the chandelier and watched as there was a pause in movement before the chandelier started falling apart and screams and yells were heard. I slid the gun against the floor and watched as people trampled over it.

It was lost somewhere in the crowd. It couldn't be traced to me anymore.

I looked around to try and find any of my girls, but all I could see were blurs of people. People were pushing others, and there was so much movement that my eyes couldn't comprehend what I was seeing. I had to act now. I had to get out of here. I had to find my girls.

I immediately started running and pushing people too. I felt someone step on my gown, and immediately I lurched backward. Falling, it felt like a domino effect as people tripped over me. I had to push someone off me to get out of here. I crawled until I was able to get on my knees and then ripped my dress from people's shoes. I felt the dress continue to tug, but I had to keep going.

Until a pair of arms wrapped around me.

I fought against the arms, but they were clasped around me. Too tight. I stopped fighting to look over at the guy who was giving Jaycie a hard time before. Phillip, I believe his name was.

"What's your name?" he asked.

"What?" I yelled. I looked around to see other people were getting stopped too. I tried to fight to get out again, but all the doors slammed shut. What was happening? "Someone has a gun! I don't have time for this! Why are you locking us in here?"

"What is your name? I need to make sure that you are on the list."

"Someone has a gun!" I yelled. I kicked him hard to get out of his grasp, but still he wouldn't let go. I heard similar yells of protest from others. "Get off of me! Let me go!"

I continued to kick, but as I continued to stare out the doors I saw a glimpse of my muscular, tall friend. We made brief eye contact before I sighed and calmed down. Briley escaped with Trinity. That's all that needed to happen. Now, I could focus on leaving. I didn't need to distract anyone anymore. I did enough to make the mission successful.

"That girl has Trinity!"

I was dropped to the ground, and I watched as all of the security officers and police officers who were outside the building chased after her. I ran out with everyone, and as I watched the van start up and the back doors open I saw Briley throw Trinity in there. I didn't care what else happened. I wished for her and Jaycie to be in the van, but I turned around and walked the other way.

There was no way I could get in the van now, but at least I could still escape this scene.

I am Y. I am happily married, have been a part of this operation for ten years with four hundred and one successful missions, and am the FBI's third-most-wanted criminal. I am usually a team lead in missions. I was usually the reason the girls got caught. I was the reason they never escaped.

------Chapter 5

As I exhaled, I could see the fog that escaped my mouth. I tried not to focus on the dropping temperatures as I walked through the dead streets. The only people who were out right now were criminals and people trying to find a place to squat for the night. Was I one of those people now? I shook my head and convinced myself I wasn't. I knew where I had to go but as my heels clicked on the sidewalk and rubbed against the skin on the back of my foot, I knew that my damaged body may not make it much farther.

Slipping through the crowd after the incident was easy. People were so riled up and were no longer looking for who shot the gun. Nobody was looking for me anymore. However, if the policemen were good, they would know that those two events were connected. The gun would eventually be found, and my fingerprints were the ones on it. It would only be a matter of time before they realize that my fingerprints were faded and very... damaged if at all recognizable.

In my second year in this organization and we first started our new groupings and the makeover. I got the least valuable member and was tortured for it. Although I have chosen to forget most of what went on in that session, I remember the searing pain of them burning my fingertips which had ultimately, destroyed most of my fingerprints. They were damaged and it was hard to get a real read on them. I remember the excruciating pain and I remember yelling out. I remember the smell of burning flesh. I remember being held there and watching as Emmanuel chose to continue with my torture. I remember how I started to try after that. I remember actively participating instead of being a passive member. I remember that was my climb uphill.

I shuddered at the thought of the burn on my fingertips but maybe that was because of the cool air surrounding me. Even though it's been years, I couldn't help but look at my fingers as I passed by a light. There was no fire there. So why did I feel like I was burning? Why could I smell my flesh burning like it did that night?

I shook my head. I couldn't go crazy now. I needed to get back to my team and help them get Trinity where she needed to go. If they wanted to, they could have already gone. However, they needed to keep a low profile. They couldn't be speeding through lights with cameras. They had to be secretive about where they were going. Their van was caught with Trinity in it. If they were smart, they would have changed the license plate. If Sloane was smart, she would edit the license plate on any photos that could be seen.

I knew they were smart. They could survive without me. They would be chaotic. There would be fights over who got to say what. There would be fights over who had the power. While Briley was very capable of her strength, she didn't know that much about strategizing a plan. Jaycie was perfect for that, but she didn't have the muscle or the technical superpower that Sloane had. Those three needed to work together.

I hoped that Mattie just listened to what they said.

As the wind picked up around me, I couldn't help but wrap my arms around each other. Such an inappropriate dress to walk around here with. I looked around to see if anybody else was on the street, but everything seemed deserted. It figures, I didn't want to be seen and knew which streets would be abandoned. However, there was more chance of something going wrong. I knew I shouldn't be afraid because I was much worse than some of these lowly criminals down here, but I couldn't help but long for my girl's protection.

As soon as I saw the illuminated sign in the sky that read there was a vacancy, I hobbled faster to the motel. I eyed all the cars in the parking lot until a familiar van made me stop. I cocked my head to look at the license plate but was disappointed to see the exact same one. Would I have to do everything? They were better than that. I shook my head at them and knew to do it now.

I reached up and under the slit of my dress and felt for the top of my pantyhose. Despite how thin they were, they came in handy for where I could store all my gadgets. As soon as I found my pocket knife, I unhooked it from my waistband and took it out. Kneeling next to the car, I slowly turned my knife into the screw and watched as the bolt came loose. Turning it the rest of the way, I put it on the ground where I would continue to see it and eventually, managed to take the plate off it.

Okay, now I just needed to switch this with another car. I looked around in the parking lot to make sure that nobody was watching me and when I felt confident in the car next to the van, I swapped the plates without making too much noise. Probably wasn't smart to do the car that was right next to the van. At least it was smart enough for now. We could switch it to the next safe house we would go to. Or if he needed to make a pit stop somewhere else.

I just wanted to sleep and make sure my girls were all right. I wonder how Trinity was behaving for them. I wonder how they were dealing with Trinity.

Walking into the lobby, a sense of familiarity came over me. The empty desk and empty lobby were cozy. A sign on the desk said to ring if nobody was there so when I tapped the bell, I wasn't surprised to hear a commotion coming from a closed door next to it. The area was small around here with one light on the wall and one bench. Nothing else. No coffee, no cups, and no space for people to wait their turn. While it felt cozy, it smelled musty and old in here. There was probably mold somewhere in this building. It was a motel after all.

"I'm coming, I'm coming!" I looked at the door that was behind the counter and watched as a short man came out while fixing his shirt. "Oh! You look very familiar!" he said as he put his glasses on and stood in front of the computer. "Have you booked with us before?"

                    AMY KULP

"No," I lied. I felt his eyes start crawling up and down my body and I suddenly felt a creepy vibe coming from around here. "I need you to tell me what room a group of girls may have checked in at." I stepped back and did a twirl in my dress. "Clearly, they would be wearing something similar to me. We were just at a dance."

"Seems like a lot of dances happened around here," he said.

"It is New York City," I drawled on.

"Did you hear the news though? Hold on, maybe they're still playing the reruns of it." He grabbed the remote that was next to him and aimed it at the TV. Quickly turning it to a news station, we both watched as the news anchor announced that Trinity was still missing, they have the gun that was used to shoot at the birthday party and watched as she announced the prize. I felt my eyes go wide at the thought of the cash prize. As the news anchor paused to read her prompter, the screen screamed at us as breaking news overtook the screen.

"Breaking news and our top story of the hour," they announced. "Detectives have been working fast with clearing the crime scene and finding out-of-the-ordinary clues. After finding evidence that is not yet available to the public, we want you to keep your eyes out for this girl." On the screen was a very blurry picture but it was unmistakably me. You could see the blue sequins shining as I pulled out the gun. "This suspect is known as the notorious, Y. She is a leader of a human trafficking ring that has been unstoppable these past years. Keep your eyes out for her and call this number if you have any information."

Shit. I slowly turned to the man who was behind the counter, and he shakily turned the TV screen off. Not meeting my gaze, he quickly scanned the computer before looking up at me.

"I guess that's how I look familiar."

"I won't tell anyone you were here," he said. He backed against the wall, and I just shook my head.

"Damn right, you won't." I reached my hand up from under my dress again and grabbed my Taser. I held it out to him, and he backed up against the wall. Should I kill him? Or let him live? "I know that your operation here isn't one hundred percent legit. So, I think it would be in your best interest that once you wake up, you pretend this conversation has never happened."

"Once I wake up?"

I didn't give him a chance to think more than that question as I quickly hit him on top of the head with my Taser. I watched as his body flailed to the floor and waited for any moans or groans that might have escaped from his throat. After a few seconds of silence, I walked behind the counter and quickly swatted his hand away from me. Scouring through the computer, I could see exactly who was in what room and if they had already paid. I just had to find one that looked familiar...

Briley

How stupid was this girl? You don't say your name if you're a criminal! I immediately clicked on her name and edited it to say, Sarah. We didn't need

                    AMY KULP

anyone to know that we were here. Looking at their room number, I turned around to get a key with the same number on it. Stepping on this guy's ankle, I quickly dragged his body back into the room he was in and paused when I felt another presence in the room.

"I would leave if I were you," I said loudly. "Because we both know that you are not with him for his looks. Grab whatever money he owed you from his pockets and then scram."

I didn't wait to see if they listened to me. I closed the door behind me and tried to find the room where my girls were at. Thankfully, it was on the first floor.

As I walked along the edges of the green doors, I knew that I was getting closer to the room where I needed to be. If I could track these girls down, how hard was it for police officers? I felt sweat beginning to pour out of me in anticipation. I just wanted to be able to get out of this dress and heels. I wanted to be surrounded and knew that we were temporarily safe. I just wanted to finish this mission. I wanted to go back to our base.

Knocking on the door, I waited a few seconds before I realized I wasn't going to get an answer. Good. At least they weren't stupid enough to answer the door. I did our secret knock and waited a few more minutes. The breeze chilled my legs, and I knocked once again. I couldn't wait any longer. I jiggled the handle to give them a warning that I would be coming in. I scraped the keys against the hole in the door until they found their way in, and I was able to turn the knob to get inside.

Something was off about this room. I closed the door behind me and scanned the darkness around me. I wasn't attacked yet. I should have been attacked. They didn't know if I was a threat or the real deal. I quickly scanned the room as much as I could while in the dark but had to feel my hand along the wall until I found the light switches. I turned it on and was completely blind for about half a second.

To find an empty room.

I already knew something was wrong, but it would have to wait for me to go to the bathroom. I scuffled through the one bedroom to meet myself in the tiny room that had a sink and a tub with a toilet attached right next to it. I shut the bathroom door behind me despite having the room empty and quietly did what I had to do. As soon as I shoved the toilet paper down the drain, I got my knife out and peeled back the shower curtains. Okay. Nobody there.

Opening the bathroom door, I expected to see someone peeking out from the curtain. When I pushed the door further out, still, nobody was there. I peeked my head around to look at the entire room and cleared it as nobody was in there. I sighed for a moment before I ran my hands under the water and quickly dried them off.

Okay, if my girls weren't here, where were they?

I looked around the bedroom again and this time, I looked at varying parts of the room. It was disheveled: blankets were tossed around the bed, a chair was flipped over, bags of supplies were left

                    AMY KULP

open, and the alarm clock was left ringing. With my urgent search for the bathroom, I must not have heard it.

I stepped over clothes and blankets to make it to the bedside table with the red glowing numbers on it. I grabbed the little red box and immediately pressed snooze. I needed to first drown out the noise before I could figure out to turn it off. However, when I pressed snooze, the sound didn't shut off. It was a rapid beeping that was a single ping with a slight pause between each sound. It was becoming annoying fast and as I pressed every single button, slid every switch, and adjusted the dials, I couldn't turn the blasted thing off. Out of desperation to turn the noise off, I unplugged the stupid piece of plastic and listened to the beeps continue.

They weren't coming from the alarm clock.

I stayed perfectly still as I continued to listen to the noise. It sounded close to me but as I stepped closer to the door, it got softer. Okay. So, it was definitely in this room. That was concerning. Beeps... What could a beep mean? My head ran through multiple ideas before I felt my pulse quicken, my skin grow clammy, and my stomach began to turn. Was it a bomb?

The beeping wasn't increasing but do bombs notify someone when they are about to kill them? I stepped further from the door and heard the noise become louder. Okay. So, it wasn't near the entrance. So, it had to be something from my girls or from the cleaning staff. The cleaning staff didn't know we would have been there though. So, this had to be a message from my girls.

Crouching down, I listened to the beeping intensify and I quickly scoured the dark floor. My hands reached all around until my fingertips touched the fabric of the bed. Scruffy and thin but at least it would have been somewhere to sleep. I gripped the material in my finger and shook it fast. Hearing something bash against the wall, I quickly dropped what I was holding and ran toward the beeps.

A little gold bracelet was held in my hands. I walked closer to the bathroom so that I could see what it looked like, and I could feel the blood leave my face. This was the bracelet that Trinity was wearing at the party. Well, that was a good thing. My girls had made it here with the target. However, I didn't know a bracelet could beep. I looked at it again and saw a small inscription on the band.

GPS Enabled

I have never dropped the bracelet faster. I didn't allow myself time to think and instantly searched around the room for my shoes. When did I take them off? Not being able to find them under the mess I had made, the first pair of socks I found, I slipped onto my feet and ran out the door.

I had to separate myself from this scene as much as I can. Walking past the parking lot and the van, I began my journey along the sidewalks and looked for signs to point me to the nearest subway.

That explained so much! Trinity had a tracker bracelet. No wonder the security guards knew where to find her when we had her outside. It explained where my team could have gone. They knew to get out of there. They knew they needed to leave once they found that out. Why would it beep though? Wasn't the point of that to be secretive? If it was me, I would have thrown it out on the road and kept traveling.

If it was GPS enabled, I bet that Sloane buried it under the blankets. If you couldn't find the GPS, then there was no way to track her. I cursed myself as I thought about how I just dropped it. I didn't bury it at all. Now I was the stupid one.

Where was I going now? We were planning to meet at that motel. Where did I have to go now? I closed my eyes as I found my seat on the subway cart and had to think. There was a safe house not too far from here if I road it about four more stops. That wouldn't be too long of a wait.

I opened my eyes again and tried not to look around the cart. There was someone over in the corner and if I didn't bother them, they wouldn't bother me. However, I couldn't help but get goosebumps at the thought of being alone in a dress at night. I had traveled New York at night by myself before and I knew I could harm others, but it still freaked me out. I would prefer to travel in groups.

I would prefer to not have to think like this. However, I knew what kind of sick people there were in the world. Technically, I was one of them.

"What do we have here?" some random man asked as he got on. He turned to me, and his eyes lazily traveled up my dress. I rolled my eyes immediately and looked at the man from the far end.

"Touch me and I'll break your hand," I said loud enough for the guy to hear on the other end.

Would he help if I was in danger? Was I in danger? Or was this guy just drunk and stupid? Regardless, he laughed at me and shook his head. Stepping closer to me, I immediately lifted my leg between his thighs. He jolted at first and I just raised my eyebrows. Did he really want to continue this? He inched forward again, and I sighed.

Time to get up. Pushing roughly into his shoulder, his balance wavered and before he could try to grab onto me or the pole next to him, I pushed my leg out to hook behind his knee. He fell flat on his back and just looked at the ceiling. I smirked as I leaned back in my seat.

"You're crazy!" he yelled. He turned over and scrambled near the guy in the corner. "It's always the ugly ones who think everyone is hitting on them."

He continued to mumble under his breath at me, but I was too pleased with myself. He backed off so I didn't need to hurt him anymore. As I stared smugly at him, I noticed that the man in the corner was now actively staring at me. I averted my eyes immediately and when the subway doors opened, I moved out.

This wasn't my stop, but this would be good enough. I wasn't stupid enough to see what the silent man on the subway was going to do. I shook my head and immediately darted up the stairs.

Okay, I just needed to get to the safe house. That wasn't too far from here, but I knew that I was going to regret it. My feet were already frozen from the cold concrete. I sped up my walk but even as I got outside, I knew that the air had gotten colder.

                                      AMY KULP

My breath was more noticeable, and I had to pause to acclimate from the temperature change. As I leaned against the building and breathed in heavily, my ears picked up a distant noise. I tried not to make my turn noticeable as I watched a figure come up the steps from the subway.

The silent man.

I closed my eyes but knew to book it. He better not be following me. I sped up my walk to get farther than him and immediately took the first right I could find. I walked down the small alleyway and could hear his footsteps behind me. Okay, he was following me.

I took a random left now. I stared at the dead end and walked slower until I reached the dumpster. I crouched behind it and waited to listen for him. I closed my eyes and made myself as small as I could. Maybe I could blend in with the other trash behind the dumpster.

I could hear his footsteps. If he was trying to be quiet about the situation, he was doing it wrong. After a few seconds of silence, I peeked my head around the corner and noticed he was gone. I sighed in relief and stood back up.

It was probably too risky to go to the safe house right now. I needed to just find a random hotel for my stay tonight and hope that I could get a good night's sleep. I had to get to that safe house eventually. I couldn't let my reputation hang on the line for this mission. She would be just another successful case, or I wasn't me. It didn't fit my reputation.

I am Y. I am happily married, have been a part of this operation for ten years with four hundred and one successful missions, and am the FBI's third-most-wanted criminal. I am usually a team lead in missions. I was usually the reason the girls got caught.

-------Chapter 6

I wish I could say that when I opened my eyes, I was refreshed and peaceful. However, I woke up to a cart rolling past my door and the sunshine glaring through the window. I instantly panicked and tried to feel for my gun on the nightstand. As I looked around, I noticed it wasn't there and couldn't help but remember that I shot that gun last night. I threw that gun. I wondered if they were able to get the fingerprints from my gun. I knew they would barely be viable but what if there was a small patch of skin that was unharmed? Could there be?

Instead, I grabbed my knife that was under the pillow and slipped it up my pantyhose so that I didn't have to keep my grip on it. I felt a pain in my breasts and knew it was time to get up. I had to dodge around the mysterious and gross stains in the carpet and crawl so people couldn't see through my window as I went to the bathroom because of the broken curtain. I instantly closed the dividers so that I had a bit of privacy.

Since I was separated from the van, I was forced to stay in my dress and dirty socks. I was tired and I felt gross but after escaping my silent stalker, I ran to the first motel I could find. Unfortunately, they were the dirtiest motel I have ever stayed at. Served me right for getting a room so late. However, as I came in here last night, I did manage to notice that the cheap owner had a gift shop.

If anything, I could buy some clothes there.

First, I had to get rid of the pain that was developing. I knew what it meant. If I didn't follow the schedule that I had laid out for myself every five hours, I got the same exact pain. It was easy for me to follow it before we captured Trinity, but now it was proving to be difficult. I grabbed toilet paper from the bathroom roll and applied pressure. When the pain started to relieve itself, I flushed the paper down and quickly excused myself from the bathroom, and went back to the sink area.

Splashing my face with water, I patted myself dry and continued to splash more on until my face was makeup free and rubbed raw. Next was my hair: I took the bobby pins out that held my hair together and then stuck my hair under the faucet of the tub. I needed to somehow wash this hairspray out and this motel was too cheap to provide little shampoos, conditioners, or soaps. They didn't even provide clean towels. I already threw the towel they provided onto the ground from the suspicious stain that was on it. I didn't want to know what had caused it and I wasn't willing to take any chances that it wouldn't give me some sort of disease or wart.

Letting my hair drip down my back, I knew there was nothing more I could do. I wanted to finger-comb it but that seemed like it would be a difficult task because of my thick mane. I attempted but when the first knot snagged around my knuckles, I grimaced and gave up. I just needed to

    AMY KULP

go to the gift shop and buy some clothes now. Hopefully, they had some sort of shoes too - I have no idea where I put my heels, but I did not want to wear those even if I found them.

Tripping through the battlefield that was my room, I shoved the keycard into my bra and immediately pulled out my emergency card. Hopefully, Sloane added more money to it. I knew that the funds would be running out because of how expensive they made my last-minute reservation. Definitely not worth the price.

"Morning," one of the cleaning men said as they came out of the room next to mine.

I gave them a weak smile and tried to not glance too much at them before I felt a shiver of worry run through me. I walked faster to the gift shop and looked over my shoulder once to see that the cleaning man had now gone into my room. Nothing suspicious. Nothing weird about that.

Except that was the man who had followed me last night. He was on the subway, and he was the quiet man. I was sure of it. I was sure that was the man who had freaked me out. I hurried out of sight until I made it into their small shop to look around. I had to get a better look at his face the next time I saw him.

Stepping into the shop was very disappointing. It was barely bigger than the sizes of the rooms. However, I could see T-shirts. I immediately walked over to the overpriced materials and scoured for my size. Once I found it, I scoured the rest of the area for any pants or shoes that I could find. Rummaging through blankets and other useless gifts that they had, I knew that this place didn't sell shoes or pants. I had to get out of this dress though. I already saw the attention of the gift shop cashier. I didn't want to cause any more attention. Walking back over to the hoodies that they had, I dropped the shirt off on that rack and looked at their largest size. Grabbing it, it might be large enough to cover me up. I had to take that risk.

"Can I help you find anything?" the cashier asked as she came over to me. I nodded my head and looked at the tag again on the hoodie. Way too expensive. I smiled over at her as she looked me up and down again. "Do you want a smaller size?" she wondered. She scoured through the rack and pulled out what she thought my size was.

"Actually," I mentioned as I stared down at her face. "Can I buy your shoes?" She stopped for a second before looking down at her dirty, busted-up shoes. "I can also trade this dress," I offered. I looked at her as her face went through a mix of emotions. "You look young, I bet you could use this for prom."

"It is pretty," she mumbled as she looked at it longingly.

"And it's worth more than those shoes," I mentioned. I grabbed some money that I had stuffed in my bra and brought out a crinkled one-hundred-dollar bill. "And I can give you this."

"I don't know, I can get fired for not following the dress code." She looked at her shoes again before looking over my dress again. I felt myself becoming impatient with her indecisiveness but knew to remain quiet. However, as she thought

　　　　　　　　　　　　　　　　　AMY KULP

it over, I saw her glance at the door as the chimes came on. She smiled at me, but I knew that she was going to leave. After all, she had to greet the new customer. I looked behind me and felt my face flush instantly.

"Do you have a bathroom?"

"Yes, in the back. Merchandise can't go there though."

I nodded my head and when she walked away, I knelt and grabbed her ankle. Tripping, she landed with a thud, and I frantically untied her shoes. I could not go around New York without shoes. Who knew how many times my feet would be stepped on? Who knew what I could accidentally step on?

"I'm sorry, I really need these. Here's the money and the dress will be in the bathroom on the floor," I whispered. I forced the bill into her mouth and watched as she became repulsed by it. She gagged and spat it out, but she only watched me with wide eyes. I thanked her secretly and rushed to the back of the store.

I had no idea where this bathroom was. I opened random doors until I got to the one that read for employees only. I closed it quietly and tore the dress from my body in an instant. I threw the oversized hoodie on and felt it reach just below my thighs. I had to be very careful. I chose to keep my nylons on and forced my foot into the too-small of shoes. I tucked the dress neatly away under the sink and looked at myself once in the mirror before opening the door.

I forced my attention to go toward the front of the store and saw the employee behind the register again. She kept nodding her head and barely added anything to the conversation. There was no way I could exit through the front without that man seeing me. Who was he? Why was he following me? I already spent too long just watching them though. I had to get out of here.

Maybe there was some employee exit that I could manage to go through. I walked around in the backroom and went through another restricted access area. My toes felt tight the more steps I took but I knew that I needed to keep wearing the shoes. I needed to look as normal as I could. Clearly, this quiet man was following me.

He could have been anyone: a cop, some weird stalker, a rival gang, or even worse, he could be someone sent to check up on me. After all, I am separated from my group. They can't take any chances that I will leave and rat them out. After all, I don't have the privilege to leave and go as I please. I wouldn't have anywhere to go anyway. My home is this organization.

"Is there anyone back here?" the cashier yelled. I ducked behind some boxes and could see her looking around. I had to stay quiet. She wasn't suspicious and didn't seem like a threat to me. However, the guy she was just talking to did feel like a threat to me. "It doesn't seem like she's here."

"Is there another exit back here?" he asked.

I squatted even lower and kept my vision blocked. I didn't want to risk looking at them and having them see the top of my head. I listened to

                    AMY KULP

them look around the room and I could hear them get closer to me. I closed my eyes shut but knew that sitting there would lead them right to me.

I needed to bolt but I wasn't sure where they were. I focused for a moment and listened to their murmurs coming from the right of me. If I just stayed left, I should be fine. I needed to avoid them until I could find the front. Once I got to the front, I just needed to run. I was athletic, I could do it. Especially now that I'm wearing shoes.

Leaving the safety of my box, I stayed low as I made a left. I found myself behind a tall stack of merchandise and could see the man walking around. I had to assume the girl was now back up front. He was on a mission to find me. Why would the girl tell him that I was here though? Did he threaten her? Did she know him? When he started moving toward where I just was, I moved forward.

Walking briskly, I cut myself off to go back toward the front. He didn't seem to see me since his back was toward me, but I heard the girl yell for him. Running out of there, I tipped over a display of shirts and ran through the front. I just needed to get to the front and blend in. I could blend in. I have been doing this for ten years. I could do this.

Allowing myself to fit in, I went at the same speed as those around me. The sweatshirt was grey, so the dull color of the crowd helped me to blend in. I was cold without having pants on, but I tried not to make it that noticeable. I walked about fifteen minutes before I heard my stomach growl.

No way that man was still following me, right? I wasn't even sure he saw me turn out of the store. He just heard the cashier yell after me. Did she see which way I went? It didn't matter though because I went every which way after that turn. I had no idea where I was. I just knew that I was hungry.

Along with that, I felt the pain in my breasts again and knew I had to go somewhere. I would have to use my card though. Maybe if I used my card, Sloane would be able to find me. Although, their main goal was to get Trinity where she needed to be. Hopefully, they were worried about me too.

I knew that I would probably not work with any of these girls again, but I was beginning to care about them. I did it with every group I worked with. I wanted to make sure they were safe. I worried about all of them. It's why I was possibly the weakest link in every group. I would never be able to leave anyone behind. They were my team. This team specifically was making history. We were proving that we didn't need any males. We were just fine working by ourselves. This had to be one of the most important missions too.

Stopping in at the first cafe I saw, I was astounded at how long the line was. I waited though. I would much rather get food than go to the bathroom right now. Even with the tenderness of my skin, I knew it could hold off for a little bit. Until I got my breakfast at least.

"Excuse me," a male voice said from behind me. My back immediately tensed up. "My table is over there." There was a nudge that sent everyone scooting closer to the person ahead of them, but I didn't move. I allowed the person to bump into me

                                      AMY KULP

and scoff that I wasn't polite enough. However, once again, that man was in the cafe.

That man had found me again.

My eyes wandered where he was and when I was able to stare forward and see him from my peripheral vision, I could see he sat down with someone else. Another male. This one looked eerily similar from the back: his hair was dark black and was greased to stay exactly like he styled it yesterday. Too bad I couldn't see the face though.

"Ma'am?" I shook my head to see the smiling face ahead of me. Oh, it was my turn. I stepped forward and gave my order. Within five minutes, it was out and as I turned to see who the man was talking to, I was disappointed to see that he was gone.

Okay, well, I couldn't dwell on it. I took a seat far away from that man. He couldn't do anything to me while I was in public. I would have to make sure that I was able to get away though. Maybe slip out without him knowing. I went near the entrance and found the closest seat. I sat down and took a bite.

His back was to me, but I could see him. I could stare at him without worrying. I did. I'm sure he could feel me staring. I'm sure he wasn't just enjoying his drink in this particular cafe. He was following me. I wanted to know why but that wasn't my goal. I had to lose him. Every time I thought I did, he was still right behind me. How could I not lose him?

I dropped my sandwich on the napkin I placed on the table and felt another pain shoot through my chest. I grasped the area and cursed myself. I waited too long. I kept my eyes on him as I got up and scooted to the bathroom. Maybe he wouldn't notice I was gone.

Thankfully, the bathroom was completely empty. I grabbed some paper towels and instantly stuffed them in my shirt for a second. After a moment, I pulled them out and shoved them into the garbage can again. I reached my hand down and made sure to keep it low in the can. I didn't want anyone to find those paper towels.

Holding the door for someone to enter, I was able to see that the man was gone from his table. Confused at first, I let go of the door and almost started walking back to my table. I quickly stopped when I saw the greasy hair of the quiet man's friend who was putting my breakfast sandwich into a baggie. I crinkled my eyebrows and continued to watch. He grabbed my cup too but just swabbed it with a cotton swab. Leaving it on the table and a small fraction of my breakfast sandwich, he dodged out of the cafe within a second.

Not wasting any time, I followed the man out but by the time I was on the pavement, I could not figure out where he was. I looked around but the crowds of New York made me start walking. If I couldn't find them, that means they were good at what they did. Putting my things in a bag? He had to be a cop. Same with the quiet man.

I turned around causing a little stir in the people around me. I couldn't wait though. I had to go back to my motel room and pay my bill to leave. If they were cops, I would certainly be arrested if I

                                    AMY KULP

went after that. Why else would they put my stuff in a bag? It had to be an evidence bag. They need my DNA.

Pulling my key from my bra, I slammed the door behind me and looked at the mess of the room. I definitely did not leave it like this. I don't think I left anything important in this room but if I did, it would have been found by that man. I sidestepped all the garbage in my room before going to the bathroom again. I closed the door behind me and paced in the tiny available space.

I didn't know what to do. I opened the lid to the toilet and bent down instantly. Coming out of me was a mix of bile, nerves, butterflies, and the breakfast sandwich. I flushed as soon as I was done and felt my face lose its color. I shouldn't be this nervous. I have had close calls before. But every time I've had close calls, I've been with my group. I'm alone.

I knew this mission wasn't a good idea.

That thought vanished from my brain when I listened to the noise coming from outside of the bathroom. I knew that I had the 'do not disturb' sign on my door so it wasn't housekeeping. That's why my room was still a mess. They haven't been able to see it or clean it. I didn't want anyone in this room. I should've known this morning. Why didn't I think about that sign this morning? More warning bells would have gone off in my head.

I opened my door and grabbed the knife that I had on me. I wasn't going to get arrested. If anything, I was going to fight to my death. That's what I was told to do. If anything, I can harm them and then they wouldn't be able to work. The fewer people trying to take us down, the smaller chance that we'll get caught.

When my door opened, I charged at the figure in the door. Knife out, I swung it and knew that I connected with someone. However, this figure caved and let me continue to hit them. That was unusual for a cop, right? I tried to look at the face, but it was too dark in here. When I felt another pair of hands on my arms, I felt my nerves race through me. Looks like it was going to be two against one.

"Y, stop!" My movements slowed for a second before I blinked and could see Mattie underneath me. I looked up and saw Jaycie hit me. Crashing on top of me, I got off Mattie and felt her scramble up. She closed the door so nobody could see what was happening and after a few seconds of catching my breath, I smiled.

"I never thought that I would see you guys again!" Even though Jaycie was on me to protect Mattie, I ended up hugging her. "Where are Briley and Sloane?"

"In the van," Jaycie mentioned. She got off me and I instantly moved to Mattie.

"Are you okay?" I asked. She didn't move but she did look at Jaycie. "Come into the light." She followed my direction, and I could see a slash that I had made on her cheek. "Let's get some cool water on that." I brought her over to the sink and ran a towel under the faucet. She didn't need to know it was dirty. I placed it on the cheek and could see her wince. "I'm sorry. I'm being-"

　　　　　　　　　　　　　　　　　　

"Followed?" Jaycie asked. "We know." She grabbed the bag she had and took out hair dye box. "We're going to change what you look like." I looked at her. "They were following us. We need to give you a makeover and fast. I bought a random dye and at least that way, they won't be able to find you in the crowds."

"I saw your guy's hotel room," I mentioned.

"Trinity had a tracker on," Jaycie replied as she poured some water over my hair. "Get your head wet. Mattie is here to help as well. I've never dyed hair, but she has."

"Sloane and Briley?"

"Sloane is watching cameras for a sight of any of those guys that were following us. I'm sorry, you walked right into their trap. We had no way to warn you. Briley is there to keep Trinity under control. She's tired so she's not fighting much anymore."

"You didn't take her to a safe house yet?" I asked as I felt the hair dye being applied to me. Looks like I would be a blonde for a while.

"We couldn't risk being followed to the safe house," she replied. "Besides, if we did, we would still have gone back to try and find you." I nodded my head as both washed their hands. "We're glad you're back. Sloane pinged your card use so we followed you from the cafe to your motel room. You're slick between crowds."

"Apparently not slick enough," I remarked. I looked over at Mattie and watched as she just stared at me. "How are you holding up?" She barely smiled at me. "Are you hurting anywhere else?" She nodded her head no but did leave my side. When she came back, she shoved a bag of clothes at me. I looked in them and saw some jeans, a black top, and some boots. I would fit in perfectly. "Thanks." I changed right in front of them and was careful not to get the dye all over me. When it was time, I washed it out in the bathtub and Jaycie helped me style it after cutting it.

"At least for now, you look different."

"It's not enough," I whispered.

"It's not." Jaycie shook her head and grabbed the bag. "Pay for your room and come to the van."

I nodded my head and did that. As soon as I knocked on the back door, I heard the lock and crawled in. It smelled bad and I had to assume it was because of Trinity. I could see the fear in her eyes, but she didn't struggle or move.

"Hey, Y," Briley said. I looked over at her and without any warning, her fist flew to my face. I immediately covered my face with my hands as the blow cracked my nose. "I've always wanted to do that."

"Sorry," Jaycie said as she came over to me. She put her hand on my back and I straightened up. She handed me a cloth to help with the bleeding. "But now, you won't be as recognizable."

"Jeez, thanks," I said. I looked up and was able to see Mattie in the front seat again. Her gaze was fixed out the window. "How are you, Briley?"

"It's been pretty boring without you. I want to fight."

"Well, our main goal is to get Trinity out of here. If that means we don't fight, we don't fight." I turned to Sloane who had her nose up to the computer screen. "Sloane?"

"We're ready to transport," she finally said. She pushed her glasses up her nose and smiled at me. "You look good with blonde hair." I only nodded my head. "We have a car that we want you to take separate from us."

"Oh?"

"When we realized Trinity had a tracker, Briley was able to hotwire a car. We just want to make sure you are not being followed," Sloane mentioned.

"And if I am?"

"Our mission is to get Trinity to a safe house. We have had someone following us since you have been gone. When they found you, they stopped following us in favor of you," Briley mentioned. "You're our leader."

She didn't have to say much else. I understood. I had to think about the group. Not myself. I only nodded as my answer. They didn't need anything else from me. I had led them and trained them on our mission, and they were ready to implement it. They didn't need me. I nodded again and saw all their eyes on me - even Mattie's through the mirror.

"Well, what are we waiting for?" I asked. Briley nodded her head, and I opened the door again.

Hopping out, I looked around the parking lot to see if anybody was in their cars. However, it was dark once again. I couldn't see anything. I did know that the car running was the one for me. I got in and watched Mattie back out. I knew that I needed to follow them.

Putting my foot on the gas, I slowly followed them. Mattie knew not to go directly to our location. She knew to take multiple circles so that it was easier to see if someone was following us. As soon as we went around the block once again and we passed the motel, I watched a car start and pull out.

Instantly, my nerves were killing me. Were they going to follow me? My eyes darted to the road and then to my mirror about fifty times. I got in the lane next to Mattie and made a quick glance. We both started and as I cut in front of her, I watched the car that was following me get in front of me. Speeding ahead, my breath caught, and I changed my lane again. I allowed Mattie to get in front of me and as I cut in front of another car, I looked back to see just how close they were to my bumper.

Assholes.

I rolled my eyes and forced myself to pay attention to the road. We only had two more lights before we were on the freeway. However, as the light turned yellow, I watched Mattie floor it and cursed. I would have to speed to catch up with her. I stopped my car though and felt my rage boiling in me again. She was a new driver, but we needed to be together. I didn't know the exact route of the safe house - only Mattie did.

This light was going to take forever too. I popped some gum in my mouth to ease the tension and looked over at the car next to me. They were blaring their music too loud and were revving their engine. They weren't going to impress anyone like that.

Turning green, I forced my car to speed up. I had to catch up to Mattie. I could see the van because she was stopped at the second light, but it was going to be a pain to get right behind her. Chewing the gum faster. I slipped my car between two that were too close. If you're in the fast lane, you need to go fast.

Seeing red and blue flash behind me, I cursed. However, when I moved out of the way and they didn't pull up behind me, my breath caught. They were following the van. I could see Mattie pulling off to the side and knew that I couldn't allow them to be pulled over.

"I am Y. I am happily married, have been a part of this operation for ten years with four hundred and one successful missions, and am the FBI's third- most-wanted criminal. I am usually a team lead in missions, and I can do this."

I pressed my foot harder on the gas and felt the entire car accelerate. I turned the car so that it was aimed right at the cop. I closed my eyes when I felt the impact of the accident. When my world stopped spinning and I opened them back up, I could see the van speed away before my vision was filled with red.

--------Chapter 7

Waking up, I knew something was wrong when I couldn't move my arms. Every time I tried, I heard a jangle of metal clinking together. I popped one eye open to try and see what was happening but was blinded by stark white walls, roof, and flooring. From the beeps around me and small chatter, I knew that I was in some type of hospital. While I didn't feel the pain my body was in at first, I could feel it as I struggled to get comfortable - bruises were probably all over my body, maybe I broke a bone or two, there were gashes on my face, and I was just sore.

"I don't think she should get any more time in this hospital. Clearly, she's faking her sleep!" someone said. He sounded angry, but I wasn't sure if it was directed toward me. However, I knew to just keep my eyes closed. "Is there a way to see if she's faking?"

"Sir, you are not allowed in this room," a calming voice soothed.

"Hell yes, I am! She crashed into my patrol car on purpose! I have a right to give her a piece of my mind."

"Sir, do not make me call the security guard."

"On an injured police officer? She is a criminal! She ran into me on purpose!"

"Sir," the calming voice said again. I could hear the agitation and was surprised that they weren't slowly losing their minds with this man. Despite the nurse defending me, I knew he was right.

I did drive right into him. However, I wasn't sure he knew who I was. Maybe none of them knew that I was the notorious human trafficker. I opened my eyes just in case they were going to test me. I wasn't exactly sure if they had the tools to be able to tell if someone was faking asleep or not. However, it wasn't very comfortable having both of my hands handcuffed to the bed. I deserved it though. After all, I ran full speed ahead toward a police car. They probably feared for their lives.

"You're awake," the nurse said. I looked over at her standing in the doorway and just nodded my head. Maybe I could play the innocent game. "Dearie, what's your name?" she asked. I crunched my eyebrows down and looked at her. They didn't know who I was. That was good. "Do you know where you are?" I looked around like I was confused. "Do you know why you're here?" she questioned. I nodded my head. I could really play this up if I wanted to. They had no idea if I was guilty or not.

"My foot got caught on my gas and I tried to veer off the road so I wouldn't hit anyone." I coughed to show that I was in pain but for once, there was nothing there. I wasn't hurt there. Just everywhere else on my body. "Did I hit someone?" I asked. The nurse must not have been good at poker because her face said it all. I forced tears to crawl up to my eyes by pinching part of my bruised thighs. "Are they okay?"

"Well," she started.

"I knew she was faking it!" I looked toward the door and saw the policeman I had hit roll up to me. For an instant, I felt guilty since I must have hurt his legs. After that instant, I knew I didn't feel sorry. He would try to take down the entire organization I was at. He probably thought something was wrong with it. Let's be real, if those girls wanted to escape it so bad, they would kill themselves when they had the chance. Trinity wasn't even fighting anyone when I was in the van. She gave up and was okay with what was happening to her. "You are a criminal!"

"We are going to need security here," the nurse said on the phone. She looked over at me as I struggled to fend off the hits of this policeman. I wanted to brace but every time I tried, the handcuffs dug harder and harder into my wrists. I cried out to try and get sympathy points from the nurse but truthfully, it did hurt. Everywhere he hit seemed to be a bruise.

I was surprised we were both alive, to begin with.

"Sir, you need to calm down," a security guard said as he came into the room. He restrained the man and wheeled him right out of the room. When the security guard came back in, he escorted the nurse out and came back in. Was it my turn to leave? He came up close to me and when I thought he was going to release my wrists, he bent down closer. "You hurt one of us," he mumbled. "Next time, I won't be here to protect you."

"I don't know what you're talking about," I mentioned. "Did I hurt him?"

"I got it from here, thank you." I looked over at the doorway as a doctor came flitting in. Next to him were two police officers. My face dropped as I recognized one of them, but I tried to stay composed. "You came out remarkably safe after your incident," the doctor said as he sat down on his chair. He signed into the computer and looked over my chart. "We cannot pinpoint who you are but as of right now, you just have a few bruises and cuts up and down your body. Do you have any questions?"

"Why are they here?" I nudged my chin toward the two officers. One of them kept a stone face but the other that I knew just smirked at me. I felt myself gulp but looked back toward the doctor before I gave away that I knew him. Maybe I should never play poker either.

"We do not know what your intentions were with your accident. I recommend lawyering up when you get out of here because as of right now, it is considered an act against a police officer."

"What are you talking about? Did I hit that man in the wheelchair?"

"Save it for your lawyers," one of the officers said. "The doctor has cleared you to go to jail and we are here to transport you."

He was rough with me and didn't seem to care that I was just in an accident and I had just woken up. Once the handcuffs were off me, I didn't have much longer before my hands were behind my back with the attached metal wrist warmers. Being pushed around, I could feel the anger radiating from him. Same with the security guard. They all seemed to be on power trips. Maybe that's why they wanted to be police officers.

I knew to keep quiet though. The less I said, the less that could be used against me. However, I didn't plan to be in prison for long. Especially if they didn't charge me with a crime yet. That means I would be in holding. Holding was probably the easiest part of prison. From all the seminars I have done, it has been said that it was much easier to escape holding than it was to escape jail or a maximum-security prison. I had to make my escape soon and I knew exactly how to do that.

"Will you be fine in the car with her?" the police officer asked as I sat down. He slammed the door behind me, and I watched them as they had a quick chat. I wish I knew what they were saying but it didn't seem to be important as the police officer waved goodbye to me. Obviously, it wasn't the usual, friendly wave. He seemed sarcastic with it. I watched as he got into his own patrol car before my police officer came into my van.

"Reggie," I whispered under my breath. He looked back at me and smirked a bit. His mustache hair prodded his nose, and he adjusted the mirror before following the other car. "Why are you posing as a cop?" I wondered.

"Not here," he grumbled. He pointed to various equipment pieces that were on his vest and in his car. There was a computer, video camera, and

                                   AMY KULP

what seemed to be a walkie-talkie system on his bullet-proof vest. I just nodded my head. I understood.

Right now, Reggie was infiltrating the police system as a cop. I'm not sure how he got the credentials to become a police officer but knowing his background, I knew he was trusted. He enjoyed causing people pain at our organization. I could only imagine what he would do if he was a police officer. He would be the bad one who used his power to get what he wanted. After all, that's how he was in control of Mattie.

We must've driven for what felt like an hour before he started pulling away from the other patrol car. After getting behind them in the lights, he took an odd turn and stopped the car. He took off his walkie-talkie and immediately exited the car. When he got out, it only took him about a minute to come over to my seat and open my door. He ushered me out and I have never been so grateful to stretch my legs.

"Why would they trust you to be a police officer?" I asked. He shrugged his shoulders and brought me closer to the end of the alleyway. When he turned around, I could see an evil look on his face.

"You know," he mentioned. "You have always been a thorn in my side."

"And I want it to stay that way," I promised. The hairs on my arms started to stand up and suddenly, I felt goosebumps raising up too. "How am I going to get out of this? I'm on a mission right now."

"And I'm on a mission too," he replied. "I can't just let you leave."

"So why am I here?" I wondered. "Why not take me back to the prison?" I watched as a wicked grin spread across his face. I looked back to the car and noticed how it blocked off the entire alleyway. When I looked back, Reggie was already right next to me. "There has to be some sort of tracker to know that you are not en route with the other car."

"They know," he said. "What do you think we were talking about when you were inside the car?" he wondered. "I'm a man, I have needs," he replied.

"Which you get from Mattie," I replied dryly. It grossed me out to even mention her name in front of him. Nobody deserved to be put through that.

"I forgot about my precious assistant," he said. He emphasized assistant in such a nasty way that I felt bile climb up my throat. He had a mischievous grin on his face and got closer to me. I refused to allow him to think that he frightened me though, so I stayed put. Eventually, he placed a finger on my cheek and dragged it down. "You see, the other officers hate people who purposely try to kill their brothers and sisters on the force." I just watched him as he dragged his finger to my lips. Repulsed, I shooed his finger away. He lightly tapped me on the cheek. "And a lot of girls are willing to do more because they are misled into thinking that doing me favors will reduce their sentence." He put his hand back on my cheek and started tracing my lip again.

　　　　　　　　　　　　　　　　　　AMY KULP

"Do not touch me," I said. I moved my face but this time, he grabbed my hair so that I faced him. "How dare you touch me? You know that I am married."

"I don't see a wedding band," he mentioned.

"It's your boss!"

"What happens if I told you that your husband gave me permission to torture you if you weren't doing your job correctly?" His finger began tracing my lips again and he slowly inserted a finger in my mouth. I bit down hard and felt a sting across my cheek. "Listen to me." He pushed me against the wall and for once, I realized how strong he was. He was right though; my husband wasn't here to protect me. I had to fight this myself.

Maybe it was a test. Maybe I had to defeat Reggie and get to my girls. My husband would never allow me near Reggie. He was vile, disgusting, sleazy, and creepy. The only reason he was kept around was because he listened and did whatever was asked of him. Granted, he did usually get physical with the girls we brought in, but it made them listen. That was usually the breaking point for some of them. However, it wasn't for me. I listened. I did what I needed to. I was rarely ever the weakest link. I had a hard time believing that my husband would give him permission to touch me or teach me a lesson.

Whatever delusional comment Reggie wanted to believe my husband made to him.

"I don't believe you," I finally said.

"So, why aren't you fighting back?" he asked as one hand stayed on my neck and the other traveled down my body. I tried to bring up an arm to hit him but was struck with the realization that I had handcuffs on.

"You are a pig!" I shook my head. I can't believe he did this to his female prisoners too. I lifted my leg and kicked him away from me. His body barely moved. "Help!" I yelled. I tried to yell louder but he squeezed my throat harder.

"Nobody will hear you," he whispered to me. I tried to yell out again but this time, I didn't have enough air to yell. "If you comply, this will be so much easier. If you don't, I'll tell them that you tried to kill me in the squad car."

"Where's the proof?" I asked. He looked at me like I was crazy. "You pointed to the camera and the laptop when you were telling me to shut up." He let go of my throat and I was able to gasp. The air hurt when it came in, but I was thankful that I was given the opportunity to fill my lungs again. "They shut off instantly when you turned the car off." I paused as I watched his confusion. "I saw the light turn off."

"Who would believe you over me?" he asked. "I'm a police officer-"

"With a sketchy past!" I interrupted. He let go of me entirely and watched my movement. "I don't know what credentials they made up on your resume to get this job, but someone has to be wondering how you were hired." He opened his mouth to argue but I beat him to it. "And all of the female prisoners would start talking if one person spoke up." I shook my head. "Don't underestimate girls when we work together."

"And how's your little experiment with your girls?" he asked. "How's Mattie? Jaycie? Briley? Sloane?" He paused. "Oh, wait, you wouldn't know. You aren't there with them! Instead, you were stupid enough to get caught for the dumbest reason."

"It was me or the group."

"And if you return, you will be labeled as the weakest link," he mentioned. "Which means you will get tortured. Do you want to be tortured by fifty men? Or would one suffice?" he wondered. "Given the choice, of course."

"Neither because when I get back there, they will be so impressed that-"

"Do you want to be tortured by me or fifty men? I won't ever tell anyone you were here. You can get out of here. Start a life out of here."

"I love my life here," I whispered. Reggie could sense the little bit of hesitation I had and smiled. "I love my husband!"

"Do you ever wonder what your life was like before this organization?" he asked. I stopped trying to argue for a moment and stared at him. "Do you remember?" he wondered. I stood there for a moment. "If you get out of here, you could learn what happened to you. You could learn about the life you had before this." I shook my head no. "Why not?" he wondered.

"I like my life here. Clearly, my life was bad if I left it to come here."

"You..." Reggie stopped for a moment. "You really don't remember?" he questioned.

"Remember what?" I felt tears start forming in my eyes. "All I remember is every time I ask

Emmanuel about it, he hurts me. I figured I didn't need to know."

"That's not love," Reggie said. He stepped closer to me and put his arms around me. I allowed myself to be taken in with his hug. "I can show you what love is, Emily."

"Emily?" I wondered. I stepped back and looked at him. "Did you love an Emily before coming here?"

He looked at me for a second with a look of pity. He shook his head and put his hand in his pocket. When he brought it back out, I could see a tiny key ring. He stepped closer to me and undid my hands. I instantly flexed my fingers and started stretching out my wrists. He stepped closer to me, and I allowed him to hug me again. When we broke apart, he leaned down to kiss me on the lips and I allowed it.

At least for a second.

I used all my strength to push him away from me. He was taken aback and quickly lost his balance. I made sure to jab him in the throat as he made his descent down and only knew I was successful when he began coughing uncontrollably. I crouched over him and thought it was a good time to smirk at him. I knew that I could have run and probably gotten away but that didn't feel good. I wanted to rub it in his face that I was able to take him by surprise.

Grabbing the handcuffs that were on his belt, I wrapped each around his wrist. I made sure to strangle his wrists by tightening them a notch too much. Maybe it was his turn to wear the handcuffs.

"You're making a mistake," he warned.

"I'll make sure to let Emmanuel know of the betrayal to him," I mentioned. "Have fun being the one tortured."

"You have to finish your mission first," he yelled. "I doubt that it'll be that easy to take a famous actor's daughter out of sight of all of New York City."

"We've done it for three days already," I mentioned. "We can do it even longer. I told you to stop underestimating girls, Reggie. Maybe now you'll start to listen."

He was shouting other things, but I didn't listen as I made my way out of the alleyway. Quietly, I jumped from the top of the cruiser and debated whether I should take the cruiser for a joyride. It would be a lot faster to get to my journey to my group. They were supposed to be at the safe house already and I knew that they could have left me behind if they were advanced enough. I was hoping they weren't though.

If they thought that I had disappeared and abandoned the mission, they would send people after me. They would return me alive - most likely, barely alive - and then I would be a prisoner. Nothing would be able to save me from that. Not even Emmanuel or Jaycie or Briley or Carlos or anyone. I would be tortured. They would practice torturing techniques on me and I would be the guinea pig.

*Hey, how much do you want to break the law?" I asked as I came across a group that was hanging outside of a restaurant. I threw them the keys without a second word. "It's the patrol car blocking the alleyway. Don't ask any questions and you can keep them."

I continued walking forward without a care in the world. They would either try it out or think I was crazy and throw the keys away. Either way, I would not associate myself with the crime. I had a place to be.

As I walked with the different crowds of pedestrians, I listened to sirens coming toward me and smirked. They took me up on that offer. Before I could see the damage, they could cause, I started heading down toward the subways.

I just needed to blend in and get to where I was going. I didn't know where I was though and knew that would be my biggest mission. I couldn't ask anyone though because then I would stick out. I wasn't a tourist. I needed to know my landscape well and while I did study the map before going on this adventure with my girls, I didn't memorize it. Now I had to try and remember exactly what subway took me where and if it could lead me mostly to my safe house.

I didn't let myself relax until I got onto the crowded subway though. I found myself a seat despite people already standing and allowed myself to take a calming breath. Nothing about my life allowed me to be calm. Nothing about my life allowed me to be normal.

So why did I think that my marriage with Emmanuel was normal? He loved me and I knew he did. However, did any of Reggie's comments mean anything? Was anything he said useful? What was my life like before this? Every time I have ever tried to ask Emmanuel, I was shot down. However, I had access to the internet and other resources. I could simply look up stuff.

In the ten years I have been here, I have always thought that I was here because I wanted to be. Now, I was here because I needed to be. What if I could escape this place? Would I stay? Would I go? Maybe I could ask Emmanuel again and he would tell me. Because while my curiosity has always been squashed, Reggie knew something I didn't. I didn't like when anyone knew something I didn't but if they could use it against me, it sent red flags through my head.

I am Y. I am happily married, have been part of this operation for ten years with four hundred and one successful missions, and am the FBI's third-most-wanted criminal.

But was that all there was to me?

---------Chapter 8

I put my ID into the slot for me to enter our base and waited patiently for it to accept my admittance. It took a moment for it to beep and then welcome me back. I grabbed my ID from it and rushed to get to the living space that I had shared with the girls. To my horror, I was failing as a team leader. I was temporarily forgetting where our safe house was. I was hoping that all my girls had already given Trinity up and that now, they were waiting for me to return.

When I entered the quiet, empty living room, I knew that they weren't there. The untouched welcoming gifts that we were usually treated with were still in their wrappings. I skirted around the room to see if, maybe, they just needed to take a shower or nap first. Sometimes these missions were very exhausting to everyone's mental well-being. Sometimes, they didn't have adequate time to eat.

Unfortunately, I was coming out of each bedroom without anybody following me. I sighed to show that I was resigning and went back to my room. My mission wasn't over until I knew what happened to all my girls. I was the lead so if anything happened to them, it was all my fault.

However, I didn't know where they were. I quickly plopped open the manilla folder on my desk and scoured through pages upon pages of our assignment. I had written so many notes and blacked out so many words that I found it almost impossible to read what we were originally going to do. The plan had changed as we learned about Trinity and I couldn't predict what would happen. We had gone over twenty scenarios about what might happen but none of them were if I were to get arrested. I didn't think I could be arrested.

I thought I was invincible. I forgot that I was human and could make mistakes because most of our missions, I didn't. I had to be perfect. Everyone did. I had to always think on my toes, but I always knew the result, our mission was to bring the girl home. I did my part: I crashed into the cop car to get them away. Hopefully, Mattie started going the speed limit afterward. There was nothing more I could do. It was in their hands.

Yet as I continued to scour our pages, I knew I wasn't turning my badge in to be evaluated. Maybe it was for selfish reasons, but I did not want to be labeled as the least valuable member. I was the one who spent most of my time away from the group and the target so it would only be fitting if they named me it. However, if they were in some type of peril and I saved them, it might bump me up to be the MVP.

I could not let my ranking go down.

I could not let these girls suffer.

I had to find them.

If they weren't back yet, something was wrong.

Almost on a convenient cue, I looked at the last page and saw a scribbled note in red. I covered it up with a black marker but if I shined a light directly over it, I could make out what I had said.

Safe house 57.

****

****

I made my fourth right in a row and watched as the headlights behind me vanished. The breath I had been holding escaped me and I could now stop tapping my knuckles on the wheel. That car had been following me for fifteen minutes and I was starting to get nervous that I was being followed again. Now I could get back to driving the route I was planning to take the first time.

I sped the van I stole from our headquarters along the darkened roads beside me but refused to put on music or try to relax. Who knows if my girls were even there? Maybe it was one of the plans that we had ruled out. Regardless, I had to try it. If anything, I could always return to the base and scour over the papers again. It would be easier to keep the papers on me, but I wasn't stupid enough to make that mistake. If those were ever lost or stolen, our entire operation would be in jeopardy once they figured out the code.

I watched the New Jersey sign welcome me into the state and found myself smiling for a brief second. My turn was only a little bit away. I drove down three more miles before putting my hazard lights on and pulling off the road. I waited until the highway was black with darkness before driving

                    AMY KULP

with my lights off on the grass. I didn't turn my lights back on until I hit a bumpy road.

Swerving to the right before I could hit the major pothole, I lined my car back on the path until I could see a very small, rundown house. Pulling up to it, I could see that some vandals had found it from the spray paint tagging and the windows being busted out but other than that, it didn't provide much else unless you were homeless. Unfortunately, if you were found to be squatting in this house, we had commands to take you away with us. I wasn't sure if these people were to be tortured, trafficked, or recruited but either way, it was a better life for them.

Once my engine cooled down, I hopped out of my car and walked around the front. I held my knife in my hands and twirled it as I made my way to the other side of the house. Obviously. if they were to get this far, there would be some sort of transportation. However, they had to be smart. They couldn't park it in plain sight especially if it was a car they had stolen.

Spinning around in my spot, I was disappointed that I couldn't find a car. This didn't mean they weren't here though. Maybe they conned someone into dropping them off. Maybe they walked. Anything was possible and I knew not to count them out just yet.

Walking up the porch steps, I saw the alarm box off to the side. It was just there for decoration, of course. Nobody needed to know that though. I quickly unlocked the door with my ID card and stood still in the darkened room. I forgot how everything was menacing here.

The fact that I couldn't see anything told me more than enough. There were no light switches. This was not one of our most known safe houses. This was one of the very few that is no longer monitored. I only remember this safe house from the beginning of my years here. I was warned multiple times to stop using it because of how wrong everything could go but this is one of my favorites.

I don't like safe houses with their new technology. I don't like that they were camera monitored the entire time in every room. I like my privacy. If someone wanted to be a double-crossing agent here, then they would be killed by me. I wouldn't let them leave. I was trained on how to fight and if they didn't believe that I could kill them, then why would they make me the team lead?

Unless they suspected me too?

I caught a glimpse of moonlight coming in from one of the busted windows and kept my glare on it. I could have sworn it just moved. Staring at the beam of light on the floor, I moved my eyes until I saw a speck of blood. I walked forward and quickly smeared my sneaker to see if it was a stain or fresh. To my astonishment, it smeared with my shoe; it was fresh which meant someone was there.

I had my knife ready in my hand as I followed the trail until it was too dark for me to see. However, since I couldn't see, I had to rely on my ears. I listened in the room for any movement but was only met with my own breathing. Maybe if I

                                    AMY KULP

held my breath for a moment, it would allow me to hear the rest of the room.

Holding my breath, I could hear air running through the room. Maybe it was from the outside world or maybe it was from someone breathing. I opened my eyes and looked to the right of me to see another broken window. So much glass here. I bet whoever was here had stepped on it and if their shoe was thin, has cut themselves with it. I grabbed a large shard for a second before keeping it in my hand.

At least now I had two weapons.

"Are you one of us?" I asked to the open air. I stood elsewhere in the room and sighed. "¿Eres una de nosotras?" I waited for the needed response back and moved. Someone was here but I didn't know where they were hiding. What other languages did I remember this question in?

When I listened to a floorboard creak, I slowly turned to the side of me. If they were stupid enough to make noise while I was down here, I had a feeling that they belonged here. Maybe they didn't remember the response.

"Mattie?" I dropped the shard of glass onto the ground and brought her into my arms. I squeezed her small frame hard and when she let go, I looked down at her foot. A sock was wrapped tightly around it and I could see the dried blood. "Where are Jaycie and Sloane?" I paused as I looked around her to see just darkness. "Briley?" Not seeing anyone, I looked at her again and was confused. "Trinity?" Mattie shook her head. "Where are they?"

I knew Mattie couldn't talk but I still expected her to offer some way to communicate with me. She didn't move her facial expressions and remained still. I took my hands and placed them on her arms. I held onto her tight and shook her while repeating my question.

"Where are they? Where are they? Where are they?"

I shook harder and more vigorously each time I asked the question. Still, she stayed there without helping me. She didn't try to write down anything and she didn't try to communicate by speaking. Of course, her voice would not come out correctly nor would I be able to understand her, but it would've showed me she was trying. I shook harder and harder and soon, she was barely able to stand.

"Mattie, where are they?" I yelled. I threw her body to the ground and watched as she squirmed on the floor. She didn't try to protect herself as my hands formed into fists and came down on her. "Mattie, where are they?" I hit her harder and forced my fists to come down harder. Some of them were in identical places and some of them were in new places. Yet every time I punched her, she didn't flinch, and she didn't try to protect herself. "Mattie!" I felt tears shoving into my eyes from frustration and I got down to her and pulled her shirt with my fists. "Where are they?"

She wouldn't meet my eyes and I shoved her back. She closed her eyes as I kicked her body into the wall. I stomped harder and harder and felt my tears starting to build up. Where were they? Why was she alone? What had happened that she wasn't saying anything?

"Mattie!" I yelled. I bent down to her again and caught sight of her bloody nose and winced. I just did that. "I am not a torturer," I said. "But if we go back to the camp and they find out that you were the only one who had survived then they would torture you." She remained emotionless and I watched the blood seep out from her nose. She didn't try to fix it or clean it up. She just let it run. "And they would torture me too." I waited to see her reaction and saw a flicker of movement in her eye.

Mattie didn't care about herself. She thought that she deserved nothing. She would have been fine by being homeless but wanted to help provide for and spoil her sister and niece. Mattie cared about others, but she didn't see her own self-worth. It was sad but I was able to use that to my advantage.

"Are you willing to make me suffer too?" I asked. I rubbed the blood that was on my knuckles onto my pants and watched as Mattie looked at me again. "I guess I deserve it. I did take on a group of girls and I guess Jaycie, Briley, and Sloane just were not a good fit. I'll make sure to mention that in the report so if they do come back, they will get retrained." Mattie looked at me again and this time, I could see the fear in her eyes.

After all, Jaycie seemed to be her best friend.

She wiped the blood coming from her nose and looked up at me. She moved her hands for a moment, and I sat down beside her, defeated. There was only so much torture I could use, and I did not want to implement it on Mattie. She has been through so much. I really didn't want her to go through much more.

When did I become such an easygoing person? I was going to get screwed over if I kept thinking like this. I couldn't be soft just because I cared about Mattie. I couldn't be soft on any of them just because they were my first all-girl group. I had to be tough or else they were going to take advantage of me. I had to keep up my power act until I could rest and let my guard down. I could not let my guard down with her.

With a new encouragement, I stood up and balled my fists up again. I could see the new emotion in Mattie's eyes as she moved her fingers and hands more. She fidgeted and when I let my rage take over for a second, I couldn't help but stare down at her. Why was she moving her fingers at me? They weren't shielding her face. They weren't shielding her from my blows. Why was she moving her fingers?

Do you sign? I asked with my fingers. I could see her pause for a second and I signed again. I may have been signing a bit wrong, but I remember learning it. *Do you sign?* She balls up one of her hands into a fist and nodded it up and down. *What happened?*

Mattie adjusted her body next to me and she wiped at her nose again. With the blood shimmering on her knuckles, she made sure I could see her. I squinted in the dim moonlight and paid close

                                    AMY KULP

attention. After a brief second, she repeated her signs at a much slower rate.

My niece is deaf. I practice for her. I nodded my head but I'm sure my face showed everything. Mattie looked at me for a second and asked, *What*?

What happened?

Mattie thought for a moment before stretching her fingers. *We were being followed after you crashed.* I grimaced and nodded my head to show her that I understood. *I left the girls at a stop.*

"Who was following you?" I asked. She shrugged her shoulders and I thought for a moment. "How did you lose them?"

I'm smart. She paused before wiping her face again. She looked at me and this time, I could see the worry in her face. *Niece?*

"What's her name?" I asked.

C-A-M-I-L-L-A. Camilla. Is she okay?

I didn't say anything to Mattie and her fingers began going at a super speed. I couldn't read that as I haven't had practice in forever. I barely ever signed because almost no one knew sign.

Except for the victim that I got to trust me before I kidnapped her.

When I opened my eyes back up, she was no longer signing. Instead, she was staring at me as if I held all the secrets. And I did. I did hold all the secrets. At least the ones that were important to her. The most valuable one.

"It's too late," I whispered. I could see Mattie's face breaking up, but she held it together. *They lied.* I repeated the sign so that she could see but she never stopped staring at me. She saw it the first time I signed it. *I lied.* "Mattie, they sold your sister and niece already."

Mattie stayed still as she processed the information. I could see it working through her brain and when it finally processed, she hid her face from me. She was making noises I never thought someone could make - she sounded like a whale, donkey, and a zebra all in one. I put my hand on her back for just an instant before she straightened back up. She gave me her wrists without a warning and acted like I was going to arrest her.

Instead, I shook my head.

I never saw you. She looked at me and I could see the confusion in her face. *Go.*

Thank you.

I only nodded my head and watched as she left. I knew that I would never see her again and I was hoping that nobody would ever learn about this interaction. Nobody would ever know that I let Mattie go. Mostly because, if they did know, I would be tortured for the rest of my life.

Was I willing to do that?

All my family was here. Everyone I knew was here.

As I sat there, I had to contemplate if everything I had was here. Reggie's comments were making me think but I was also questioning it.

Every single time I have tried to find an answer about my past life, my husband shut me up. He never wanted to talk about it. Why? Why couldn't I remember? Who was I?

I closed my eyes hard and set my head on the wall behind me. I was trying to will myself to

AMY KULP

remember but as I sat there, I knew I wouldn't remember. I had been tortured to forget certain details about missions even now. If someone didn't want me to remember something, they would make sure I didn't remember it. If my husband didn't want me to remember, then there would be no change for me. However, I could try to annoy it out of him. I knew his weaknesses.

But he also knew mine.

I got up from where I was sitting and looked around at the empty house. Now wasn't the time to be sulking about my life. I lived a good life. I have lots of money saved up and I get to see my husband after each mission if time allowed for it. I was usually always the team lead anymore so I didn't have to follow orders from other people. I had a good life. I didn't need to think about my past life.

Even as I got back into my car, I couldn't help but think about how ridiculous that was. I had a right to know about my past. All I knew was that I am Y. I am happily married, have been a part of this operation for ten years, and am the FBI's third-most-wanted criminal. And right now, I was aiming for another successful mission, and that started with finding the rest of my group.

-----------Chapter 9

Okay, where would my girls be? I stopped my car at the rest stop Mattie had noticed someone was following her at, but there was nothing near it except the highway. How could three girls go down the highway without raising suspicion about their activities? They didn't know where the safe house was. I chose to only tell Mattie because I knew she was my driver. It was supposed to make her trust me more because I only told her. Look at how that screwed me over. Sloane was pretty much useless too because all her computers were in that van.

Going into the bathroom, I was surprised by how empty and clean it was. If it wasn't the middle of the night, I was certain that this area would be bustling. Now that it was dead, I knew that they were smart enough to stay in here: it was warm, there were snacks and drinks you could buy in the vending machine, and you could freshen up here.

I had to put my feet in their shoes though. If I felt good enough to stop here, they must have arrived at night, right? They wouldn't risk anybody recognizing Trinity from the news, would they? I shook my head at the thought. Jaycie and Sloane would ensure that wouldn't happen. What happens if they left her in the van though? I knew that was wrong because she wasn't with Mattie.

Okay, so they all went to the restroom. What did Mattie see that she knew she was being followed? She wouldn't risk the mission like that, would she? Once again, I physically shook my head as if the thoughts would leave my mind. My priority was not Mattie right now. After all, I just let her escape. She would probably be hunted down in no time. If she were to be brought back, they would torture her for the rest of her life.

What would I do if I came out of the bathroom and saw that Mattie was gone? I walked out and looked around the parking lot. If they arrived at night and the parking lot was as bare as it is now, they wouldn't have to look around the parking lot in case she moved. They would be able to see that there was no beige van. Okay, so that eliminates any chance of them getting picked off by whoever was following them. Or would those people have followed Mattie? I shook my head. Speculating wasn't going to help me.

If I had no idea where I was, I would find a map. I walked outside of the bathroom and followed all the sidewalks around. I was going up and down on different hills before I caught a glimpse of a barely illuminated map. Rushing over, I stared at the faded map to figure out where I was. There were little flyers pinned all over the map to show where they were. There were two very close to here—a halfway house in one direction and a homeless shelter in the other. I grabbed a flyer from both and immediately jumped when a voice behind me started to talk.

"You're going to have tough luck with both of those." I turned around to see a lady flicking out her cigarette. She looked to be a lot lizard. "The homeless shelter is almost always full."

"And the halfway house?" I asked.

"It's not a thing anymore," the lady laughed. "Every now and then, I'll see people grabbing at it. It's just a building now. It's been about three months since it closed." She took one final drag of her cigarette despite it being dead.

"And how would you know?"

"Honey, look at me." She stepped back and fanned her arms back. She didn't look like she would handle living in prison very well. Looking at her face, I could see varying shades of scars. Looking at her body, she wore tight clothing that didn't fit, and her skin was aged with discolored spots. She looked like she either did drugs or was dependent on them. "I can see what you're thinking." She did a hearty laugh before coughing. "Don't be like me. Get yourself some help. The homeless shelter is where to start."

"And you give everyone this advice?" I wondered as I looked at the two flyers in my hands. She nodded.

"You don't want to end up like me. If you go to that halfway house, this is what you become."

"Thank you," I whispered as she moved away. I looked down at the two flyers in my hand and took her advice into consideration.

On one hand, I do believe the girls would have gone to one of these, as they are the closest. Which one though? Would they have rather taken her advice? Or would they go to the halfway house because they knew it was shut down? I looked at both and quickly folded and stuffed them in my pockets.

As I got into my car to prepare the drive off, I felt a sharp tenderness in my breast and groaned. Okay, first I would need to go to the bathroom. Running back to the bathroom, I closed the stall door and quickly grabbed the toilet paper that I would need. When I was done, I flushed it down the toilet and quickened my way out there. I felt a lot better now and didn't have the tightness anymore.

Hopping back in, I sped off, and once I got onto the highway I followed the GPS toward the homeless shelter. All the lights were off, and I had to assume everyone was sleeping. However, this didn't mean that I couldn't knock and try to get in. Would they let someone in who had a car? I shook my head because I knew that I had to try.

Knocking on the door, I waited patiently until I heard something from the other side. There were people in there who were sleeping. I grimaced because I knew that they would all rather be working and having a nice home than this. Maybe I should recruit here.

"Hello?" A piece of the door slid, and I was able to see a pair of brown eyes from behind it. The bags were so puffy that I knew this person worked hard most of their life. They could have been in the same situation as a lot of these other people and decided to open it. "What do you need?"

"I was just wondering—"

"We don't have any room for anyone new, and you woke up a lot of people," the voice grumbled.

"I'm sorry. Do you happen to have—"

"I don't give out who is in here for the safety of my people," they warned. I nodded, and when I opened my mouth to talk they already shut the hatch.

Okay… That didn't help. I knew that they probably weren't going to have vacancies because of what that lady had told me. However, I wasn't sure if it was because they already had no room or if four of my girls were trapped there. I shook my head at the thought and knew that I would have to drive the other way to get to the halfway house.

If they weren't there, I would have to try again at the homeless shelter. Maybe even threaten them if they needed me to. I didn't want them to risk calling the cops though. That would be the last thing I needed. I was now the girl who had kidnapped Trinity, shot off a gun, and outran a cop. I didn't need upsetting the homeless to be on my rap sheet too.

Shaking my head, I got back in my car without another word. I wanted to scream, and maybe it was because I picked the wrong choice but maybe it was also because I wasn't leading my group correctly. I couldn't pinpoint what they were thinking or how Trinity would react. Why couldn't I lead them right? What was going on?

Speeding down the highway, I didn't stop until my GPS told me I was five minutes away. I would have to walk this distance because I wasn't sure exactly what was going to happen when I got there. I didn't want this car to be tied to anything that would ensue. Best-case scenario, it would be empty. Worst-case scenario, I was walking into a trap. Either way, I had to check it out.

Locking the car with the keys inside, I started walking further down the sidewalk until my GPS had told me I reached my destination. Putting my phone in my pocket, I knew this had to be the building. It was rundown with only a few windows busted out of it. Walking up to the door, it easily creaked and opened for me. I closed the door behind me and could already hear noises from people snoring, turning over, or waking up from my loudness. I grimaced because the last thing I wanted to do was bring attention to myself. How was I going to find my girls though? If anything, they were probably sleeping with one person as a guard. How would they see it was me? It was pitch dark in here and despite it being dangerously cold outside, the walls seemed to keep most of it out. Maybe there were more people here than met the eye.

As I walked past different groups of families, loners, druggies, criminals, and alcoholics, I made sure to examine everybody on the floor. Some of them were wrapped up in sleeping bags, ratty blankets, layers of clothes, newspapers, and anything that they could get their hands on. Less fortunate folk had their hands wrapped around their bodies and were shivering by themselves. Those people seemed to be in the middle though, so they weren't too close to the door and weren't too close to the busted windows.

I stepped over crack after crack, and thankfully most people stayed asleep. It was awkward for me to accidentally make eye contact with them, but nobody said anything. I just wanted to get warm too. They didn't need to know what I had on me. If I didn't make a fuss, they shouldn't make a fuss. I hoped that anyway.

Getting to the end of the first floor, I cautiously walked up the stairs and avoided holes in the landings. As I walked, I had to watch the ground more than the people here. There were more holes in the floor, sunken in where it might snap, and the ceiling collapsed in multiple places too. I wasn't sure how high this went up, but it felt even colder up here. I brought my arms around myself and began to shiver. Even my heavy coat couldn't prevent the cold from seeping into my bones.

As soon as I felt arms snake around me, I froze. I knew not to kick until I was put back on the ground, but instead I turned around. I came face to face with Briley. She smiled at me and grabbed me by the wrist to take me over to where she was. As we walked, she expertly dodged the holes and was in a corner by themselves. It was probably too cold for most people to stay up here. They were smart about that.

I hugged Jaycie and Sloane quickly before turning my attention to Trinity. She was slumped against the wall in a deep sleep, but at least she was there. I shook my head at all of them and saw just how cold they were too. None of them looked good—dark, puffy circles reminded me of that.

"She was really rowdy," Briley mentioned. "We had to inject her with drugs to keep her quiet."

"We hope she'll wake up, but so far she's been out like a light," Jaycie whispered.

"And who decided this?" I asked. I looked over at Trinity and shook her arms. There was no response. I quickly grabbed her wrist to try and find a pulse and sighed when I realized she did have one. Hopefully, she would stay that way.

"I did," Sloane mentioned. "I figured—"

She didn't get a chance to explain before I slapped her across the face. She sat there in stunned silence for a second before looking back at me. When I turned to see Jaycie's and Briley's reactions, they too were stunned. I grabbed the collar of her shirt and brought her face close to mine. As I spoke each word, I could see my breath moving across her face.

"Don't ever do that again. If she ends up dead from not waking up because of the concoction of drugs you gave her, it will be you who is at fault."

Sloane shook her head rapidly up and down to tell me that she understood, so I let go of her collar. However, when I felt a tap on my shoulder, I looked at all three girls before I turned. They looked petrified and immediately backed up. That could not be good. I turned to try and intimidate them, and a big, scruffy guy was towering over me.

"Can I help you?" I asked with a bit of spit coming out of my mouth to emphasize each word. I felt a hand placed on my arm to warn me not to talk like that, but I wasn't going to back down. I had all my girls here. We could take this one man. I crossed my arms over my chest and continued to stare at him. If he needed something, he needed to tell me. I couldn't read minds.

"Why are you touching Ms. Sandra?" he asked. His voice boomed through the building, and I could already see some people tossing and turning. If he kept this up, everyone would be awake and watching the scene too. I couldn't have all these witnesses.

"Oh, it's okay," Sloane attempted.

"Touching anyone in this building is forbidden," he boomed. He looked at me again and clasped both hands around my neck. "We may be unfortunate, but we are not miscreants." I dug my nails into his hand as he squeezed tighter.

"Let her go," Jaycie said. She said it quietly and looked around. "Now!" She looked around again, and thankfully it didn't seem like anyone else was going to wake up. She jumped on his back, and he immediately loosened his grip. However, I couldn't pry his fingers off. "Briley, help!" Jaycie called as someone snuck up behind her and struck her in the back.

"There is no fighting here!" the man yelled. "Get out!"

"We will!" I yelled. "Let go of me." I took my hand and hit him hard in the eye. With a squeal from how hard he was hit, he dropped me on the ground. "Let's go!" I yelled at my girls. However, I knew instantly it would be much harder than that, as people were coming up the stairs and everyone who was already on this floor was fighting. "Briley, get Trinity!" I yelled. I watched as she kicked someone hard in the face and winced.

Blood was already spewing everywhere.

She easily got Trinity up on her back, and I punched the guy who was hitting on Jaycie. When he was on the floor, I paused for a second before getting her off. It was hard for me to keep track of Sloane, but I was able to catch her crawling through the massive crowds that were coming. We just had to dodge through everyone to get out. That would be so much harder for Briley with Trinity on her back.

"Go up ahead!" I told them. "I'll cover you."

"No," Jaycie declined. She came close to me and whispered, "I still have my gun."

"Try not to use it," I whispered. She nodded her head and instantly brought it out. I got ahead of Briley and Trinity and followed Sloane's lead. However, I could see three people picking on her and stripping the coat off her. "Leave her alone!" I yelled. I barreled at them and instantly threw a punch in there. If I could get my taser from my pocket, I could do some real damage.

However, as soon as I reached, everybody froze, and everything went silent. I could see the flashing red and blue before I could hear the sirens. Panicked, everyone rushed toward the stairs. People were pushing, falling, and getting hurt. It was getting so bad that the stairs were clogged. Nobody was coming in and nobody going out. Panicked, I looked around to the opposite end.

I pointed for Jaycie and Briley to go that way, but when I went back to stare at Sloane she disappeared. I wish I knew where she was. I bit my lip and knew that we had to make it out. If that meant leaving Sloane behind, it meant we had to leave her behind. As soon as we got to the hole in the floor, we stared down at the police barging through the door.

"Can you see how many are out there?" I asked as I came up behind Jaycie.

"Looks like two cars."

"That's not enough," Briley mentioned. "We can jump down and make a run for it."

"Okay, let's do that. My car is five minutes down the road. We need to go before any more cop cars show up." I nodded at them and watched as Jaycie went down first. She fell on top of someone but scrambled up to bust out of there. "How are we going to get Trinity out of here?" I asked Briley. Without a second thought, Briley pushed Trinity out. We watched as her body flailed to the floor and I couldn't help but nod. "It works."

"Don't overthink, Y," Briley said as she jumped down.

I followed her, but by the time I was down from the second floor I felt the pain in my ankles and in my knees. I must have landed wrong. I could see more cops had arrived, and as they barged through the building I hid behind other people. I knew I wasn't going to be able to get through the door so instead I covered my head and busted through one of the already smashed windows. I could feel the glass in my coat go down my neck, but I had to worry about finding my car.

"Y, in here!" I looked around to see Sloane driving a random van on the street. She stopped and I instantly got into the back.

                    AMY KULP

"Is everyone okay?" I asked as she started to drive again. "Drive at a normal speed," I warned. "We don't want to catch another cop's attention."

"Too late for that. We're being followed," Sloane said. She adjusted her mirrors, and I could see how uneasy she was with driving.

"Okay, if we get pulled over, everyone just needs to be calm," I stated. "There shouldn't be any reason he pulls this van over."

"Except that it's stolen," Briley murmured. I looked over at her, and she just shrugged. "I'll try to think on the bright side—Trinity is moving." I looked to her side and knew that Briley was right. Trinity was moving on the seat. Barely, but it was noticeable.

"Here's a blanket to put over her!" Jaycie said as she threw the blanket to Briley. "Cover her up, so if he does pull us over, he won't be able to see her."

"He won't be able to see her unless he opens these back doors. Those windows are blacked out," I pointed out. "Maybe put more of these supplies to block you."

"He's pulling us over!" Sloane aid.

"Pull over!" I yelled. Sloane very roughly pulled to the side of the road, and we all bounced around as she came to a stop. "Sloane, a little easier next time."

"I've never been pulled over," Sloane mentioned. "I don't know what to do."

"Do what he asks you to!" I yelled as I moved some of the supplies to cover Jaycie, Briley, and Trinity. "We'll stay quiet back here."

There was a tap on the glass, and I'm assuming that was the cop. I could feel the cold air coming inside the van, and for a moment I had to wonder how we survived in that house with it being this cold. Was it worse because so many cars were zooming past us and the wind was strong? I grabbed a mop handle and stayed low to the ground near the doors. I needed a weapon.

"We are just doing a routine stop."

"Is there something I did wrong?" Sloane asked innocently. For someone who has never been pulled over, she seemed calm. Maybe she should be the actor next time she does an assignment. "My dad will kill me if he finds out I got pulled over!"

"Nothing bad. We just have to inspect the vehicle. You came from the same place where we had a massive fight break out. We want to make sure you aren't harboring any criminals in here." He leaned in and immediately took his head out. I was crouched so low that while I could see him, I knew he couldn't see me. "Ma'am, have you been drinking?"

"And driving? I'm not stupid."

"I'm going to need you to open the back doors. Please get out your ID so I can see if you are of drinking age and can be transporting alcohol."

I sniffed the air, but nothing smelled like alcohol. However, she already unlocked the back doors, and I immediately gave her my sign that I would be taking one for the team again. This time, they better make it to the base. I whispered the location to Jaycie and waited until the back door

                    AMY KULP

was open before I threw the mop at the cop and jumped on him.

He was flabbergasted as his back hit the ground, and I waited until the van started moving before I tried to run away. With his back on the ground, I thought I would have a few seconds to begin my run, but he quickly caught my ankle. I fell back down on my wrists and knew when he landed on top of me and forced my hands to my back that I was not getting out of this one.

But, hey, at least I am Y. I am happily married and have been a part of this operation for ten years, and this was my first official arrest. I think that's a pretty good track record.

-----------Chapter 10

I glared at the policeman as he continued to drive over the speed limit to take me to jail. Every now and then he would glance up at me and roll his eyes. I refused to say anything to him despite how much he was questioning me. I knew to remain silent. Policemen just wanted it their way. They were blind leaders. They didn't understand that they were putting someone innocent away.

I adjusted my hands that were behind my back and pressed against the seat again. He didn't need to hear how much I was struggling with the metal digging into my wrists. After all, he knew he had made them too tight. He did it on purpose. After all, I'm sure he didn't want to go into the police station with the bruise that was forming on his face. He wanted to make it seem like I was fighting the entire time. However, I barely laid my hands on him.

As I pressed my hands into my back, I kept my watchful eye on the policeman. He had to focus more on navigating to the station than what I was doing in the backseat. Besides, he was probably pissed at me for hitting him. I would be mad too. I am mad. However, I couldn't show it though. I might get killed if he thought I was mad. I kept my eyes on the mirror to see if he would be looking back at me and started moving my hands closer to my back. I started to bend my back so that it arched and continued to watch the mirror. He was too focused on the road to notice my hands scooting to my butt. I carefully moved my thigh so that I was sitting on my hands until I could pull my legs up to my chest. Trying to work quickly and quietly, I had trouble moving my arms around the seatbelt. The belt wrapped along my lap and made it more difficult for me to scoot my arms underneath. It seemed the officer was braking now. When he released the pressure on the brakes and proceeded to accelerate, I snuck my arms through my legs and managed to get them into my lap.

It would be a little more comfortable now.

Now that I had my hands in the front of my lap, I was able to reach into my front pockets. Feeling in my right pocket, I could feel the small poke that meant this cop hadn't checked them. He was probably too much in a rush to handcuff me and take me to their station. I wiped the little blood droplet onto the fabric of my pants and waited a moment. Was there a typical place during an arrest where I could pull my knife out on a police officer?

"If you want to get even more time on your record," he stated. I looked back up at the mirror and could see his eyes staring at me. He quickly darted them back to the road, but I knew that he was talking to me. "Your knife?" he wondered. I didn't make any notion that I knew what he was talking about. "It's in your pocket. Yeah, I know about it."

I was tempted to ask why he left it there then but knew the answer. If I were to use it against him, I would be charged longer. If he knew about the prick on my finger, he could claim that I was trying to use it against him. After all, he was mad that I attacked him in the first place. He had to be willing to take that risk though. I could have done so much damage to him if he looked at the road for too long.

However, I wasn't going to do it now. I knew that the car doors were locked from the inside. The only way I could get out was if he were to let me out or if I crawled through the front. The best option was to wait until we were at the station.

So, as he continued to drive, I remained perfectly still. I kept my gaze focused on the mirror to see if he kept looking back at me. However, he never did. Almost as if he didn't care if I was going to attack him or not. Nothing was separating me from reaching out to him. There was no net or divider like you see in those cops' shows. It was just a front seat and a back seat.

"Police car forty-seven is about to pull in with a high-risk person. Prepare other officers at the entrance."

I could hear a mumble back but couldn't quite comprehend what was being said. It was either an affirmative or a straight denial because he didn't say anything else. He continued to drive for about five more minutes before slowing down and turning into a parking lot. He swiftly shut the car off and popped the back doors open. Before he removed my seat belt, he retracted his hand and looked at my hands.

"How did you do that?" He stared down at my hands and slowly undid the seatbelt. I stood up obediently but didn't say anything until he got behind me. He led me forward to the doors, and when he got there he grabbed my handcuffs and started putting the code into the lock pad.

This was my absolute last chance. I hurriedly yanked on my handcuffs and could see the man press a wrong number. The keypad flashed a small red dot, and he lost his balance. However, he did not let go of my handcuffs. I yanked again while I felt the metal sink sharply into my skin. With the bite of the cuffs, I bit my tongue and yanked harder. If he couldn't regain his balance, he couldn't possibly get ahold of me. I yanked again and again before I felt a hand loosen from the grip on me. I smiled but instantly frowned when I saw him reach for his radio. I kicked at his hand, and he grabbed my ankle with the one that was going for the radio. Grabbing it, I was the one who lost my balance now. As he fell on top of me, I knew I was going to be at a disadvantage if he knew how to pin me down correctly. I reached low with my hands until I could feel the knife and jabbed upward with it. However, he quickly deflected it and twisted my wrist around until I heard a faint snapping noise. I cried out and attempted to kick him off me, but he already flipped me around and held his knee on my back as I flailed.

"Let's go. I've had enough of you." I felt my hair getting tugged as he grabbed hold of the back of my shirt. I got up with him and held onto my arm so that it wouldn't move much more. However, when he noticed my pain, he made sure to push me into the shoulder blade. I had no idea where exactly my arm was popped out, but any motion or movement from him resulted in the ache appearing. "I can't wait to look at the footage later and laugh."

I grunted under my breath for a minute before he started pushing harder. I stopped when we got inside, and I already knew that I was outnumbered. This was all going to be new territory for me. I have never been in a police station before, and I've never been booked. I had no idea what I was getting myself into. However, he couldn't know that. I had to be cocky and confident. Then maybe I could find my way out. It's been done before by some previous members. However, I also knew that if I were to stay in jail they would be waiting for me to get out. I don't know how they got the information they did, but they had good hackers.

I could see Sloane being one of the top hackers in a couple of years.

"You need to change into these," he said as he looked back at me. He roughly threw a pair of prison uniform scrubs at me, and I purposely didn't catch them. As they fell to the floor, he stared at me as we both waited for each other to pick them up. "Then we'll get your picture and fingerprints. Once those are all done, you'll be waiting in that holding cell over there until we are told what to do with you." He continued to stare at the clothes that were on the ground, and I only watched him. When he had enough waiting, he deliberately hit my arm and watched me squirm. I would not give in to this guy though. That's what he wanted. He wanted my obedience. I was only obedient to my husband and his crew. They were the only ones who deserved my respect. "Let's get a move on." He started moving

                                          AMY KULP

ahead of me, and when I tripped over my shirt and looked up at him he only smirked. "We'll just have a female officer restrain you until you wear the clothes." He shrugged his shoulders. "I'm sure she'll take extra special care of your arm."

My eyes widened with fear, and I momentarily looked back at my clothes. Nothing could be worse than going back as someone who didn't put up a fight though. I would never live that title down if I got out of here. I shook my head and followed the officer as he pulled me along. When he realized I made up my mind, he opened the door and called his coworker over. Maybe she would give me a little more respect.

"Won't change," he mentioned as he shoved my body into the small, claustrophobic room.

I stared back around and watched as he made faces to the girl. I could see what he was saying and found myself rolling my eyes. Do they really think I would be stupid enough to try and escape the smallest room possible with only one entry point? I would wait for my chance to run, but it would be when I was close to the outside world. Who knew where all the officers were? They could be to the left of me, and I would never know until I took my chance to run. However, with this busted arm and shoulder, I wasn't too sure that I would put up much of a fight. My husband told me that police officers played dirty to get what they wanted.

"Hello there," a voice called. I watched as a young female officer came toward me. She smiled sweetly at me as the door closed behind her. Wasn't that dangerous for them to do that? What if I attacked her and then took her gun? I could point it at the door and then nobody would be safe. I looked down at her pants but saw that she didn't have any weapons on her. That was strange. "Why don't you want to change?" She had a fresh set of clothes in her hands and handed them off to me. When she saw the squint in my expression, her smile faltered. "Are you okay?" She stepped closer to me, and I refused to back down from her. She reached out to my shoulder and when she pressed it down, I took a huge intake of breath. "As soon as we're done, I'll make sure you go to medical, but they won't see you until you put a uniform on." I eyed her as she opened the pants for me. No way was this person trying to help me. Cops were corrupt and evil, right? "Go on I'll look away if you want." She stretched the pants and handed them to me low. Her head was facing the wall, and even though she didn't have her eyes closed I appreciated that. I carefully took my pants off and changed into the pair she had by stepping each leg into them. "That wasn't so hard, was it?" She smiled at me and then looked at my shirt. "This might be the problem." Reaching for the end of my shirt, she started bringing it up on my body until she was met with resistance from my hands. "I know this will hurt, but, like I said, right after we'll get you to medical." She paused for a second. "Actually, you have to get your picture and fingerprints taken, and then you can go to medical." She paused again and shook her head. "I can never remember the correct procedures of those things." She smiled up at me as she got the shirt over my head. "I'm new. So maybe I'm not as miserable as my partner was when he was dealing with you. Anything doesn't go his way and he's a monster." She shook her head and laughed a bit. "Not that you need to know that."

As soon as the shirt came on, she removed my shoes for me, and I followed her out. Almost as if this was a shock to the police officer I had before, he started to glare at both me and his partner. I smirked a bit and would much rather work with this girl than him. She pretended to care. She walked past the guard, and I followed behind her quietly. She loosened my handcuffs in the room, and I was grateful for that. They weren't digging into my flesh now.

"I lied," she whispered. "It's the picture, then fingerprints, then medical."

"You are not taking her to medical."

"Why not?"

"They're gone for the night." He smirked as I looked between the two. I hated this cocky guy. She seemed to be annoyed too as she led me to get my picture taken. I held onto the sign that they had and waited for the flash. When that came, I was instructed to turn to the side again. I obeyed but had to bite into my tongue to avoid cursing out the male police officer. He was so full of it. "Fingerprints. I'll supervise."

"Of course, you will," she grumbled under her breath. We made brief eye contact, but even through that I could see the annoyance. "Do you get sweaty hands?" she asked as she brought me up to something that looked like a copying machine. I didn't answer before the male police officer grumbled. "It doesn't work if she has sweaty hands. It'll say it's inconclusive or can't be read." I could now hear the annoyance in her voice. She turned back to me, and I shook my head no.

Whatever she wanted to try, I knew it wouldn't work.

She positioned my fingers onto the screen and carefully rolled them as the scanner scanned each finger. When it said it was unidentified, her eyebrows furrowed, and she tried again. It wasn't going to scan, but she wiped my fingertips and tried again. Once again, she got the same result. They couldn't read my fingerprints.

"Let me do it. This is taking too long," he grumbled. As soon as he grabbed my wrist, I felt my body straighten. I did not like this man. He thought that the uniform automatically gave him respect. As he did the same thing that the lady officer was doing, he sighed. "She doesn't have fingerprints."

"What?" the female police officer asked. She stepped closer, and he showed her my tips.

I did have fingerprints, but they were so charred and distorted that if I was in the system they would never be able to find me. I watched as the two seemed to ponder what to do next but as my fingerprints were pressed down on the screen again I knew that they were going to put them in as new ones. Or send them to someone who could get a better read out of them.

One of the various ways that we were tortured was by destroying our fingerprints. Mine had been burned off, pricked at, and then burned

                                      AMY KULP

again. I knew some people had it easier or harder depending on how easy it was to distort each of them. I remember not being able to hold anything for a week because they did all of them at once. I drank everything through a straw at that point.

It reminded me that I needed to remember who I was, because the database for criminals wouldn't: I am Y, and I am happily married.

Chapter 11

"Get up."

That's all I heard before the metal clanking of the bars told me that someone was coming into the room with me. I turned over and sat right up. I wasn't going to give anyone a chance to attack me while my back was turned to them. The voice that woke me sounded irritated, agitated, annoyed, and any other synonyms for those words. He was probably sore from the night before. I knew I was. However, that may have had something to do with the metal bench and thin piece of the mattress I was sleeping on.

No wonder I was always told that I would regret getting arrested. I did regret it. I was not going to get any sympathy from these dudes and when I stretched out my back, I heard the various cracks in my bones. How could people survive with constant body aches? Maybe the actual prison was better than this holding cell that I was stuffed in.

When I looked up at the police officer, I could tell he had a rough night. He had a shadow on his chin and despite looking well-kept yesterday, he seemed to be a completely different person. Yesterday his hair was gelled back but today, it didn't look like he ran his fingers through the swoop. I already knew that he barely had any sleep since when I went to bed, he was still here and now that I'm getting up, he is here. I doubted he went home as soon as I went to sleep. Unless there was a shift change. From the tiny blood droplet on his white shirt, I knew that he didn't change out of his uniform. That was my tiny blood droplet. However, when he came closer to me, I could smell an overpowering smell of Irish spring.

"Hands out," he commanded.

I rolled my eyes but complied. It was too early for me to fight him, and I still wasn't sure of the layout of this police station. Placing my hands out in front of me, he slapped the metal cuffs roughly. He was beginning to make me angry. Where was that nice officer? She would handle me with care. She would make sure that I was comfortable and that my arm wasn't hurting too much from the pain of having it in front of me.

"Straighten your arm out," he demanded.

I did so as much as I could but the sling that I was wearing was preventing me from straightening it all the way. He grabbed my wrist and straightened it out. I'm sure that I made a face, but I refused to yell out in pain - he would enjoy that too much. He removed the sling from my neck and tossed it to the ground. I didn't have any time to react before he nudged my back for me to start walking.

"Do you want to tell us who you are yet?" he wondered. I didn't say anything and felt his nudges grow harder. "Still not speaking?"

Did he expect me to verbally answer that? I have managed to remain completely silent during my transition from the police car to the station and everything in between. I refused to even talk to the nice officer. I was always told to remain as silent as I could when it came to the police. They have a way of setting everything up against you and they knew how to manipulate people into lying without the use of extreme force.

I would rather be dead than a snitch. Even if it was on accident. I didn't want to give them something that seems so small to me but turned out to be a turning point in whatever investigation they had. They just didn't understand our mission. We took girls who weren't pleased with their life. We put them somewhere that they could be useful. Why couldn't they see that?

"Now's your chance to use the bathroom," he said as he stopped in front of a door. I looked at him quizzingly and he let go. "If you try to kill yourself, I won't stop you." I paused before pushing the door open. "However, if you're caught, you'll only be able to use the bathroom in your holding cell."

Going in, I was surprised to see a bunch of stalls. I had expected it to be a tiny room with the bare minimum. Was I supposed to be in here? This was the first ounce of privacy that I was given. It seemed suspicious to me. However, when I heard a coughing noise come from the officer outside, I knew that I needed to run with it. What could possibly happen here?

I went in and did my business and as I stepped out of the stalls, I saw the female officer from the day prior. She smiled at me as she washed her hands, and I carefully threw the paper towel that was in my hand away. I followed her routine of

                                         AMY KULP

washing her hands and quickly wiped them off with more paper towels before exiting. I moved my head to the side to see what she was doing and could see her rifling through the trash.

Entrapment. I couldn't trust any of them. No matter how nice or stern they were.

"Took you long enough," he grumbled. He grabbed me by my handcuffs, and I winced as he steered me toward the conference room.

It was probably where I would be interrogated.

I sat down in the chair that was by itself without being asked. I watched as he sat down and closed the door behind me. Yes, this would be an interrogation.

I put my hands on the table and let the skin seep into the cool metal. While yesterday it felt as if it was biting into my bones, today it felt refreshing to have it pressed against me. It almost seemed to cool off my temper that I had. I wanted to brag that I knew more than them and that they didn't even know who I was, but I feared that they might have a vocal recognition device that they could use to figure out who I was. If they figured out my identity, they could figure out my organization. Who knew what kind of torture devices they would use on me then?

I knew I messed up big time on this mission. This was my second time being captured by the bad guys and Reggie wasn't here to save the day this time. Granted, I knew what his implications were, and I knew he was undercover. I couldn't say anything new because this may be someone undercover, and I didn't know them. I would be tortured beyond belief if I let anything slide. Besides, I knew if I went back, I would be tortured for letting Mattie go and messing up so many times. I could try to plead and say Mattie left when I wasn't around, but I was always supposed to be around. I have never had so many hiccups in a mission as I did with this one.

Maybe I was being set up with inexperienced and ruthless girls. They had to know that Mattie was bound to be trouble. After all, her file told me that. While I had Sloane and Briley, they didn't work together well. Briley wanted to be the leader of the group. It felt almost impossible to tell her anything without her dismissing my orders. She wanted to be the top dog and lead the first all-girls team to victory. She probably was too. Jaycie was great but I felt like something was going on between her and Mattie. Something I couldn't explain. Why were they so close to each other? Why did Mattie trust Jaycie so much? Why didn't Jaycie willingly give that information to me?

Was I losing my touch as a leader?

"Who are you?" he asked as he sat down across from me. I stared at the empty chair that was across from me and tried to figure out who was going to sit there. Would it be that girl officer? She didn't seem to be that experienced but I'm sure this would be a valuable experience for her. "As soon as we figure out who you are, we can send you off to the appropriate prison. Are you running from the law?" He paused and stared at my reaction. I was hoping that I didn't have a reaction for him to figure anything out of. "Are you in trouble already?" He leaned more toward me as if he knew he was getting to me.

Did he already know who I was? Was this just a game to wear me down? As I studied his body language, I knew that he couldn't be that great of an actor to know anything about me. I looked behind him in the mirror and knew that someone was staring at me. Someone I couldn't see was trying to get me to talk. They were thinking of different ways to get me to talk but there was nothing that could cause me to disobey my orders. I could never talk to the police. I could never rat out my husband and friends. This program has changed so many people's lives.

The police were just destroying them. Watching as inmates fight and lose their lives. Do they ever step in? No. They only step in when they know someone is about to lose their life. They don't care about the suicides that happen. They care about putting bad people away. Most of them probably aren't guilty. However, they need someone to blame for what's going on in the world. Everybody wants to point fingers at someone else and claim they're the problem. Now the fingers are being pointed at me.

"Why did you attack me when I was investigating your friend's van?" he wondered. I looked up at him and could see a glint in his eye. Although I couldn't tell what emotion he was feeling, I could tell that he knew they were important to me. Or whatever in that van was important to me. "What was in that van?" He slammed his hands on the table and watched my reaction. He seemed surprised to see that I didn't react at all. I was used to worse than this after all. "Were there drugs?" He continued to tower over me to try and intimidate me. It just made me sit with a straighter back and a smirk on my face. "Were there people in that van?" I cocked an eyebrow and stared at him as he got closer to me. He wasn't allowed to touch me - that much I knew. He got close to me and bent down to whisper in my ear. "Do you really think I can't hurt you? Who would believe a criminal?" I let him breathe harder in my ear and he placed his hands roughly on my shoulders. I winced when he squeezed harder on the shoulder that ached.

Their medical staff didn't seem to be any good at what they did. They just pressed my arm and constantly asked if it hurt. No painkillers or medicine was administered, and they had given me a sling to temporarily relieve any pain. However, it didn't help. That wouldn't help either. Especially with this lunatic constantly swinging my arm around. I tried not to show any weakness to him because he always thought I was faking it.

"That's enough, Brian."

I looked over to see the door open and the female officer walk in. He got up and sat back in his seat. I couldn't tell if these two not liking each other was a ploy or if they truly couldn't stand each other. In either case, I knew not to trust the female officer. She was sweet but that just didn't show me her true intentions. After all, I had caught her rifling through

                                    AMY KULP

the trash when I was done with it. She was trying to actively find something on me.

"We're not going to waste our resources on trying to figure out who she is. If she wants us to know, she'll tell us." She crossed her arms as she walked closer to me. "I think we should just take her to the general room and wait for the boss to interrogate her. After him, we can call in for help or just send her off."

"Who says you can call the shots?" he asked. She made brief eye contact with me, and I could tell that she knew more than she was letting on. Maybe she was playing dumb and naïve on purpose compared to him. He reminded me so much of my husband always trying to be on top. Sometimes, he was derogatory toward me and acted as if I didn't know anything. However, I didn't and that was on purpose. They only ever told me what I needed to know. Most of the time, it wasn't a lot. "Whatever, you're keeping her at your desk and if there are any problems with her, you're taking the blame."

"Sure."

Without another word, he left the room, and I was escorted by the female officer. She was gentle as she guided me toward her desk. I could feel stares as we entered the land of cubicles. Any chatter near the water fountain was ceasing to exist and everyone dispersed to do the paperwork for their jobs. The lady officer pointed for me to sit in a chair, and I watched as she began typing on her computer.

I didn't care what she was typing about though. I cared more about myself and as I felt my butt getting used to the flat cushions, I found my eyes wandering around the room. I would be outnumbered if I made a scene here. If I were to escape silently, I could probably make it to the front without getting caught. All of the cubicles faced away from each other and most of the officers' backs were to the opening of their space. It was a stupid design choice, but it didn't seem like a lot happened around here.

Especially since they weren't good at interrogating people. Had I been a regular criminal, Brian's tactics would have worked against me. Since I was used to being tortured, I could tell that he was losing his confidence. I wouldn't be surprised to see him looking up interrogation techniques right now. I'm sure they would consider that studying up on the job and not wasting their time.

My eyes continued to wander over this girl's desk, various coffee bottles, and finally out of the cubicle. I could see a TV playing some daytime show loudly and knew that it was easy to drown out. When they weren't talking about anything interesting, my eyes wandered back to the computer in front of me. It seemed to be a dinosaur. I wondered how it ran so smoothly as she typed - I would expect it to be delayed and lagging. I stared longer at it to try and see if it had a webcam but was surprised to see it didn't.

That was good information to know.

                                    AMY KULP

I could possibly plan my escape that way if she left the room. I still had to wonder how new this girl was. There could be a chance that she was fresh out of the police academy. Or there could be a chance that she was experienced and purposely pretended she wasn't because she knew I would let my guard down. She picked up the phone that was next to her and quickly dialed a number with frustration evident on her forehead.

"Holy shit, I'll call you back." She put the phone roughly down and stared up at the TV screen. I followed her gaze and could see the astonishment of what was playing. On the screen, were my face and Trinity's face. There was information and a phone number to call if anyone has seen me. I was a very wanted person, and they made sure to mention that I was on the FBI's Most Wanted list. "You're Y?"

"I am Y," I finally confirmed.

------------------Chapter 12

I kept my stare at the wall as another hour ticked by. There wasn't a clock in this black, dull room, but I kept track in my head. Nobody talked, so I didn't lose any of my concentration. I have just been counting down time in here as I glared down the two police officers who have been in this room with me since they found out my real identity. I'm sure there were calls made and they were just following their orders, but it felt like they were babysitting me. How much damage could I possibly do with handcuffs on and constant surveillance? Besides, I was hungry, and I hadn't slept that much with how uncomfortable the bench was that they had me sleeping on. My eyes must have drooped for a moment from the exhaustion because they perked back up when I heard Brian moving very urgently.

"Maybe you could sleep when you name all of the locations of those innocent girls you took."

"Brian, we have orders not to talk to her," the female officer grumbled back. She had her arms crossed on her chest, and this was the most irritated I had seen her. I guess nobody liked to wait.

"We could be interrogating her right now," he said. "Instead, we're just glorified babysitters."

"Clearly, she won't talk," the female said. "She's said three words in total since she's been here. The FBI probably knows more useful tactics to get her to talk." She rolled her eyes and stared forward again.

I couldn't help but watch the reactions between these two. I couldn't pinpoint who was in charge, the girl or the guy. However, I knew in this type of field men did not like to take orders from females. So, she might just be dealing with some sexist asshole who wants to make her look bad because he doesn't follow her orders. However, she could be new and still want to follow direct orders. Even I know that sometimes you must break a rule or two to get the result that you wanted. Although I'm sure that they needed to do things more legally than myself.

"Why would we want to wait?" he asked as he stood up. My eyes stayed trained on him since I felt like he wasn't a reliable person. He was overworked and needed sleep. All of us did, but he didn't seem to be able to handle not getting it. This was possibly his first real assignment since he started. He was jumping at the opportunity to show the world that he was a great cop. I had to assume that he had led a long, boring career and that his police work wasn't what he thought it would be. This assignment was probably the biggest thing he'd seen, and he wanted more of it. I was glad to supply this to him. "We can probably get information out of her if we keep pestering."

He circled around me, and I'm sure he thought that was intimidating. However, I was used to this. I was used to my comfort zone being poked and prodded by sleazy dudes. I got paid for dealing with these creepy men and women. I didn't know how to be uncomfortable anymore—that feeling was tortured out of me. I wanted to let this guy think he was getting to me. I think it would be hilarious.

I flinched purposefully when he touched the back of the chair. I'm sure he smirked. but I knew that I had to keep my face frozen. He wasn't supposed to know that I wasn't actually breaking under his leadership. I had to force him to believe that he was breaking me. Men tended to be better with body language than facial expressions, so I knew I needed to react more physically. However, I needed to keep that girl on my mind. She would be able to sense this was a ploy just from a wrong eyebrow movement.

I closed my eyes and made sure to rattle my handcuffs when he bent low to my ear. His mustache seemed to graze my skin, and it took everything in me not to shudder. Although I'm sure that would've been better for his ego. As if he thought I was creeped out by him. He just wanted some sort of reaction out of me.

"Her mind works in ways that you will never understand," a voice said as they entered the room. Brian jolted back away from me, and my face fell flat when I looked at who it was. It was the guy from the subway. The one who had followed me around in the motel room when I originally lost my girls. I had to wonder where his greasy-haired friend was. "I cannot have someone on this team who does not want to follow simple orders." He opened the door wider for Brian, but Brian stayed still behind me. He was a little farther away, but I

                    AMY KULP

could still feel his presence. "She was going to manipulate you. You would not scare her. She has had so much worse. Y is a victim."

"Y is a criminal," Brian corrected.

"She is right in this room," the girl officer mentioned. Her eyes darted toward me, and she stopped crossing her arms for a second. "If you want to continue this conversation, go somewhere else. There is nothing more demeaning than talking about someone while they're in the room." She scoffed and shook her head. However, she wasn't looking at me as she said this. It felt genuine. Maybe she was bullied in school. "No matter what she did, she—you—are still a person." She looked blankly at me, and I stared back too.

Brian grumbled on his way out, and I felt satisfied when the door shut roughly behind him. Nobody went after him and each of the two who were left in the room got comfortable. They shifted in their seats until I could see the girl swing her legs into a crisscross position and the guy scoot closer to the table. He seemed to like the cool metal feeling underneath him. I did not.

"I am Agent Navarro," he finally stated. I didn't do anything but look him up and down. He was older up close, and I could see why I thought he was originally homeless. The wrinkles in his hands and eyes aged him, but I could tell that he had a good rapport underneath his belt. Why was he still doing this? I wasn't sure but I had to commend him for it. His shirt was uneven and wrinkled so I knew that he didn't have anyone to help him at home. There was even a small stain near his neck that was slightly bleaching the stripes. He didn't seem to notice and normally I wouldn't, but it made me realize how perfect of a role they gave him. With his short height and lazy eye, he seemed almost as if he was homeless. By ratting his hair and adding a touch of scent to him, he would be the perfect passerby. He blended in with his environment, and that was the best part for him. He was used to watching people. He was probably more dangerous than those who initiated the fight. "My partner will be in shortly."

"Until then," the girl started, "I'll be standing in to make sure he treats you like a human being." There was a glance between the two, and for a second I was suspicious that this was a setup. However, this girl seemed sincere. She didn't seem to take an immediate disliking toward me despite knowing who I was. Maybe she didn't research my name after she found out who I was. Maybe she was just clueless as to what my actions were. People never seemed to understand why we did the things we did. I was convinced because of the good deeds.

"Our main focus is trying to find Trinity," Navarro stated. I carefully watched as he brought out photos of the girl. Some were when she was a younger child. Some were where her instrument was bigger than her, and more recent ones looked to be taken by her. Jaycie was in one of the pictures, and I had to wonder if they knew she was in on this. "Cooperation with us will lighten your sentence and send you into Witness Protection once you are done." I continued to stare at the pictures as he talked nonsense to me. "She's been gone for more

                    AMY KULP

than twenty-four hours. We know the statistics that she is most likely not alive." He paused to see if I would give a reaction, but I knew that my face didn't move. I would not be telling them anything. There was so much more than this girl's life on the line here. "Your face was spotted multiple times when looking back through security footage and news coverage. After all, you are the reason that we knew that we—the FBI—had to be involved." I still didn't say anything, and he slid the pictures closer to me. "Before today, whenever your name was attached to an assignment, you have not gone after big-ticket people. Why did that change with Trinity?" My lips stayed together as I stared straight ahead. My eyes were now between Agent Navarro's head and the girl officer's head. I was just staring at the see-through mirrors, wondering if Brian was watching all of this from behind that glass. "We followed that van for a very long time."

He took out more photos from his pocket and slid them facedown toward me. I stared at the black sides of them before looking at Agent Navarro. He nodded at me to look at them, and despite everything in my head yelling at me not to touch them I turned them over. My eyes got big as I adjusted to see that they had pictures of Sloane, Briley, and Mattie all chilling in the front seat. I quickly forced a stone-cold expression on my face again as I stared at Mattie in the front seat of the van, just a glimpse of Briley's face as she loaded herself into the back, and Sloane's face was mostly covered by her coat as she was walking toward the restroom with Trinity by her side. Despite all these pictures, Jaycie wasn't in any of them. Maybe they didn't know she was part of this yet.

I could, at least, save one girl from a terrible fate.

"We don't know who these girls are yet, but if they are in any criminal database our programs will be able to find them within a couple of months." He leaned forward and scooped the pictures away from me.

I wanted to beg him to keep them on the table but knew that he would know that those girls were important to me, despite how much I wanted to deny it. My mission didn't just end because I was caught. My mission was never going to end. I owed those girls so much. They had my back, and I needed to have theirs. I couldn't say their names or hint that I knew who they were. So far, the only safe one was Jaycie. Unless they were using that to really hurt me.

"The dad is willing to offer a cash reward to you if you give us information," Navarro stated. I continued to stare at the table where the pictures had been. Almost as if the cash didn't matter to me anymore. It had always been about completing the mission. The cash was always an afterthought to me. Mostly because my husband had always bought everything I needed. What did I need cash for besides getting food before and after? "Any information you have would help us." Navarro stared at me for a moment, and despite how much I wanted to stare at him and tell him I couldn't say anything, I continued to just stare at the table.

More than my life was on the line here.

                    AMY KULP

"What is the price for giving us your information?" the girl officer asked. She leaned forward and put her elbows on the table. She seemed to be almost fascinated with me, as if she was trying to figure out how my mind worked. I knew she would never be able to get that answered though. I, myself, didn't know how it worked. My thoughts weren't my own thoughts. I did things because I had to. Would I still be doing this if I was told I could walk free? "Because from what I've been told over the phone and what I've seen on the TV, I feel like you'd be making more money by returning her."

I knew what she was trying to do. She wanted me to argue to try and figure out who our clients were. Maybe she didn't even know she was asking this question to help them with the investigation. Having them narrow down the list of rich people versus poor people would help them get closer to finding that client list. I wasn't sure if there was a client list. I didn't know how they informed people of their auctions and how they sold them. Did they pay upfront? I didn't know any of this, but they thought I did. That meant I couldn't let them know that I didn't know a damn thing.

I was just a follower.

"Are you curious about the number at all?" Navarro asked. He took the pen from his pocket and wrote a number on the sticky note. He folded it once and put the pen back into his shirt pocket. He slid the sticky note toward me, but instead of staring at the mirror or table I stared at him. He kept his eye contact, and I made sure not to waver. He needed to know that I couldn't care less about the money. I cared about my name being ruined and what would happen if people thought I snitched.

I would be looking over my shoulder forever. They would send people to come in and kill me if I was in prison. Even if I was by myself. They could send in other prisoners and guards. They could figure out how to conveniently cut the cameras so there would be no evidence. They knew how to make people disappear without a trace. But they definitely wouldn't kill me. They would bring me back and torture me. They would find new tactics to hurt me. They would perfect their tactics to get information out of other people. They would use these tactics to hurt other girls. They would never kill me though. I would constantly be left to die and then recover. I would be going in and out. They would never get tired of me.

They had specific people now to torture those who were questionable.

I did not want to be tortured.

"It's not about the money," the girl officer stated. She looked at Navarro and brought her legs back up on the chair. She seemed to cradle her knees as she brought them closer to her chest. "What is it about then? Why would you torture people willingly?"

I wanted to object to her. She didn't need to know my exact position though. I did not torture those girls. I would never hurt a fly. I was just doing what I was told. I knew how to fight, but I rarely ever did. I defended myself, and when someone was going to hurt our chances of completing the mission

　　　　　　　　　　　AMY KULP

I had to show them who was boss. I never tortured anyone though. She had to know that. I wasn't that much of a monster. But I needed to complete my mission. I didn't have a choice or else I would be tortured.

"What aren't you telling us?" Navarro asked as he slammed his hands down on the table. I jolted from the sudden anger coming from him, and from the corner of my eye I could see that the girl officer did too. She brought her legs down from the chair and stared at him. "You need to face the consequences of what you did to these innocent people!" He stood up, and I could see the nervousness radiating from the girl officer. Either she was an amazing actress or she really was new. Navarro came closer to me, and just like Brian he got close to my ear. I knew not to flinch, and as my eyes clouded over I knew that I wasn't going to hear him if he yelled anything at me. I had to protect myself. "We should not even be giving you choices on how to help! You should want to help Trinity! You got her into this mess. You need to get her out!" He grabbed the handcuffs that my wrists were in and slammed them on the table.

"You can't do that!" the girl officer yelled as she stood up. My knuckles banged down on the table, but I refused to wince. I have experienced worse than that. "Agent Navarro, you are getting out of line!" She yanked my handcuffs away from Navarro, and he immediately started pacing around the room. The officer just stood near me as if she could stop Navarro. We all knew that even if she was experienced, the FBI was trained differently than normal police stations. "Agent Navarro, you need to calm down."

"How can I calm down when there are millions of girls who are being trafficked every day because of her and her crew?" he asked. He put his palms behind his head and sat back down. I could tell that he was angry though. "Why do you get to live a happy life when they are suffering in their own nightmares?"

"Are you okay?" the officer asked. I didn't react, and she carefully flipped my hand over on the table. I could see that my knuckles were beet red, but only one was busted open. She winced at my pain and ushered me out of my seat by pulling on the cuffs. "I'm going to take her to get cleaned up. Try to think of something else to get her to talk."

Navarro only nodded his head in response.

I walked out with the girl officer and felt stares coming from the other room. I refused to do anything but stare straight ahead. I was brought into the exact bathroom that I was in yesterday when I saw this officer digging through the trash. I couldn't tell if this was a coincidence or if this was the closest bathroom to the interrogation room. Either way, she followed me inside and started running the water on warm.

"What's your name?" I whispered as I repeatedly ran my knuckle under the water. I didn't look up at her until the bleeding stopped and I needed to start sanitizing it. The soap burned the cut as it crept its way into my skin, but as soon as the pain started I forced my hand under the water again.

"Kolleen," she finally answered. I only nodded and when I was done, I flicked the water onto the floor. A paper towel was probably a better option, but she was looking for something when I last threw the paper towels away. I couldn't give her that opportunity again.

She grabbed my shoulder initially, but when I nodded to use the bathroom she allowed me to go. I just needed a couple of minutes by myself. If I had to go into the stall and fake my bladder antics, that was one way I could get it. I locked the stall door behind me and pretended to fiddle with my pants before sitting down. I just wanted to get a couple of minutes of rest. I leaned back into the wall and felt my eyes close for a solid minute. As soon as Kolleen made an uncomfortable coughing noise appear from her throat, I flushed the toilet and rewashed my hands.

She carefully led me out and then proceeded to poke me in the direction of the interrogation room. Walking back in, I could feel the pokes intensify, so when I looked back at Kolleen her face seemed to show a different emotion. It looked guilty. I tried not to think about it though. I wasn't supposed to see that emotion. When the door swung back open and I took my seat, I saw that Navarro was also straighter and more pristine in his appearance. It wasn't until I sat down and could see that there was an additional figure near the door.

This familiar face smiled creepily at me and didn't stop until he sat down in Kolleen's chair. He played with the sticky note from Navarro and ripped it up happily in front of me. Blowing the pieces at my face, I didn't allow myself to flinch except to blink when a scrap got a bit too close to my eyes. I had to fight myself to stop from sneering and looked over at Navarro again. He seemed to enjoy the game that I was playing in my mind, fighting myself on what to say exactly. How do I voice my disgust with a traitor? Someone who was part of the company for so long and that I have known briefly on missions we had together? This person was like an older brother. But here he sat without handcuffs on displaying a smirk and a flirty attitude. This time, I couldn't help but feel betrayed.

"I missed you, Y." He leaned backward in his chair, and I made sure to put my hands on my lap so that he couldn't see I was balling my fists up. "Haven't worked together since our previous mission. I was surprised when they called you in as soon as we came home. Have you had time to rest?" I didn't say anything. "Aw, Navarro, she's playing hard to get." He sat up now and smiled delicately at me. As if his charm would work on me here. "Maybe you got caught because they were overworking you. We all know how that feels." I felt my glare intensify. I couldn't control my face right now, but I was hoping that it wasn't too readable. I pulled at the beige shirt I was wearing and continued to clasp and unclasp my fist. "After all, I was working a double shift, one as an FBI agent and one as—"

"A mole!" I yelled. I popped up and dove across the table. I had his shirt in my hands before I could convince myself to let go. "You are a dirty rotten spy!" I could hear commotion from around

                    AMY KULP

us, and I knew that I hurt my hip from landing on top of him. "Carlos, we trusted you! Why would you turn your back on us when we needed you?" I tried to push his shirt up and down so that I was banging his head on the ground, but it seemed to just shake him like a worm. No real damage was happening. I felt tugs at my own body, and when they started lifting me off him he smirked again at me. "How could you betray us?" I yelled as I swung my hands toward his face. I winced as the knuckle connected with his cheek. It reopened, and I could already see the swelling. He deserved it.

"Sedate her!" Navarro yelled.

"No," Carlos protested as he scrambled up. "Sit her down." He stood up tall as I struggled against Kolleen and Navarro. "I have some explaining to do." The other two seemed to think he was nuts, but as I sat down I instantly calmed down.

I trusted this man. He was someone I always enjoyed working with. We constantly played around and joked with each other. He was always pestering me with questions that I didn't know the answers to, and now it made sense. He wasn't asking to know more about the mission; he was asking because he needed to take our team down. He was asking so that he could really hurt me. I always told him it was classified when I didn't know an answer, and he must've assumed that I actually knew the answer. He thought I was important to this crew. Why else would he show himself to me? He would never show himself to Mattie if she was caught. I was furious that he betrayed us, but I wanted to hear the explanation he was giving me. He was clearly a good actor, so I knew I couldn't fall for his trap.

"Hands off of her," he stated. Kolleen and Navarro instantly removed their hands and stared at us. Navarro reclaimed his seat, and Kolleen stood menacingly close to me. "Ask me any questions you want, and I'll answer them honestly."

"What's your real name?"

"Carlos," he mentioned. He shrugged. "I never lied about that. I wouldn't lie to you, Y." He paused as I sneered at him. "Have I ever lied to you? Think back to all of the times we worked together." I refused to follow his commands. "She's always been stubborn," he mentioned as he realized I wouldn't do what he said. "You are the most caring leader I have had in the missions that we worked together."

"So you targeted me?"

"You were vulnerable," he restated. "They were overworking you. You barely had any time off." He paused again, but I refused to think about what he was saying. "You were making mistakes left and right. You didn't train your new group as much as you did any time I was with you."

I clenched my fists at the thought that he would insult me. Kolleen must've seen it because she was right by my side. She stood in a stance that told me I would not make it over the table if I tried something. I glared at her, Carlos, and Navarro until I set my eyes back on the mirror. Not knowing who was back there was so much better than knowing about this double-crossing snitch.

"Y, you need to tell us where Trinity is." He put his hand on my knuckle, and I flinched away from him. I didn't want to talk to him. I didn't want to look at him. I hoped that nobody else would find out about this. I didn't want them to associate me with anyone who couldn't be trusted. I was reliable. I don't care what Carlos thought—I was not vulnerable. I did my job right this time and every single other time. "Where is Trinity?" I could hear the anger rising in his voice but continued to stare at the mirror.

"It looks like your plan is backfiring," Navarro commented. "She doesn't seem to trust you as much." He paused and studied me. I didn't have to look at him to be able to see him out of the corner of my eye. "Alright, so let's cut to the chase, Y." He spat at my name. I couldn't help but stare at him. "Nobody but you knows about Carlos. Nobody knows where you are except us. Nobody knows anything." He paused. "However, Carlos is free to go back undercover and report back that you are the double-crosser." I arched my eyebrows but quickly put them back down. I closed my eyes for a brief second and felt my hands start to get jittery. "Do you want to talk now, even though Carlos is going to tell everyone all of these lies about you?" He paused again. "Carlos, now."

Carlos immediately rose out of his chair and smirked as he left. I didn't stop staring at him until he left the room and Kolleen took her place back in his seat. I knew that he was just staring at me through the mirror, but I could feel my eyes starting to look around the room.

What if he did go back and tell everyone? I would be on everyone's hit lists. They would send so many people after me. All my nightmares would be coming true. I would not have the protection of my husband if he thought I was a spy. He would personally instruct everyone on how to torture me. He would use my deepest fears against me. I would be electrocuted, medieval torture devices would be used, I would be starved, sleep deprived, and I wouldn't be able to think without begging for my life. They were animals. They liked the sadistic torture. They liked to hear screams.

They cut Mattie's tongue off!

They would do so much worse to me. They would pull my hair out of my head, one by one. My throat would grow raw from screaming and begging for my life. My cheeks would be stained with tears as they raced down my face in a desperate attempt to have them feel bad for me. They would smash my teeth in one-by-one. Leaving me with hideous sharp pieces. Crushing each morsel until there were bruises in my mouth. My mouth would be so damaged that I wouldn't be able to talk. The screams would be intensified since nothing would be blocking the noise from coming out. There wouldn't be a place on my body that wasn't covered in bruises, cuts, and wounds. All my bones would be broken, and none of them would heal properly. I would be deformed to the point that nobody would know who I was. I wouldn't even know who I was. I would be humiliated.

I would beg for them to kill me so that I didn't have to suffer anymore.

"Are you okay?" Kolleen asked.

I shut my eyes for a second and felt my mind shut off. I could not give in to their lies. I could not trust someone who was against our system. If they wanted to lie about my reputation, then they could lie. I could not give up information. I would be just as bad as Carlos. I would be worse than Carlos. I have been doing this longer than him, and I was trusted more than him. He needed to ask me and interrogate me because he couldn't go up the ranks fast enough.

They wouldn't tattle on me because he knew to fear their power. They wouldn't have any information if I was found. They would never get any information if I escaped here. Carlos knew better.

Unless he was stupid.

"Kolleen, I need you to go out there," Navarro commanded. When I looked back over at him, his eyes were scanning a phone he was on. Kolleen obeyed, and I knew that she was more experienced than what she let on. They needed her. Her caring attitude was an act. As soon as she left, Navarro just stared at me. Nothing was being said, and I found my eyes going back to the mirror.

I knew not to think. So, I blacked out my mind, and for a moment, I felt the exhaustion hit me. However, I couldn't show them I was weak. I stared at the mirror, and for what felt like an eternity Navarro and I were stuck in silence.

Until the door opened back up and Carlos stepped back in.

"I have something I think you would be interested in," Carlos said. I could see that Brian and Kolleen were also in there and another set of shoes too. Carlos paused for a second and looked at Navarro. Without saying a word, he nodded and left the room. "Or someone."

He moved to the side, and I was faced with Brian and Kolleen again. Turning around but still not showing me who else was in the room, I heard the rattling chains on their hands and on their ankles. I was curious, but I knew I couldn't show it. I could feel Carlos studying me.

"I figured since you weren't going to tell us with anger and anything else we were throwing at you that I would try something else. You have been tortured and prodded for ten years," Carlos mentioned. "Anything we do to you legally would not be anything compared to there. So, I figured—"

"Just shut up already," Kolleen said. She moved to the side and grabbed Carlos and Brian before exiting the room. Looking back at me, she winked for a second, and my eyes landed on the person who was left in the room with me.

I looked them up and down with disinterest. They brought me some sort of criminal. The red jumpsuit was a color that I wasn't expecting on this man. I wasn't sure where this prisoner was from, but red usually indicated they had more serious charges than the average criminal. Maybe he was in maximum security? He crept closer to me, and I stared at the chains around his ankles. It looked uncomfortable since he didn't have room to move his wrists. However, he kept rattling them. His body

                                    AMY KULP

was muscular with his biceps poking from the short sleeve of the jumpsuit. While not as muscular as Carlos, I could see why Kolleen thought there might be something more. This person was attractive until you got to their face. Crawling up his neck seemed to be various cuts and scars that healed horribly. While just small bumps now, it looked like they were deep and hurtful. They were old, but some newer, lighter scars seemed to dance from his eye to his chin.

Something about the cut rang familiar to me.

"Do you remember me?" he asked as I continued to stare at him. My eyes continued to scour his face for a hint of something familiar about him. I could feel the thoughts racing through my brain about who this was. Who was so important to me that I was expected to snitch on my entire group? My entire organization? My husband? My friends? My life? As soon as I saw a smile form on his lips and could see his teeth, I felt my face change. It went from a stone-cold expressionless statue to my forehead wrinkling, my eyebrows crinkling, my eyes closing in happiness, my nose scrunching up, and my lips broadening in a smile.

"Murphy?" I asked as my voice barely escaped my throat.

He nodded, and without thinking if this was actually him, I crashed my body into his. He stabilized us, and I threw my arms over his head. I squeezed into him tight and felt tears brimming up in my eyes. Neither of us let go, and it wasn't something sexual—this was my family. He was my brother. He showed me the ropes. He was the reason I survived. He was the reason I was doing so well.

Once the organization split up, I didn't see Murphy too often. My husband felt threatened by him. Even though I could swear nothing was going on, he didn't believe us. Murphy was my brother and mentor. He has lived here since he was born; he was able to do his job while also complaining about the faults. Nobody but Murphy had enough confidence to do that. He took me under his wing for some reason. The past is a bit blurry, but I do remember Murphy. When the split first happened, we would find times to hang out whenever we were in between jobs. However, those started becoming less frequent. Then after a while, I went to check in on him in his room and he wasn't there. He didn't come back. Eventually, they filled it with someone else. I never learned what happened. I figured he died or was killed. Going to jail was so much better.

However, he grew up so much since I last saw him. He sprouted taller than me. He had more cuts, bruises, scars, and wounds than I have ever seen on him. His hair was cut differently, and despite being in jail it looked better. He was fit now instead of being lanky. However, he looked older. Time was catching up to him. I'm sure he had to fight in jail. I'm sure he didn't snitch during his trials. How he failed a mission, I will never know. I don't want to know and don't care. Murphy wasn't Carlos. Murphy wouldn't put our organization under—no matter how much he hated working here.

I put my hands on the back of his neck and released from the hug. I kept close to him so that I

                                          AMY KULP

could whisper and not be listened to by the police officer and the FBI agents. I didn't know what to do, and I felt like Murphy would help. Murphy always knew what to say to make me feel better or to avoid the torture. He knew his way around the game. He knew his way around the missions with barely being involved.

"What do I do?" I whispered to him. I put my forehead on his and just closed my eyes. It felt good to be near someone who I have known for so long. He moved away and opened his eyes to stare at me. I knew that he would be taken away after he gave me the advice. He had to do his time, and I didn't know how long that was for. "Thank you," I whispered. He nodded and stared at me. As soon as the door opened, he wiped the tears from my eyes. He smiled sadly at me, and I could see his lips moving, but Navarro, Kolleen, Brian, and Carlos were too noisy for me to hear what he said.

"I'm not coming back, Emily."

"Stop telling me I'm lying!" I yelled. I wanted to slam my hands on the table and felt like that would have been an excellent choice. In my predicament, I couldn't lose my cool though. I didn't want them to get any type of emotion out of me. They just saw me at my most vulnerable and they took the most precious thing away from me. The most annoying thing in the world was when someone accused you of lying when you weren't. How do you prove you are not lying? There is no way. They will always just believe that you are lying. There is no way to fix that. "I don't know where they took Trinity." I shook my head and made sure to enunciate each word. I had to act like they were preschoolers because of how dense they were. "Hook me up to a lie detector test, Carlos." I could hear the rage in each word becoming stronger and stronger.

"We both know that you would pass regardless of if you were lying," he said. He looked at me and just blinked his eyes. "I know you passed multiple lie detector tests." He paused and stared at me.

I had no idea what he was talking about. Yes, we were trained to pass them. Yes, we were trained to lie. However, I do not know what lie detector tests he was talking about. I took one once and that was it. That was how they knew I was ready to start being the leader of the group. How would Carlos know that? Carlos wasn't higher than me in the ranks. However, that didn't mean he wouldn't have gotten special privileges for being male. I had to work twenty times harder than him to get where I was.

"Every time you came back and saw the doctor," Carlos stated. He leaned forward and licked his lips. That was his tell that he was nervous. I'm not sure if he knew that but from working with him so much, I came to realize it about him. "He hooked you up to wires and asked you questions." I blinked at him. "That was the lie detector test. They wanted to make sure that you could keep lying. They knew not all our missions went over well. They always had someone from the uppers in a group. They always had eyes on us. They always had cameras in our vans and on the computers we used. We were always being watched. They just had to make sure you were a good liar."

"How do I prove that I'm not lying?" I asked. I could feel the metal handcuffs dig into my wrists as I pulled them apart underneath the table. I needed to feel the sting in my wrists. It felt good and I knew that I was betraying the only people who have been there for me. The only consistent group and the only consistent friends I had. I was betraying them and if they ever found out, I would be tortured. I was just preparing myself for what was to eventually come. "Carlos, I promise you; I was never told where they keep the girls. Why are you pushing this so hard?" I looked up at him and then over to Kolleen.

She's been silent this entire time. I could feel the judgment from her but wasn't sure if she was leaning against me or for me. Her face was as cold as mine was. However, she didn't start acting like this until Murphy left. What did she know that I didn't? What did Murphy tell them?

Why would Murphy be transferred down here? He would have had to agree to it. How did they convince him he wasn't going to be killed? Maybe he had a great place in jail, but I knew that in the back of his mind, he was worried that they would find him. He was always worried that if he did ever escape, he would be brought back. I don't know if his entire plan was for him to escape or if jail was the ultimate goal but how did he not think this was a setup? Did the organization tip him off that he was not needed? That he was useless? Why was he not worried? Did they give him a lighter sentence? Did they-

"A partial fingerprint was found from what I got from you," Kolleen stated.

"And there was a match in our system," Carlos continued.

He remained still in his seat with his arms crossed. He wasn't looking at me at this point. Kolleen got up but I wasn't looking at her. When she left, Navarro came back in with a stack of papers. I had to assume it was me in that file. What did they know about me that I didn't? Did I have a last name?

"What did Murphy call you when he left?" Navarro asked roughly. I stared at him for a second before returning my gaze to Carlos. He wouldn't

                                   AMY KULP

look at me still. "Your name is not Y. What did Murphy call you?"

"My name is Y," I stated. I shrugged my shoulders at them as if they were crazy. "I have always been Y."

"Are you trying to convince us or yourself?" Navarro asked. I looked at him intently as he shared a glance with Carlos. "Do you know who Emily Washington is?" Before I could answer, he held up his palm and stopped me for a second. "Think really hard. Do you know who Emily Washington is?"

I stopped my anger and frustration with both and thought about it. I racked my brain for possible answers to this riddle. It seemed impossible. Could she have been one of those girls that I kidnapped? I didn't remember most of their names. I just knew them as statistics. They were the reason that my rank was so high. Was it a family member of a victim? Most of the time, I did get to know those close to them. It was how I fit in. It was how I gained their trust. It was how I betrayed them.

Was Emily someone I worked with? While I didn't work with too many girls, there were still some names that I didn't get to know too well. I would remember them and swear that I would but as the months passed, I would forget. I would see them as we passed in the halls and all I could do was smile at them. I couldn't say hi because I couldn't remember them. They were not important enough for me to remember.

Who was Emily Washington?

I shook my head and opened my eyes. I didn't want to say it out loud because I felt like they would tell me I was lying again. I didn't know who she was though. Why couldn't they just tell me? Clearly, she was important to them.

Navarro slowly opened the manilla folder he had. With a glance toward Carlos, he showed me the picture of a girl on his paper. It was a 'missing' sign with the name scrawled in deep red at the bottom. The picture looked like a girl who was smiling and looking forward to her life. When I squinted, I could see that this picture looked like a younger version of me.

"That's not me," I stated. I shook my head and looked back at Carlos. I didn't like this game. I didn't like what they were insinuating. "I am Y."

"You are Emily Washington," Carlos mentioned. He made eye contact with me for a second before looking down at the paper. I shook my head at him, but he didn't seem to notice. "You were kidnapped ten years ago." I shook my head again. "You were trafficked ten years ago." I shook my head again. "For some reason, you were kept as a team member. You were one of those girls. Emily, you were sent to where those girls are being sent now." I shook my head again and felt tears in my eyes. This was a sick joke. "Emily-"

"My name is Y!" I yelled. I sniffled back the snot that was coming out of my nose and flicked the tears out of the corners of my eyes. "I don't know who Emily Washington is, but she is not me. I am Y. I don't like this. I don't like you lying to me, Carlos." I could hear the strain in my voice, and I shook my head again.

The room was different now. We weren't yelling at each other for lying this time. Instead, they seemed to pity me. Even Navarro wasn't saying much. Carlos had to think about what he was saying to me.

"Does the name Ellis ring a bell?" Carlos asked. I sniffled but ended up shaking my head. I didn't know anyone they were talking about. "Ellis was an FBI agent who worked on your case." I stared at the table and shook my head again. "I don't know what happened, only you would be able to tell us but-"

"I don't know Ellis," I stated. The name didn't even ring a bell to me.

"We don't know what you've been through," Navarro stated. "We don't know why they picked you to stay." He pushed the flier toward me again. "But you have a family out there. You have people who care about you."

"My husband is the only family I need."

"Your husband lied to you," Navarro stated. "He's been lying to you since you have been in the organization." He shook his head. "You are our only hope of finding Trinity and stopping the human trafficking horrors of these girls." He paused and opened his mouth to talk. However, he didn't get another word out without me talking over him.

"We are helping these girls," I stated. Carlos and Navarro both shook their heads. "These girls don't have a purpose in life and once they are captured, they are being put to use."

"Is that what your husband told you?" Navarro asked. I looked at him before nodding my head. "Emily-"

"Call me Y," I begged. I shook my head. "I am not this girl."

"Who are you then?" Carlos asked. His voice was loud and aggressive and surprised me. I looked over at him and could see the anger on his face. I could see the annoyance.

"I am Y," I stated back. "I would like to use the bathroom." I got up without their permission and waited for Kollen to open the door.

When she did, she barely smiled at me. She looked at the two boys and warned them about questioning me any further right now. I didn't listen to her warnings though because I wanted to go the bathroom. I was exhausted and knew that I was allowed to rest soon. I just needed to get rid of this pain in my chest and another gnawing pain.

As soon as I got in the bathroom, I ran to the stall. While it was important for me to get the pain out of my chest, I knew that the weird urge on my thigh was for something. I pulled my pants down and spread my thighs apart until I could see my inner thigh.

There was a faint scar there that said the name "Emily". I traced my finger over it again and again. As I stared at the light-pink scar, I couldn't help but close my eyes. I couldn't remember how I got it, but I did remember that I was the one to make it a scar. Maybe the earliest memory I have, but I know it was written in pen or marker or something. While I was being tortured to be able to stay in the organization, I kept scratching it into my thighs. It was so I didn't forget who I was. But I did. I did forget.

I forgot that I am Emily Washington.

-------------------Chapter 14

I could hear the metal creak underneath my body weight as I turned to my side. Despite how exhausted I was in the interrogation, I couldn't sleep now. My mind was racing with thoughts while my body ached from sitting all day. Who knew that if you remained in the same position repeatedly that your body would become sore from that? Who knew that your thoughts could keep you up even if you were exhausted?

The pain in my body radiated throughout with thumps of hurt. I had a small indent around my wrist where the handcuffs had laid all day. Over time, they had gotten tighter and every time they were taken off, the next instance they hurt more. I placed my fingers around the small indent to try and see if it was a cut or a mark. It was itchy and felt like it when you wore too tight of a sock. Caressing the skin was making it sorer though so I stopped. My hands traveled down to my breasts and I felt how swollen they were. Closing my eyes, I now moved my hands down to my knees. Whenever I was exhausted and couldn't sleep, my knees were weak and sore. I massaged them but knew it wasn't going to help at all. Giving up on that task, I put my hands down my pants and traced over the scar again. It was still puffy and I don't think it would ever go down, but it was comforting. It felt familiar.

My name was Emily apparently. For ten years I went by Y. Everyone I knew called me Y. I fully embodied that my name was Y. While having Emily scrawled onto my leg, I assumed she was someone important to me. Someone I had forgotten. Turns out, it was just myself I had forgotten. How does someone forget themselves? When did I stop being Emily and when did I start becoming Y?

Who was Emily Washington? Did I have a middle name? Did I have parents? A family? A dog? Were there people who knew who I was? Why did I run away to join this organization? Or was Carlos truthful when he said I was a girl who was kidnapped? Was I someone that went through the program and wanted to join the organization? Did I have a choice?

Why couldn't I remember Emily Washington? We were the same person after all, but I couldn't remember anything about her. Did she look exactly like me? Or was my hair dyed? Did I like my hair long or short? Was I girly or a tomboy? My mind was racing with so many possibilities that my forehead started to sweat from the stress.

I was not Emily Washington. I was Y.

Turning over, I closed my eyes and forced them to stay shut. I couldn't keep thinking. I had to sleep because as soon as they came back in from their shifts, I would be interrogated. I would be investigated for twenty-four hours. They would run me wild until I begged to go to sleep or eat something. Although, they knew that I would never beg. However, I knew that they couldn't withhold sleep or food from me. Did they have to give me a lot? Absolutely not. Did they have to let me get a full eight hours of sleep? I didn't know. So, I shouldn't be taking what sleep they are giving me for granted.

I used to be able to shut my mind off but as I turned over again, I knew I was too distracted. As soon as I commanded my body to sleep, I used to shut my eyes and drift off. Why couldn't I follow those directions right now? I turned to my stomach and put my arms underneath the pillow that was provided. It was as flat as a board and smelled gross. I wasn't sure if it was from my hair or if they just didn't wash it. After all, prisoners usually weren't sentenced to a holding cell. Normally, I would be whisked off to a prison to hold me. They just didn't want to move me because I could possibly escape.

Carlos knew not to underestimate me.

From down the hall, I could hear someone obnoxiously swinging their keys around on the ring. Hitting together used to soothe me but now that I was irritable from exhaustion, I wanted to rip them apart. I sat up and stared down the long hallway to see if they were coming for me. Of course, they were. Where else would they be going? Nobody was drunk overnight and needed to stay there to sober up. There was nobody who fought their spouse last night and was waiting for the paperwork to move to a different prison. I was alone and I think they were doing that on purpose.

"Rise and shine," Brian said as he put one of the keys in the cell to let me out. I held my wrists out in front of him and he clasped the cuffs on too

                                          AMY KULP

tightly. He did it on purpose. He always did. "We're going to give you breakfast and then I'll take you to the bathroom."

"Can we go to the bathroom first?" I asked.

"Who's in charge here?" he asked. I blinked as I looked up at him. I didn't mean to say it in a challenging way, but I was sore and didn't feel that good. "Let's do as I say and be grateful that I'm even feeding you. I can say I did and not do it. Who would believe you?"

"Carlos," I said.

"I think Carlos is still getting his beauty sleep."

"Jealous?" I asked. He tugged hard on my wrists to get me moving and I tried not to visibly wince when he did it. I've had worse than some guy who had an ego problem. "Is that how you feel manly?" I wondered. I slowed my speed and felt his finger prodding me in the back. I knew where I was going but I was sick of this man. "You have to assert dominance over the stupidest little things?" I tried to turn around, but his palm quickly clasped onto my shoulder. He wouldn't let me get away with anything easily.

"I'm doing my job," he growled.

"You're pissing me off," I retorted. "Why don't I have this problem with Kolleen?"

"Her name is Officer Caquatto," he retorted.

"Maybe to you." I rolled my eyes. "Seems like she doesn't have a lot of respect for you either. Are you pissed that, maybe, you have to take orders from a female?"

"Are you kidding me?" he asked. "Are you that stupid?" His laugh was so fake that I knew he was going to insult my intelligence. "Officer Caquatto isn't part of the police force - she's part of the FBI. They've been playing you this entire time."

"I don't believe you," I simply stated. "You didn't know who I was until you saw it on the TV."

"Because it was an act," he stated. "Everybody knows who you are. We wanted confirmation with the fingerprints, but we saw your wanted poster. We are trained to know these things. While we were in the car, I had people call for you." He pressed my back so that I faced him and stood taller than me. He did it on purpose. "When you do eventually get booked, I'll make sure everyone knows you kidnapped little girls and-"

"I would never do little girls," I stated. I stared at him in disbelief. "These girls were almost all eighteen. They wanted something more in life, so we gave them that purpose. If they wanted to leave, they could have."

"Screaming, crying, and yelling for help wasn't enough?" he asked. He rolled his eyes as he refused to look at me. That was a bit insulting to me, but I didn't need respect from him. I needed respect for the future inmates and prisoners that would be with me. I needed respect from my husband and everyone I worked with. "You didn't care. You just wanted a paycheck."

I opened my mouth to argue but knew to shut it. He wouldn't listen. He didn't know. He would never know that I did what I had to so I would survive. Yes, I made those choices but the

                                    AMY KULP

alternative would have been so much worse for me. Morally, I did not care about those girls. Once they were out of my hands, I forgot about them. Maybe it was on purpose. Maybe it was because I was focused on my next task. However, I could never do what Jaycie did. I could never befriend them and then tear that trust away. It would break me. Maybe I wasn't as good at my job as I thought I was. But I did always command respect and when I didn't get it, I didn't throw a hissy fit. I put my chin in the air and trudged forward. I could lead anyone to a successful mission.

Apparently, even an FBI agent. I can't remember how long I had known Carlos, but we did have multiple missions. He allowed those girls to get captured and tortured and trafficked just like I had. So why am I the bad guy? Why isn't Carlos in trouble too? He can claim anything he wants but now he's just going to be known as a snitch and he's going to have to look over his shoulder for the rest of his life.

If anyone ever found out.

Depending on what happens to me, I wouldn't be ashamed to let loose that secret. Carlos was my friend. Maybe he still is. I'm not sure but I knew I shouldn't trust a cop. Or an FBI agent. Or whatever he was. But to him, I was just a mission to get closer to. Maybe not even me. Maybe I got in the way at some point. Maybe I wasn't supposed to be involved at all. But how could I not? He said that a previous agent was working on my case. I didn't know an Ellis unless he used a false name. Honestly, it would have been much smarter than using his real name. But if Ellis was watching after me, why couldn't he help me? Why was I still stuck in this organization?

I hated it at first. I remember that. I remember crying and my husband having to hold me at night. He would soothe me. He would relax me. When he couldn't, I went to Murphy for comfort. Although he wasn't helpful ever. He just grumbled and said one day he would get out of there. I always told him to shut up about it because if anyone were to overhear, we would be tortured. I would guilt him and say he would be responsible for my torture. After a while, I stopped going to my husband and just went to Murphy. It was rewarding to have a friendship where we had the same mutual feelings about this organization. I think that's when my husband started to get jealous. He didn't know what happened behind closed doors. When he came back from his missions and meetings, he started working his way up the ladder and he made sure that Murphy and I never worked together once the organization grew.

"Let's get going," Brian said as he snatched me by my handcuffs again. This time, I groaned out loud. I wasn't sure if I just momentarily fell asleep or if I was daydreaming, but either way, I felt a tad more refreshed. Although maybe it was because I was allowing myself to think without caution. "Eat." He sat me down near his desk and threw a banana in my lap.

I just looked at it before nodding my head. I wasn't going to argue right now. I was too hungry. My teeth clanked so hard when I started chewing

                    AMY KULP

that at first, I thought I chipped a piece off. A banana was so much better than the cold, unidentified piece of meat that they gave me yesterday. It could have had mold on it, and I would not have cared. I was too hungry yesterday and that hunger seems to have multiplied when I saw the banana. Maybe it was because it was something I haven't had in forever. Did Emily like bananas?

As I savored the taste on the tip of my tongue, I watched as Brian peeked over to the next cubicle with a smile on his face. That was interesting, I haven't seen him smile since I've been here. I always assumed he was a grumpy man. He peeked over and for an instant, his playful nature made me realize that maybe he was a dad. Maybe he was only grumpy when he was at work. It had to be depressing in this line of work. Gratifying though.

"Oh, she's adorable!" he said as he kept his foot inside the cubicle. He would probably get in trouble if he left all the way. This was his compromise. "How old is she?" he wondered as he leaned closer to the coworker. "I remember when my little Connor was that tiny. She's adorable. I bet you can't wait to go home to her." I didn't hear a response but listened to Brian say hi again.

However, the mood instantly changed when I could hear a baby crying over the phone. With a swift goodbye, I could hear the phone hanging up and Brian came back in. He went back to his desk and started typing on the computer as I sat there with the banana in my hand. Those little cries instantly made me drop it on the floor and I did my best to clutch my arms around my chest. Being handcuffed, it was a little difficult, but I needed to hide my shirt.

"I really need to go to the bathroom now," I stated. Brian looked over at me and then at the banana on the floor before he stood up. It must have been something on my face because instead of yelling at me, he picked up the banana and tossed it in the trash. He nodded his head and I thanked him profusely as he walked behind me.

I tried to go as fast as I could, but Brian seemed to saunter on the walk over. He didn't want to walk me to the bathroom because he hated babysitting. However, he knew fighting me over this was going to take forever. If anything, I would have pretended to pee myself just so I could get what I wanted. How could he refuse me bathroom privileges? In an actual prison, did they have to ask or could they always go? Wasn't there a communal bathroom?

"Thank you," I whispered as he removed my handcuffs. I barged into the bathroom and looked under the stalls to see if anyone else was in here. Thankfully, it looked like I would have my privacy. I was sure that Brian saw everything when I gave him my wrists, but I didn't care. I stared straight at the mirror and could see the wet marks leaking from my breasts. I cursed myself and immediately started dabbing paper towels over them. Maybe it would help with what liquid was already on the shirt.

Hearing the bathroom doors open, I rushed into a stall and started dabbing the toilet paper onto myself too. How could I make this look like something it wasn't? I turned around and sighed as I investigated the toilet. Desperate times called for desperate measures. I scooped my hands into the water and quickly splashed myself. The officer in the stall next to me paused for a moment before flushing her toilet. I immediately splashed more on myself and waited for her to leave. I could hear the drips of the water come from my shirt but was hoping this officer didn't care. Hopefully, it wasn't Kolleen.

I waited patiently and when I heard the dryers going off, I splashed myself again. When they finally left the room, I opened the stall door and found myself sliding against the tiled bathroom. Going to the sinks, I splashed more water that way and dunked my head under the faucet. I could say I was taking a shower with the fastest method I knew how. Throwing the hair further into the sink and putting the nape of my neck right under the water, I felt a little freshness coming about. Maybe I would wash my hair.

Looking through my hair, I was able to feel for some hand soap and began dispersing that in there. I dug my nails into my dirty scalp and didn't rinse it until I was sure the grime in there was cleaned. I didn't know if hand soap was going to work but at least it was something. I was tired of smelling and fearing about how I looked. While it was usually the farthest thing from my mind, I knew it would eventually creep up into my thoughts.

Until I heard Brian's yell and out of reaction, I hit my head up into the faucet of the sink. I fell instantly from how hard I moved and had to take a moment to look up at him. He didn't seem mad but instead, his face was soft as he picked me up. I was a bit dizzy, but I allowed him to move my body under the hand dryer as my hair began to stop dripping. He rung it out for me and when I wasn't a sopping mess, he moved my body. He could see the mess in the bathroom that I had made from the toilets to the sink, and to the soap. However, he didn't yell at me.

"What happened in here?" Kolleen asked as she had her hand on her belt and her eyes moved from all the water everywhere. "Are you okay?" she asked as Brian stepped away from me. Brian nodded his head and then she turned to me. "We can't just leave her in those clothes. She'll get sick. I'll go get her some new ones. Brian, clean up the mess."

"I'll clean up the mess," I whispered when Kolleen left. "I made it, I'll clean it."

"What happened?" he asked. "I think that I can guess but..." He shook his head.

"I wanted to be clean," I answered as I grabbed the paper towels. I would probably be using all of them, but I methodically wiped any excess soap from the sinks and began drying up the water on the floor. "There isn't a shower here," I commented.

"I didn't realize," he said. "We're used to just shipping people away to prisons that do have showers." He thought for a moment as I started picking up the paper towels. "You could have said something, and we could have arranged something for you to clean yourself."

"You wouldn't even let me go to the bathroom this morning," I commented.

He stayed quiet after that and I was glad. I didn't want to continue lying to him especially if he thought we were having a heart-to-heart. Maybe he did see me as a human now. He wasn't one of those cops that thought they were better than us but he didn't believe in letting me slide on any crimes I committed. I knew it didn't help that when we met, we were fighting each other. He probably assumed that I didn't have respect for police officers.

He would be correct.

"Alright, I found more uniforms," Kolleen offered. "Change in the stall and then I'll make sure these get washed."

I nodded my head and headed into the stall. As I took the wet shirt off, I was proud of my work. There were minimal stains on the inside or outside and it did just look like one liquid to me - not two separate ones. I quickly changed and when I came back out, I handed her my stuff. She left in an instant and Brian just stared at me as he got ready to put the handcuffs on. I offered my wrists and he put them on again; this time they were even tighter on me. I tried to flex my wrists but I could barely move them because they were so tight. When I looked back at him, he just poked me with his finger to start moving.

I'm sure that Navarro and Carlos were waiting for me.

"Looks like you got into a mess this morning," Navarro commented as I sat down in the chair. I didn't say anything to him but quietly roamed my fingers through my hair. "We're not playing games today. The longer that Trinity is out there, the more likely we won't be able to find her. It'll be on your head." I just arched my eyebrows and continued to comb through my hair. If I didn't comb it while it was still wet, it would tangle into a massive knot.

"Can I have my handcuffs removed?" I asked. I looked between the two to see their completely different reactions. Navarro was disgusted that I would even suggest such a thing to him. Carlos, on the other hand, looked like he would agree to anything at this point. "I have proven that I'm not going to attack anyone."

"You attacked Officer Brian-"

"When I first came here," I interrupted. "That was my last chance at freedom. You already know who I am and I already know that I'm going to jail. There is no reason to add more time onto whatever sentence I will be given."

"So, you admit it?"

"I have not admitted to anything. I'm just telling you what you want to hear so you'll get these suffocating handcuffs off me. A little too tight there, Brian." I made sure to point my face to the two-way mirror and hoped he would be there. I waited patiently until Carlos got up and removed the handcuffs from me. When he sat back down, Navarro was glaring over at him.

"Sorry to interrupt," Kolleen said over the intercom. "I need to speak with one of you immediately. It's urgent."

I raised my eyebrows and stared at the two. Eventually, Navarro got up while shaking his head. He probably wanted to continue to harass me. Out of the two, he was definitely the bad cop. I'm not sure what Carlos was but he wasn't the good cop either. He seemed to have more empathy though. He sat back down and I just stared at him again. When I moved my hands to comb out more of my hair, he flinched hard and I only smirked. Good to know that I still had that power of fear over him. Wish I had more of it with those three other guys too.

"Where would they have taken Trinity?" Carlos asked as I flipped my hair upside down to comb the underside. It was probably making him mad that I wasn't just sitting like a normal criminal. I was more fixated on the mess that my hair would be though. Just because I was a criminal didn't mean I didn't care about my looks. "Emily-"

"Call me Y," I stated. I flipped my hair back over and glared at them. "I might be Emily Washington but I don't know who she is. I don't remember who she is. I don't know her family or her story. Care to enlighten me on any of that?" I asked. Carlos stared at me for a moment before he licked his lips and flexed his muscles. He was definitely not the cocky and playful guy that I used to work with. Right now, it seemed as if that personality was completely faked for when he was working there.

"I don't know specifics," Carlos started. "I was only given notes from the previous FBI agent who worked with you. His name was Ellis." I shrugged my shoulders to indicate that I had no idea who he was. "To be honest, there aren't a lot of notes. He couldn't risk blowing his cover. He did send us a message that he was so close to finding out who the leader of the organization was." I didn't say anything because I wasn't going to give them any of that information. I was not going to risk myself for that information. "All I know about you is that you were kidnapped and you were trafficked."

"How did I end up in this organization then?" I asked. "That doesn't make sense. You know just as well as I do that they don't keep girls they plan to traffic. They break them and torture them until they are broken into being submissive. They have never taken a girl for their own organization."

"I-I don't know," Carlos admitted. "But what I do know is that you can help us. You have been to all of the places that they are currently taking now."

"How do you know?" I asked. "How do you know that? They have done a complete break and reconstruction of how our organization works. We are so much bigger now. They can have millions of locations."

"I know because your husband told me," Carlos said. I looked at him and shook my head. My husband wouldn't have said anything to him. He knew not to leak that sort of information to anybody but the leaders. He was one of the leaders but I wasn't sure who else was. It was hard for them all to get together as they were around the world and their schedules often didn't match up. "Emmanuel pulled me into a meeting and discussed my future with the company." He paused. "He told me that their secret was that they changed the front end, but all of the back end was the same."

"I don't believe you. He wouldn't say anything unless you accepted the position as a lead. He's smarter than that."

"Apparently, not."

"Don't do anything stupid, Y," Kolleen said as she came into the room. She had a cloth in her hand and slammed the door shut behind her. "Shut up, Carlos. Stop making things worse." She sat down in the seat beside him and he looked offended for a second. "This poor girl's entire life just went up in flames. She found out she's someone else and now you're telling her that her husband didn't trust her?" She rolled her eyes and shook her head. "Men, right?" I didn't move as she put the cloth on the table. "I figured out why she won't spill any details despite Murphy telling her to." She spread out the cloth and I could tell that it was the shirt that I was wearing. "She has a baby."

"What?" Carlos asked. I remained silent and he looked from the shirt back to me. "No, she doesn't. I would remember if she was pregnant or had a child. No babies were running around."

"Well," Kolleen said. "She has to go to the bathroom every couple of hours to pump out the milk from her breasts. While I may never have been pregnant, my best friend was. She would become extremely sensitive and sore if she didn't." Kolleen paused. "I started digging through the trash to see what you were doing in the bathroom. You were taking too long." She turned back to Carlos. "I saw a white substance in the paper towels. At first, I thought it was drugs." She shrugged her shoulders. "We started putting the substance through testing and our forensic scientist found it was milk." She paused. "When I took your top, I could confirm that once it dried, there was a distinct smell mixed with water." She looked at me and then back at Carlos. "I think that she won't tell us anything because she is trying to protect her baby." Kolleen paused for a second and smiled. "If we can get you your baby, will you help us find Trinity?"

"Yes."

I'm Emily Washington, and I have a baby.

"Like I said, we might be going on a wild goose chase," I replied as they removed the cuffs from my hands. I smiled a bit but completely erased it when I hopped into their van. Navarro was driving up front with Carlos giving directions. They should probably invest in GPS or get designated drivers who know the area. Even we were better than pulling out a physical map. I was squished in the back with Kolleen next to me. "They move the babies periodically."

"How do we know she's not setting us up in a trap?" Navarro asked.

"I wouldn't risk my child," I retorted. It felt like my eyes turned into slits as I stared at him. He had every right to think this way, but I wasn't going to risk my child getting hurt.

"Tell me about your child," Kolleen managed. She looked at me and smiled. I could tell that she didn't feel threatened by me. Her demeanor was too calm. Despite her telling me she wasn't a mother, I knew she would be a great one. "How come Carlos didn't know you had one?"

"They keep pregnancies secret," I replied dryly. I shrugged my shoulders and tried not to get emotional about it. Even the day I found out I was pregnant, I was emotional.

I had been sick for about three weeks: I was throwing up constantly in the morning.

Unfortunately, even if we are sick, we do not get shipped to hospitals. The uppers feared that new people would start to fake their illnesses and then find a way to escape without anyone knowing. So, we had a doctor who wasn't really a doctor - these people may have studied to become one, may have helped their younger siblings, or some had their licenses revoked. However, they were all that we had. Emmanuel had been mad at me for laying around in bed and always being hungry and puking at the smallest things. He thought that I was faking it so that I didn't have to do a mission. We fought about it until finally, he forced me to go to the hospital wing.

I found out by myself that I was pregnant. Emmanuel told me he had some sort of meeting, but I think he just didn't want to be there. He didn't want to find out that I was right and something was wrong with me. He wanted to believe that he was right - that I was faking this nonsense. I had to wonder what would happen if the doctor couldn't find something wrong with me. Emmanuel was a manipulative person, but he loved me. Even if I wanted to leave him, I couldn't. He would spread rumors and lies about me that would certainly get me tortured and killed. I liked being with him too because he was protective against the other men there. They knew to leave me alone. They knew not to harm a hair on my body or look at me the wrong way. Just like Emmanuel, I could lie to protect myself too.

The emotions that I felt were overwhelming and when I was told, I just nodded my head. I had

                                           AMY KULP

gone so long without showing emotions that when I had a flood of them, I knew not to say anything. If I reacted wrong, they would hold me somewhere less comfortable, so I didn't kill it. Of course, I knew the procedures for finding out I had a child. The doctor told me even if I wasn't listening too well - no matter what, they had to tell the uppers.

Being pregnant had its perks. I was in one of the most comfortable rooms I have ever been in. I got fed amazing meals and was allowed anything I wanted. With regular checkups and constant monitoring, I was the healthiest I have ever been. I didn't have to go on missions while I was pregnant either. It was the best rest I ever had. It was the best rest I would ever get from them.

I remember telling Emmanuel too. The doctor, at least, let me do that. Emmanuel was ecstatic. He was so excited and wanted a boy so badly. He was ensuring that I was getting better treatment than the other pregnant moms in the room. He was ensuring that he knew how to rock the baby and put them to sleep. He was picking out baby names for them and telling me all about his family history. Of course, he would be excited though, he couldn't wait to raise a prodigy son that could follow in his footsteps.

I was the complete opposite. As soon as I found out and I was alone, I began to cry. I didn't want to have a baby. I didn't want to grow attached to it and then have it ripped away from me as soon as it was born. The only use I had was providing the milk, but they tried to wean the babies off of it as soon as possible. They wanted them detached from their mothers and they wanted to start raising them to become soldiers. Only Uppers could see the children and the moms could occasionally. Sometimes, I would be extra good to Emmanuel, and he allowed me to see our baby.

The only time I was happy about getting the news of our baby was when we found out it was a boy. Emmanuel hugged me so tightly that the doctor worried the baby would suffocate. He let go and cupped his hands around my cheeks and kissed my nose. I smiled back as tears fell down my face. Everyone thought that I was happy for this child. I was just happy it was a boy.

"His name is Manny," I finally stated as tears began to collect in my eyes. I wiped them away and noticed everyone shifting uncomfortably in their seats. I wasn't sure how long I was lost in my thoughts or how long they were trying to talk to me. I was in my own little world remembering him growing up.

"Did you get a say in that name?" Carlos asked.

"No."

He nodded his head and coughed uncomfortably upfront. Carlos instructed Navarro to cut the lights and for the first time, I looked out the window. It seemed we were at the first place where the babies might be. Carlos looked over at me and I just nodded my head. My hopes were high, but I wasn't exactly sure if they thought this through. They were going to fight for the children and if they hurt any of them, they would have to answer to me. I would kill them all.

"We're not giving you a gun," Navarro commented. I nodded my head. I understood completely why they wouldn't give me a gun. However, I wouldn't shoot regardless because if it ricocheted anywhere and hit one of those kids because it rebounded, it would haunt me. Who would hurt innocent children?

I watched as they all put their vests on and prodded me forward. I didn't have one which I thought was stupid. If they were to lose me, they would lose all possible other locations. They would lose the location of where Trinity was. They would lose everything. I was valuable information, but they were treating me like dirt right now.

"It doesn't look like anyone is here," I whispered as I looked around. We were the only van but we parked a little away so that they wouldn't hear our tires against the rocks. "They tend to keep protection with the children minimal. Do you have backup?" I asked. I looked at Carlos, Kolleen, and then Navarro but none of them answered me. That's okay because that was an answer too. "You need to call for backup next time. As I said, whoever is guarding the children is an Upper."

"Which is who is most valuable."

"They'll most likely not kill the children, but they will try to kill themselves. They were trained to do that," I whispered. I looked at Carlos. "I don't believe that you were going to be an Upper. You are more hands-on when fighting. Uppers tend to take the easy way out and have other people do their mess and then fix their mess."

"Now is not the time to argue about that," Navarro mentioned.

"You guys talk about trusting me but what if I can't trust you?" I wondered. I stopped dead in my tracks and felt someone's body run right into me. I turned around to see I had caught Carlos off-guard, but Kolleen and Navarro were a bit behind us. "What happens if we find the children, one of the Uppers, and then you force me to tell you where Trinity is and then I don't get my child?"

"Well-"

"You are a criminal," Navarro spoke. "You are still going to have to do the time before you can see your child."

"What will happen to my child?" I angrily asked. I looked at all three of them and no one spoke to them. "While I am in jail, for who knows how long, who is going to watch my child?"

"Foster-"

Without letting them finish that sentence, I grabbed Carlos's gun from his hand and swiveled it at all of them. Navarro immediately pointed his at me and Kolleen fumbled to get hers out. Carlos just held his hands up in surrender. My hands were jittery, and I stared at them intently. I knew that Kolleen was the negotiator of the group. Every single time I have gotten upset or mad, she has been the one to calm me down. She was always the one to ease the tension but now as she had a gun pointed at her, she didn't seem to know what to say.

"My child will not be put in foster care," I said. Navarro moved first so I instantly pointed my gun at him. However, I knew that I was going to

                              AMY KULP

lose this if I kept having to point the gun at someone else. I looked at Kolleen and with a surprise move, I grabbed onto Carlos and had my arm around his neck and the gun to his head. He awkwardly shifted into my body as he was taller than me. He kept his hands up in surrender and I watched as Navarro faltered. Clearly, they were closer than I thought. "There are so many people who have come from foster care into our organization - some were trafficked, some worked for us, and many of our clients fostered." I put more pressure on Carlos's neck and listened to him gag for a second. I knew that he could easily get me off of him, but he had no idea about my target skill. If I wanted to shoot, I could shoot him and one other person before everyone else reacted.

"Put the gun down," Kolleen tried. I rolled my eyes at her attempt and plunged it deeper into Carlos's temple. I could feel his breath become shaky and I knew he was nervous. Despite how much we worked together, he still couldn't read me like I could read him. Like I could read his betrayal as soon as we made the deal about my child. "We can work something out."

"Now," I commanded. "We'll work something out now."

"If someone is here, they'll surely know that we're here by now."

"Those walls are soundproof. They can't hear anything," I said. To prove a point, I yelled at the top of my lungs and we waited. Nothing. No movement from the house that was a little far off and no movement from the surrounding areas. "Next time, you should probably bring backup."

"We trusted you," Carlos said. I tightened my hold around his neck and listened to him gasp for air. I lessened the hold as soon as I felt his body stop fighting me. I couldn't kill him if I wanted my child.

"Stupid decision, huh?" I wondered. "Do you think I'm stupid enough to fall for something where I don't get a deal?"

"We don't have a negotiator," Navarro stated.

"Kolleen," I mentioned. I looked at her and could see the fear grow in her eyes. "I'm sure she was trained to talk down people. You aren't the rookie I thought you were. This entire time you have all been playing me."

"What do you want?" Kolleen finally asked. Her voice caught in her throat and she squawked out her question. I still think she was new but she wasn't as new as I thought she was. After all, she was here taking down everyone and Brian wasn't. "What can we get you so that we can work as a team again?"

"What?" I asked. I shook my head.

"We are a team," Carlos muttered. I stood there unable to focus on what they were doing. "Don't let your new team down, Y."

I lowered the gun and as soon as I did that, Carlos headbutted my face and pushed me toward the ground. He spun me so that when I hit the ground, I landed on my stomach. I could feel a knee in my back and the pounding of Navarro running

                                    AMY KULP

toward us. Carlos knelt down closer to me, and his hot breath filled my ear.

"I will make sure your kid is safe."

I wanted to believe him, but I wasn't sure I could. I just fell for the stupidest trick in the book. These guys weren't my team. They didn't care about me. They cared about finishing their jobs. As I sat up, I looked between all three of them - none of them looked mad, none of them were going to sock me in the face, and none of them were pointing their guns at me anymore.

"I want a vest," I stated. I looked at all of them as I was given material to soak up my bloody nose. All three looked at me before Kolleen ran back to the van. I could hear her huffing and puffing for a lot longer than she appeared. "Are we an actual team?" I wondered. Carlos nodded yes and when I looked at Navarro, he resisted answering that. I stared at him though. I couldn't help it. He didn't like me so I would only know if we were working together if he admitted to it.

"Unfortunately, yes." He stared at me and gave me a hand to help me up. I took it and when Kolleen returned, she put the vest on me. "We're still not giving you a gun."

"We're not making a deal with you," Kolleen said when she secured the vest. I looked at her and then at Carlos, but he wouldn't meet my gaze. "However, we will pretend that you didn't just try to kill Carlos."

"I think-"

"Navarro, shut up."

I stifled a minor laugh as we started walking toward the house again. I still couldn't be too sure but at least I had a vest on now. I felt more secure, and I felt like if I was shot, I could survive now. Of course, they would have had to shoot me in the chest. My forehead was a huge target.

As we got up onto the porch, I started walking softer as a light came on. All three agents behind me moved to cover but I just shook my head. This light was a motion detector light but didn't have a camera attached to it. When their fears and suspicions made them feel stupid, they followed me up and I opened the door.

"No passcode?" Carlos asked in disbelief.

"Don't need one when you're not afraid to kill people who show up unannounced," I said. I looked back at the three and they seemed to be shocked. Even if there was a miscommunication, they were told to shoot first and ask later. Besides, there were always backup plans that they had. "I was only here once," I admit. I look back at them and I think they could see my uneasiness to step back inside.

"We'll do a sweep first," Carlos mentioned.

"With just three of us?" Kolleen asked.

"You wanted to be more involved with the field," Navarro commented. "Here we are. I'll go in first."

"I'll be the butt," Carlos said.

I nodded my head as I let Navarro get in front of me. As soon as I turned the knob, the second door opened, and Navarro scooted in with the gun held at eye level. I wasn't sure how I could help so I followed him in with Kolleen touching me. I could tell that she was nervous. She was too afraid of being torn apart from the group. I let her skin press against mine as I followed Navarro. While Navarro walked forward, Carlos took the first right as he entered and Kolleen was torn between following who. However, she had to make a choice. Carlos couldn't be by himself.

When Navarro turned around, my heart skipped a beat for a second seeing him point the gun right at my forehead. However, he swiftly pushed me aside and followed Carlos and Kolleen. I didn't though. I looked around in the kitchen and was surprised to see some dishes were left in the sink. Some dishes were put in the strainer. As I ran my hand along the counter, I could feel some stickiness and sugar covering the tops. I opened the fridge and could see the formula bottles that were left there. Some fruit that would go bad and some milk that was already expired.

"Nobody's here," Navarro said as he came back in. He watched me as I closed the fridge doors and then opened the trash. There was nothing in there. He switched a light on and looked at the scene on the table. There were eight high chairs and four regular chairs at the table. One of the highchairs wasn't cleaned up and as I went closer to it, I put my hand on the tray hoping that it was ketchup. I brought my fingers up to my nose and when I took a whiff, I felt myself beginning to get emotional. "Hey, you don't know that something happened!" He came close to me as I bent over with my hands in my face.

What happens if this was Manny's blood?

"You need to be strong," he said as he held onto me. "I'm not good with comforting people. We can't be emotional right now." He paused as I grabbed his wrist for comfort. "We have to find those kids. If they are hurting them..." He shook his head at the thought and I forced myself to stop.

I needed to turn my emotions on and off like a switch.

"There's one more place, you haven't checked," I said. I dried under my eyes and got up. Navarro was still sitting down when I started moving across the house. When I turned, he seemed to be surprised by my difference in reaction. When you're constantly being yelled at for showing emotion, you learn to mask it very well.

I ushered him up and he followed me. When I stepped foot outside of the kitchen and into the living room and spare room, I could see Carlos and Kolleen looking through things. Kolleen was bent down looking through the various drawers and desks while Carlos was holding a picture frame in his hand. When I came around to see what picture it was, he was holding my boy's birth certificate.

"How old is he?" he wondered as he flicked some dust from the frame. It was a picture of Manny, Emmanuel, and I. I smiled as I looked at the picture and found myself frowning when I could see the other pictures. While my family was smiling, some of the others weren't. Some of the other mothers had bruises around their faces or sometimes the father was hurting the baby. Some of them didn't want to be there.

"Four," I whispered. I shook my head though and moved Carlos from the pictures. "There is one place that I know you guys skipped out on." I ushered them to follow me but turned around last minute. "Can I... Can I have that picture?"

"I'm sorry, it'll be going into evidence," Navarro said. He put a hand on my wrist like I had before but I just nodded my head. I wanted something to remember how my little boy looked as a baby. "This room that you know we didn't look at?"

"This way."

We headed back over to the kitchen and I opened up the closet. I heard a protest from Kolleen and Carlos saying that they looked there. However, when I moved the jackets and coats that were hanging there, I carefully stood on my tiptoes and grabbed the top right corner of the wallpaper. Sliding down like a glove, the tearing was so loud in the silent house that I was sure alarms would be going off. Revealed there was another door a few feet away from where the wallpaper was. On the door were about fifty locks and one huge padlock.

"I have never been down there," I stated. I shook my head and looked at all of them. "I was always told I didn't need to be down there because the children were up here. They saw me watching once and I was never allowed back."

I bit my lip and looked at them. I have always wondered what was down there but I wasn't sure that I truly wanted to know. What were they hiding that they couldn't show me? What were they hiding that they had to put wallpaper over the actual door and put a dummy door there? What were they hiding that they needed five hundred locks and one big lock? What was down there?

"I'll kick it down," Carlos said. He pushed me aside before I could say anything. I shook my head and stood right in front of him as he tried to kick it. He kicked me right in the side and I fell into the door with a yelp.

"Don't touch me!" I yelled as I tried to get my hand off the door. I could see their confusion before Navarro could see something was wrong. I stayed still as I felt the electricity pulse through my body and wanted to move. I couldn't move. How do you get out of being electrocuted?

"Cut the power source," Navarro said. He immediately killed the kitchen lights and in three seconds, my body lay down and I closed my eyes. Navarro didn't give me a chance to recover before dragging my body away from the door. I just let him.

"You okay?" Kolleen asked. She looked down at me and I just nodded my head.

"I've been through worse."

I could hear Carlos kicking the door. It took about five tries before he actually got it. I could hear the wood splintering from the hinges, but I didn't say anything. I wanted to lay there more and recover, but I wanted to see what was down there first. I huffed and forced my aching joints to get up. I walked behind Navarro and Carlos and as they held their guns up, I had a hunch that they wouldn't need them.

I couldn't see much at first, but the temperature immediately dropped as we got down there. When my foot hit the ground, it seemed to be less solid and very dirty. It wasn't until Kolleen turned on her flashlight that I was able to see the room. Navarro and Carlos soon did the same and I was able to see the monstrosity of this room.

There were three big jail cells on the floor. One of them had a bucket while one of the other ones had a dirty mattress. The smell was horrendous and I could see that there was an additional bucket for each cell. I didn't have to try to guess what was inside those. As I scurried around each cell, I could hear the others talking but I couldn't stop myself from walking into one of the cells.

I looked around it as I went inside and got onto my knees. I closed my eyes and crawled around before feeling a drop on my head. When I looked up, I could see water dropping down. I took the unused bucket and put it there to hold the water. I pushed my hands against the dirt and felt my body getting dirty. My knees were starting to get covered with the mud and as I crawled around again, I looked up and saw the blue emergency light.

"Y?"

I looked at the entrance to the cell and could see some boy bringing me my food. He tossed it on the ground and when I didn't come to the entrance, he forced himself in. He forced me to eat and when he left, I felt my body getting exhausted. I felt my vision getting blurry and some girl was in the cell across from me. Telling me about how the food was drugged so we would go to sleep. I touched my face to make sure that they didn't put the sack back over but found it difficult to breathe. There was black everywhere and I couldn't see. Was it too tight against my neck? I clutched at my neck and felt my nails digging into my skin. I had to get it off. I was suffocating.

"Y!"

"Get off of me, Reggie!" I pushed so hard onto the body that was on mine that my body ricocheted into the bars.

I had to search for the pin. Where was the pin that the girl gave me? She gave me a pin to get the sack off my head. Where was the pin? I searched for it on the ground but instead, was met with the bucket. That would do. I listened to the surrounding areas and felt the vibrations of Reggie coming near me. I threw it at him and heard a gasp. I hope that was the bucket with poop in it.

"Don't touch her, Carlos!" Kolleen yelled. "She's having a PTSD episode. She can't tell what's real right now!"

"Close the door!" Navarro yelled.

"No, don't close the door!" I begged. "Please, don't leave me here to die." I crawled near the bars and felt that they were closed. "Emmanuel?" I asked as I realized they wouldn't open them. I let my back curl and felt myself begin to cry. "Please let me out? I won't tell a soul."

"Y, Emmanuel is not here right now," Kolleen said through the doors. "Please, let me help you. I am Kolleen Caquatto. Where are you?"

"I don't know. They took her already."

"Took who?" she asked.

                                      AMY KULP

"They took my friend. She didn't fight them like I have been." I felt for the hole on my wrist from the pin. "Please, we don't have much time to get to her."

"Who's your friend?"

"I-I don't remember," I said. I looked up at her and was surprised to see the black sack was off my face. Standing in front of me on the other side of the bars were Kolleen, Navarro, and Carlos. Kolleen was crouched down in front of me with a soothing face and smiled at me. Navarro and Carlos were behind her, but they didn't seem so relaxed. They almost seemed shocked and traumatized. "I was here," I stated. I looked around the cell again and shook my head. "I was here before."

"It's alright now," Kolleen stated. "We're here with you."

"Will you let me out?" I asked as I held onto the bars that were still closed. Kolleen nodded her head and yanked on the bars that were in front of her. Nothing. She looked up at Carlos and Navarro and each of them tried the bars too but neither of them could get it open. They each tried and tried, and I felt my nerves beginning to rise. "Don't leave me here," I said as they all stepped away from the cell. Carlos kicked and kicked but he couldn't get it open.

"Do you know where the keys are?" Carlos asked.

"Don't ask her anything," Kolleen said with force. "She can go into another epi-"

We all looked up at the sound of cars from outside. Why could I hear them now? This house was supposed to be soundproof. I could never hear anything when I came here. I looked back as Kolleen, Navarro, and Carlos all backed away from the bars. I shook my head and felt the tears starting to collect in my eyes.

"Don't leave me here!" I yelled as they disappeared from my view. I shook my head again and again and frantically, shook the bars. "Carlos!" I waited for a response but didn't get any. "Navarro!" I looked again and shook the bars again. "Kolleen!" I yelled again.

I could hear someone going down the stairs now and felt myself breaking down. I had to be quiet. Maybe they wouldn't see me. Maybe they didn't hear me yell. I scurried to the furthest corner and watched as the figure moved down the stairs. They slinked along the edges and their shadow curled into a demon behind them. They held a gun out and I knew that I was barely going to survive this. My eyes twitched in the darkness and as soon as they turned their flashlight toward me, their smile grew wickedly.

I wasn't familiar with this person but as they grabbed the cell to come in, they couldn't get in either. I let a small breath out knowing that none of those three were lying to me. He smiled again as he went back up the stairs and came back down with a ring of keys. He rifled through all of them until he got the door open. I felt my body beginning to shiver as I pushed myself further into the corner. Maybe if I was skinny enough, I would be able to make it through the slot.

"Who do we have here?" he asked as he walked toward me. I attempted to crawl away from him, but he grabbed onto my hair and lifted me up. I closed my eyes and he immediately slapped me across the mouth. "An FBI agent?" he wondered. He read over my vest and smiled again. "How did you get here?" He dropped me on the ground and my body faltered underneath him. When I tried to get back up, I already saw his gun pointing at me. He pulled the trigger without a warning and I closed my eyes for the impact. Instead, I felt the pain in my chest. He was shooting the vest, but it still hurt. "Who would let you down here?"

"Hands up where I can see them!" Carlos yelled. I looked over at him hiding in a random corner and found myself smiling. Whoever was here with me gasped though. "Warren, step away from the FBI agent."

"Carlos?" he asked. "They'll have a field day knowing that you are in the FBI too."

"Drop the gun," he said. He walked closer and stood in front of the entrance. While Warren was distracted, I found myself getting up from the bullet to the vest. It hurt a lot worse than I would have thought. It felt like a hammer coming down on my chest. It almost inhibited the way I could breathe. "Hands up."

He pointed the gun back at me but this time, he seemed to know that I have moved. Maybe I wasn't as quiet as I thought I was. He pointed it right at my forehead and smiled wickedly at Carlos. I sighed and just closed my eyes before realizing his back was turned to me. He was staring at Carlos and while he knew where I was, he wouldn't be able to tell what my next move was. I clutched onto my vest before I silently stood up so that the gun was pointing there. I quickly shot my leg up between his and felt him blast the bullet into my chest. However, he fell to the ground while Carlos disarmed him. I was laying down as I watched him handcuff one hand to a cell while he checked him for other weapons. Finding a knife and a taser, he quickly punched him when he tried to move and his body went still.

"We're a team," Carlos said as he handed me the knife. I nodded my head and he held out his hand to me. "There's probably people outside. I doubt Warren would come alone."

"Warren?" I asked as I hunched next to Carlos.

"Clapper."

My eyes grew wide as I recognized the name. I have never worked with him, but I remember his name from Mattie's profile. I felt sick to my stomach and while I wanted to spit on the guy, we were already busy escaping. I led the way and while I wasn't completely sure where I was going, I did eventually lead us outside.

Carlos held tightly onto my hand but as soon as we made it outside, he let go. We snuck around the house into the surrounding woods and when I thought we were far enough away, we started rounding out to where our car was. I felt my breath coming heavier and heavier and I started to slow down when I saw our car. Navarro and Kolleen

                    AMY KULP

weren't near it, but I was glad because all of our tires were popped.

"We'll have to go back by foot," I whispered. I looked back at the house that was now so far gone it only looked like an ant. "Seems you were right, there are definitely people there."

Carlos looked back to see two vans of people. Of course, they would only send one person in to check. They didn't want to risk their whole crew being captured or killed. While I was sure that they would be able to get Warren out of the handcuffs, I knew that Carlos wasn't leaving him there to die. If anything, it would have been to ensure we got out safely. He could send backup later.

"You can slow down now, Y," Carlos said. I looked back at him and nodded my head. I guess we could. Slowing down made the fire in my legs more evident and made it harder for me to breathe. I was just shot twice and while I wouldn't bleed or die, it did feel like my lungs were affected. "What happened back there?" he asked.

"I remember that place," I whispered. I didn't want to talk about it, but I knew that Carlos wasn't going to let it go. Maybe it would do me good to talk about it after all. "I remember Emmanuel being there and Reggie too."

"Anyone else?"

"Not really," I stated. I shook my head. "Just blobs of people. There was a girl with me while we were in those cells. I can't remember her at all. Her face is blurry and every time she talked, I just heard my own voice." I looked up. "There was a boy too.

He fed me drugged food. He gave me a pin to cut off the sack on my head." I shook my head. "I couldn't see and they would taunt me. They would hit me and I couldn't prepare myself. They would-"

"It's okay, you don't need to tell me," Carlos whispered. "I don't want you to relive that." We walked a little quieter as I watched my breath coming out and mixing with the cool air around us. "You are a victim too."

I didn't say anything to that and we continued to walk quietly back. I wasn't sure where we were going but when we finally made it to some sort of highway, Carlos pulled out his phone. He talked back on it and I had to assume it was Navarro and Kolleen. Did they leave me there to die? Or did Carlos tell them to go on ahead without us? I wanted to know but was too afraid to ask when they pulled up.

I wasn't sure how they got this new car, but I was too exhausted. My body was sore from the electrocution and my chest was sore from the bullets. My mind was always tired anymore, but it felt more like I couldn't catch a break. Whenever I resolved one issue with myself, a new one popped up to try and scare me. This time, it was my own memory. However, was it accurate? Did those things actually happen to me? Or was it something of my imagination? Maybe I did those things to someone else.

"Y?" Kolleen asked. I looked over at her and I realized that I must have fallen asleep. "I need you to be honest with me for a second." I nodded my head and looked up at Carlos. He was still giving

                                   AMY KULP

directions but I knew that he was listening. Navarro was still driving but he was still listening. When his eyes flicked up to the mirror and I could see them, I knew that I needed to close my eyes. I didn't want to see anyone's reactions to what they were about to ask. "What happened to the baby you were just pregnant with?"

"I killed her," I whispered.

I'm Emily Washington. While I have a beautiful growing boy, I killed my baby girl.

They didn't understand and I was okay with that. I could see their glances at each other when they thought I wasn't looking. I could see the desperation on Carlos's face, the judgment on Navarro's, and the confusion on Kolleen's. I wasn't going to elaborate though. They could make their judgment based on that last statement. They could base everything they know about me based on that last statement. It was the truth and I wasn't going to shy away from it. I wouldn't object if someone accused me of it because I was tired of lying to everyone. I had to live with the guilt and the realism. However, I didn't regret doing it.

I didn't regret killing my little girl.

However, sometimes I did feel guilty about it. I think back on how I could feel her moving around and would try to guess what body part I was feeling. I would track on the phone to figure out how large she was and watch as her size grew. I put soothing music on so that she would be calm before going to bed. I would read her bedtime stories to increase her vocabulary and understanding. I was ready for this child and I was going to do everything I could to get her ready to start the world. I knew that I couldn't change the fact that I was pregnant, so I decided to enjoy motherhood.

Until I found out what sex she was. I acted happy for the doctor and my husband. I was able to visit Manny more and tell him all about his younger sister. In actuality, I was petrified for her.

I knew how they treated females here. I didn't want her to live a life like me. I didn't want her to be tortured for looking at someone wrong. I didn't want her to be assaulted because she was pretty and some old man wanted her. I didn't want her to worry about her worth and denote it to how many guys liked her. I didn't want her to be owned like I was. I wanted her to have a happy relationship. I wanted her to be able to pick what she wanted to do without being sexualized for it. I knew that she could never do anything without being judged. I knew that she would never live a happy life here.

So, I started eating sushi and seafood. I started eating uncooked food. I wanted to drink alcohol and do drugs, but they weren't available for me. I was still heavily watched. I had to sneak some things. I had to constantly look over my shoulder. When they started restricting my diet, I had to get creative. They took better care of me because they wanted another female. They wanted me to have a baby girl to give to them. So, they could teach her how to serve the disgusting men here. So, she could be born a servant to them. So, when I went to the bathroom by myself, I made sure to trip and fall on my stomach. I made sure to constantly whack my belly off things. When little bruises started forming, they reprimanded Emmanuel for the destruction of my body.

I have never been happier than when I woke up and I started bleeding. I remember smiling and going back to bed because I didn't want to call a doctor for them to try and save my baby. I didn't want her to be born premature and suffer through possible conditions. I had put her through so much that I can't imagine she would be born normal.

I didn't ever meet her, but I have never loved someone so much. Georgia-Jean would have been her name if I could name her. I'm sure Emmanuel had a different name planned. It would have always been named what he wanted but I would secretly call her Georgia-Jean. How cute was that?

As soon as I miscarried, I was forced back into the field. Carlos, Howie, and Santiago were my next crew. I was so distraught that the distraction was needed. However, there were times I would wake up and think about how I couldn't hold her. How I couldn't nurse her or care for her scratches. I knew what I did was the right thing, but it was hard to deal with that decision. I never gave her a life. But what would her life look like if she was born? I couldn't imagine it being good.

"Where are we heading?" Navarro asked to break the silence. I looked up at him and quickly ran my fingers under my eyes. It was still dry so maybe I was used to the idea that Georgia-Jean would never be held in my arms.

"Pennsylvania," I stated. "I have never been here."

"So how do you know about it?" Carlos asked. I didn't want to meet his eyes, but I felt like I had to. I looked up and was thankful that I didn't see any judgment from him. I wouldn't be able to take it right now. I was feeling too much emotion for my

　　　　　　　　　　　　　　AMY KULP

baby girl and for whatever nightmare I just lived through down in that basement.

"I have a hunch."

"Or you're setting us up for a trap," Navarro remarked. I didn't look over at him for his snide remarks. He has shown me that he is here to protect me too. Even if he didn't like me.

"We're a team," I whispered. I nodded my head and fiddled with my fingers. "I just... I remember something else from when I was..." I stopped for a second and felt Kolleen's hand touch me for comfort. "Trafficked." I looked up at Navarro and could see his eyes through the mirror. "I have no way of knowing if this is where the babies are-"

"You're our only hope," Carlos mentioned. He sighed for a moment and I could feel that there was some sort of tension in the air. "So, we have a choice between Pennsylvania and where?"

"New Jersey," I replied dryly.

"They have really big hunting grounds," Kolleen commented. I nodded my head. She had no idea, but I wasn't going to ruin her delusion that they were only in New York, New Jersey, and Pennsylvania. There was also Maryland, Canada, Mexico, Alaska, and pretty much the entire United States. They were still expanding and their organization was on the rise. They were selling to big-time actors now. They were selling to regular people who could afford it. They sold to whoever and I don't understand how they weren't caught yet. They were always so careless in their auctions.

"We can split up," I mentioned. Navarro immediately shook his head, Carlos's entire body tensed up, and Kolleen retracted her hand back to her body. "If two of us want to take New Jersey, the other two can take Pennsylvania."

"I don't think that is a good idea," Kolleen mentioned.

"Absolutely not," Navarro stated. He shook his head and I felt the van accelerate. "As you said, we are a team. It does not matter if I want to be or not." I nodded my head. "Do you know the address?"

"Not specifically," I said. I closed my eyes and thought about the place.

It looked like any other building: it was tall, old, and seemed to be taken care of. There weren't any unusual colors that made it stand out or any weird shapes. It wasn't mysteriously dark or peppy. There weren't signs to signal what it was and there wasn't any marker for anyone to know it wasn't just a normal house. You had to parallel park to get there and half the time, there weren't parking spots. I closed my eyelids harder together in hopes that the image could stop being so blurry. I couldn't see a number anywhere on the house.

Was I just leading them on a wild goose chase?

"How do you expect us to get there?" Navarro asked again.

"I don't know," I replied dryly.

"I have an idea," Carlos piped up. I looked up at him and saw the concern on his face. That immediately sent me into a panic and I couldn't help but wonder what his idea was. Was it safe? "You said this place was somewhere you have been when you were trafficked?" he asked. I nodded my head to reassure him. "You were talking about a black sack over your head when we were down in that basement." I nodded my head again but this time, it was a little more hesitant. "How often did you wear that black sack?" I shrugged my shoulders.

Closing my eyes, I tried to remember. However, this time it was difficult. I tried to make my mind remember something that it hasn't in a long time, but instead, I was just staring at the black color of my eyes being closed. When I pressed harder, little swirls of green and purple were visible for me to concentrate on. No memories or pictures or words were popping into my head though.

"It's okay if you don't remember," Kolleen mentioned. Her comforting hand was back on my arm. She patted it once and waited for me to open my eyes. "Would you be willing to put something over your head to try and retrace your steps on how to get there?"

"Would I remember?"

"It's worth a shot but only if you are comfortable with it." She looked around. "It might bring back unwanted memories of your time there." I nodded my head. "Okay, Navarro, is there a way that we can turn around and go back to that house?"

"No," Navarro said. "They are going to surround that place now that they know we've been there." He looked over at Carlos this time. I tried to see what he was searching for on his face but instead, he looked back at the road. "However, I can get us as close as possible."

"Okay, Y, we can start getting you situated in the back of the van," Carlos stated. "I'm assuming that they didn't have you sitting in the seats."

I nodded my head and removed the seatbelt from my body. I hopped over the seat and plunked my body back onto the ground. Looking around, I knew that it didn't feel right to be back here. Yes, I would have a sack over my head but that wasn't enough. I slid over to one of their toolboxes in the back and dug my hand through it until I felt stickiness attach itself to my hand. Pulling out the duct tape, I looked up at them in the front. Carlos and Navarro were busy directing the van to where we needed to go while Kolleen was watching me.

"I need someone to put this on my wrists and ankles." Kolleen grabbed the tape but when I wouldn't let it go, she retreated her hand. "I need someone who knows how to do it."

Carlos turned around and for a second, I saw a glint of shame in his eyes. However, he had to own up to it that he was part of the story and organization. He left Navarro in the front and walked his way in the back with me. His hard boots landed in the back with a thud and for a second, he startled me. He didn't react to it and crouched down beside me as I handed him the tape. He gave me a second to change my mind but when I didn't, I pushed the tape even harder into his chest. He quickly found the end and started wrapping it around my wrists first. He swiveled the tape in figure eights before wrapping it around and around

                              AMY KULP

and around and around and around my wrists. When the tape finally reached my elbows, he wound it back up to my fingernails. Eventually cutting it off, he silently made his way toward my feet. He kicked off my shoes and rolled up my pants and attached the tape to the top of my foot before going up to my ankles and down again. When he was done, I flexed my foot and heard the ripple from the tape being moved and broken. I tried to move my arms apart and when they refused to budge, I nodded my head at Carlos. Now it was time for the sack.

"This is the best we have," he said as he took his shirt off. My eyes lingered longer than they should have and he smirked at me. "Nice to see that you are still obsessed with me despite being a mole."

"Nice to see that you are still cocky and self-absorbed despite being the good guy." I smirked back at him and felt my lips begin to frown as he wound his shirt around my head. He made it so that the transparent parts of the shirt were double stacked and I closed my eyes.

Despite not being able to see anything, it felt like I was in more control when I closed my eyes.

"Now, Y, we are going to try and simulate the exact environment that you were in when you were trafficked ten years ago," Kolleen mentioned. "Is there anything that doesn't feel right to you about this van?"

"Music," I mentioned. "We never play music."

As soon as I said that, the music was instantly halted. The silence was deafening and I slowly laid my head back on the ground. It didn't feel right though. Something was off. I didn't want to tell them that though. They were putting me through this to help me find my baby and all those innocent children, so I had to know where we were going. I wasn't sure if this place even existed. The image just kept popping into my brain.

"Okay, Y, we are as close as I can get to where we started from," Navarro called. "Where am I going?"

"I'm not sure," I mentioned. "Which way to Pennsylvania? Maybe, I'll remember when we hit our first pothole."

"Are we sure about this?" Navarro asked.

"Just drive left," Kolleen called.

The van started moving at a faster speed than before. I felt my body begin to slide and as it did, I crashed into the side. A breath was released from my back and I opened my eyes. I was afraid at first from not being able to see before I closed them again. A nervous tick was beginning to go through my body and I felt myself sliding again at an odd turn. This time, I crashed into another side and felt hands on my waist.

"Don't touch her, Carlos. We want to make this experience as authentic as possible."

The arms retracted themselves from me and I felt my nerves shooting through the roof again. Why did that make me feel better? Wouldn't I normally feel worse if someone was constantly touching me? Especially if I couldn't see whose arms they were and couldn't see what they were going to do. Unless I had someone that was

                                    AMY KULP

constantly touching me. Was it this Ellis person? He was a mole and he was supposedly helping me get away.

"No, come here," I commanded.

I crawled closer to Carlos when I felt where his body was from. I laid my body on his and positioned his hands on top of my stomach. This made me feel secure and safe. It felt familiar and despite how anxious I was previously, it felt like they were melting away. I breathed in once through my nose and let it out through my mouth. The shirt that was around my head was too tight though and the hot air just surrounded my face awkwardly.

I don't know how much time had passed before the van sharply turned to the right and stopped. Carlos and I started sliding forward and thudded into the back of the seats before he could properly brace. His breath got heavier as I positioned myself off his chest and I forced myself to sit up.

"If you come to a y in the road after this stop light, take a right."

I refused to breathe until after we started back up and could feel the car moving. It should be here any day now and when the van slowed and he took the right, I breathed out. While I didn't remember the way there, it just felt right. It felt like that was supposed to happen. Maybe I was paying more attention than I originally thought.

I moved away from Carlos this time and managed to kick myself into the door. My nerves were shooting through me again and I wanted to rip the tape and blindfold from me. However, I stayed like that and forced out any directions that ran through my head until I let the blood drain from my face.

"Stop!" I yelled loudly. I waited to see if the van did but felt it continue to drive. "Stop, now!" I moved my legs and hands and could hear the duct tape moving in my presence. I shook my head vigorously until I could feel the shirt coming loose. "Stop, stop, stop, stop, stop!" I kept repeating it but still felt the van move. My yells became cries of pain and I felt Carlos's arms on me. He tore the shirt off of me and when I opened my eyes, he had a knife ready to cut the tape off.

I calmed down instantly and when I was free from the tape cocoon, I sat upright. My breath was heaving and my nerves were shot, but I looked around to see if we were moving. We had stopped and I closed my eyes at the realization. I must have been confused from my eyes being closed. When I realized that Navarro and Kolleen were both looking at me, I bolted for the door.

They ran after me and when I got onto the streets, I was puzzled. Navarro, Carlos, and Kolleen weren't shouting after me, but they stopped beside me when they realized I wasn't running. We all were staring at the abyss and I felt my run beginning to go cold.

There was supposed to be a long line of buildings here. There was supposed to be one that I was imagining. The one that looked normal but I couldn't remember the number to the house. The streets and parking meters were there. I turned around and it looked exactly like it should on the

                               AMY KULP

other side. When I turned around, it was still bare. I didn't move and could feel my chest still heaving. This was the correct place, I was sure of it. Why was there a random row of buildings gone?

"Y," Carlos said as he got closer to me. He shook his head and grabbed onto my arm. "There's nothing here." He grabbed my arm to try and get me to move but I refused. I shook my head and looked back at the mysterious disappearance of buildings.

My eyes traveled to the two closest buildings on the ends. I walked silently on one end with Carlos by my side and the two other agents behind me. The building on this side was charred. It was all black and looked like it may have caught on fire. When I turned around and went to the other end, it looked the same way. It was charred and there was black all over it. No damage besides that. When Carlos tugged at my arm again, I just pointed to the black markings on the buildings.

"This seems really familiar," Navarro commented. "I'll be right back." He withdrew the gun that he had in his hands and went back to the van. I looked over at Kolleen and saw that she had hers out and was readily pointing it at me. When I looked at Carlos, his hand was on the holster, but he was more concerned with grabbing me.

They still thought I was trying to run.

"I'm not wrong," I whispered. "There is something here. Why is there a random disappearance of about ten buildings?" I wondered. I turned around when I heard the van door close and watched as Navarro did his little jog toward us. "Anything?" I wondered. He nodded his head and seemed a little paler than usual. My eyes got wide and he put his hand on Kolleen's gun for her to withdraw. When it was safely in her holster, he nodded his head again.

"This was where FBI was sent ten years ago," Navarro said. "Ellis had notified the FBI to come here. They stormed the building and..." He looked between Kolleen and Carlos. I knew that she wouldn't know. She was younger than me. I was surprised that, maybe, Carlos didn't know. He was usually on top of things and was knowledgeable of what he needed to know. "They waited until FBI responders were inside and they bombed the place."

"Ellis was here?" Carlos asked. He turned to me and I shrugged my shoulders. "How did you survive a bomb?" he wondered. I shrugged my shoulders again. I had no idea and no flashbacks or memories were coming to my mind. "Well, what do we do now?" Carlos asked. "It's clear that the children aren't here."

"No," Navarro said. "Wait." He looked at me and when I noticed, I looked at him. "Y, how did you survive a bomb?"

"I have no idea," I said. "This just seemed familiar."

"No," Navarro mentioned. "How did you survive a bomb?" He looked around. "All of these buildings look like houses or businesses. The FBI would have had people guarding the entrance." He paused a bit longer and looked out at the empty spaces. "If the FBI didn't see you come from the entrance and you clearly survived... Right? She's not a ghost?" he wondered.

　　　　　　　　　　　　　　　　AMY KULP

"Nope, no ghost," Kolleen said with a smile.

"There has to be another entrance somewhere." He walked off the sidewalk and onto the dirt plot that was once where the buildings were standing. "An underground entrance," he added.

He looked at me with a twinkle in his eye and turned back around to face the abyss. Behind the buildings was a forest of woods. We all walked forward with him and as we entered, I felt my nerves becoming more alert. The goosebumps on my arms stood up and my head felt dizzy. No memories or flashbacks though.

We walked further and further into the woods and I knew that the elevation was getting higher as I felt the sting in my knees and sting in my thighs. I turned around to look at the buildings and grabbed onto Carlos's arm. He turned around with me and we looked at the plot down below. It was peaceful but it was so familiar. I looked around the area until I saw some grass that was a little lower than the other grass. Almost as if it was walked through repeatedly. I nudged Carlos again and he alerted the other two. Carlos and Navarro took the lead and Kolleen was behind me as we walked through the green grass. It verged off and got super steep before going below the land and what seemed like civilization until we saw a cave.

A cave?

I looked at all of them before I started running full speed ahead. I could hear shouts for my name and shouts for me to stop but I didn't care. If my child was in here, I was going to get them out. If he wasn't, I was going to try and find him. The further I went into the tunnel, the lower the entrance came until I had to curve my spine so I wouldn't hit my head off anything. It was so dark that I was unable to see anything and could only see the light from those that were behind me.

When they caught up to me, they all gave me dirty looks, but I forced them to turn off their lights. That was one dead giveaway that we were down here. Before we continued to walk, I forced all of them to hold hands and we started walking quietly together. The further we went along, the darker it got. Until we met the first blue emergency light. It was glistening in the darkness and a couple moths were attached to it. Further down, the emergency light was flickering until we passed it and came to the next one. I made us stop at the fourth one because the dirt ground was now becoming more solid - although I wasn't sure that it was flooring. Ahead, there was a split - one to keep going straight or one to turn right.

"We need to split," I whispered. I looked at all of them and Kolleen's eyes widened. "You have a way to communicate with each other?" They nodded their heads and I licked my lips. "We can just tap—"

"You can just put them on the ground and freeze."

I didn't have to turn around to know whose voice that was. From the corner of my eye, I could see Carlos shudder as well. He recognized the voice as anyone in the organization would. This man had overseen our mental evaluations and decided if we were sound enough to continue on another mission

                                    AMY KULP

or if we needed to get retrained. During my mission before the girls, he had even insinuated that something was going on between Carlos and me. I wish I could turn to see his face now.

Following directions, the three agents all put their phones on the floor. They raised their hands in surrender and when I finally had the heart to face Dr. Dowell, I grimaced at him. Why was he here? Why wasn't he doing the mental evaluations of the people working there anymore? Was he doing both? I guess I didn't know all the details of his job.

"You both are despicable," he said with a sneer. He instantly hit Carlos with the butt of his gun on his head. He grimaced but didn't show too much pain. He pointed the gun at me and shot right next to me. While it scared me, it was clear that he couldn't harm me. They would want their biggest traitor alive. "Oh, Y, I had so much fun with the evaluation of Jaycie." He smiled sadistically and pointed the gun at Kolleen. "Seems that she couldn't get over the guilt she carried for you. We all know how much your team means to you."

"What happened to her?" I asked.

"Oh, you know, same old, same old. The least valuable player always gets rehabilitated. Seems she wasn't much help once Trinity was captured." He shrugged his shoulders and without a warning, shot Kolleen in the leg. She yelled out in pain and when I tried to run after him, he pointed the gun directly at my forehead. She clutched onto her leg and I could see her applying as much pressure as she could. "I'll take one off of your current team since you weren't the only one not to return from your mission."

"Don't you dare," I yelled as he pointed the gun back at Kolleen. She was hunched over and crying. She wouldn't even see it coming.

"But I don't think that's why you're here," he stated. He lowered the gun but only for a second. His next target was Navarro. "You're here for Manny, right?" he asked. I nodded my head hesitantly. "I'll make you a trade." I cocked an eyebrow. "Your team for your toddler?"

"Y, don't do it!" Carlos yelled.

"Who are you more loyal to: your temporary family or the family you made?" he wondered. He taunted the gun for a second and I looked at him. My eyes darted between Navarro, Carlos, and Kolleen. Navarro was staring directly at me and was trying to figure out what choice I was going to make, Carlos already knew what choice I was going to make, and Kolleen was holding onto her leg. I could tell that she was getting weak. "I know that family is everything to you. After all, I was one of the people who watched your growth." I didn't say anything. "You always screamed for your mom and your dad. You always asked Emmanuel about your family. Until you were conditioned to forget. When you couldn't remember who your family was, your team became your family. There wasn't anything you could do about it now." He smiled. "You always took one for the team. That's what made you a good leader. So, now I'm asking, which family is more important to you?" He pointed the gun at Kolleen again.

I had to choose. Who would I choose? My team: Carlos, Kolleen and Navarro, or my son, Manny? Carlos had been part of my team so many times. He was someone I could joke with. He was someone I had always gotten along with. He was spicy when I was grumpy. However, he was the entire reason I was in this predicament. He was a mole and he turned me into one too. I was going against the organization that took me in. Kolleen had been nothing but amazing to me. She may have tricked me a couple of times, but she was there to make sure I was mentally okay and nothing would harm me. Now she was shot in the leg. She was the one bleeding and crying out. Because of me. Navarro was old and wise and he was growing a soft spot for me. He was the true leader of this team. But Manny... He was older now so if I got him out, he would probably need so much therapy. He didn't have a chance to leave the world though. He didn't-

"I'm waiting," Dr. Dowell said. He looked almost bored with me.

"What about me?" I asked. "If I turn myself in, can Manny go with them?" I asked. Dr. Dowell seemed to ponder for a second but grinned widely at me as he shook his head no. I closed my eyes and looked over at the trio who were by my side. I was doing this because of Manny. The only reason I agreed to do this was because of Manny. "I choose Manny."

I listened to the gunshot go off, but I closed my eyes hard to stop myself from seeing who was hit. I was hoping it wasn't Kolleen. I'm not sure how much more she could take. However, if it was someone else, there was no chance that we were making it out of here alive. None of us.

"Follow me," Dr. Dowell said. "You two might want to help your friend up. Y, you're in front."

I didn't look at any of them before I got up and walked next to Dr. Dowell. Although with his back turned, I crouched down to the floor and put whatever was in my hand, into my back pocket. I could hear them dragging Kolleen as they walked behind us and knew that she had to be passed out. He shot her other leg too.

We walked further down until we were at a door and the ceiling opened back up. He knocked twice and when he pushed in, I saw that this room had to be the nursery. There were tile floors and walls everywhere. It was stark white and as I walked in, I could see the cribs and little beds. Without thinking, I ran to an empty crib and checked all the sleeping children. I kept searching and searching until I searched all of them.

Manny wasn't in any of them.

"Where is my boy?" I asked as I grabbed the knife from my pocket and held it against Dr. Dowell's neck. While he was manipulative, he was not a good fighter. I squeezed harder against his neck and knew that the blade was drawing some sort of blood. From my position, I could see that Kolleen was on the floor and Carlos had his gun pointed at Dr. Dowell too. Navarro was too busy putting pressure on Kolleen's wounds. I could see that his hands were stained red. "I won't ask again Dr. Dowell, where is my son?"

                    AMY KULP

"Why don't you ask me?"

I turned around and felt my blade slice a small portion of skin on Dr. Dowell. He squealed as we turned and I saw Mr. Barnett come back into the room with Manny and one other boy. I made sure to cut Dr. Dowell more before tossing him to the side and opening my arms. Once he recognized me, he ran to me and I hugged him so tightly. However, I stopped when my hands ran over his back and felt something odd there. I turned him around and saw a huge welt against his back. I stared at it in horror before looking up at the face I have never wanted to see again.

"Why are you watching the kids?"

"I was always in charge once we split sections. You see, I'm getting old so I wanted to be able to hurt those who couldn't defend themselves," he said.

"What did you do to my little boy?" I asked. "Where is Emmanuel?"

"He's not here. He never was. Kids aren't his forte," he mentioned. I felt my anger begin to boil and my body began to shake. Manny ran from my arms to chase the little boy around the room. "But I was wondering if you brought the stuff, Dr. Dowell?" He gave a thumbs up but didn't move. His neck was bleeding, but he was too afraid - Carlos had his gun pointed at him.

"What stuff?" I asked. I gritted my teeth and clutched my knife harder.

"Oh, you know, the chemicals and poisons."

I didn't listen anymore and I didn't have to. I charged at Mr. Barnett and watched as his smug face turned to that of fear. However, it quickly changed and he brought out a whip. He smacked it against me before I could get into contact with him and I felt my hands lose grip of the knife I was holding. I wrangled around that and felt another smack to my back. I cried out but ran closer to him until he slapped my head. I pushed him over and made sure to knock the whip out of his hands. Out of his reach, I forced my body onto his and leaned over him so that I could grab it. I put the whip around his neck and squeezed so tightly that when I heard the gunshot go off, I couldn't concentrate on who got shot.

I was trying to kill this man for harming Manny.

I could hear cries from the other babies and toddlers in the room, but I didn't stop pulling. If anything, it encouraged me even more. I could feel nails going into my skin and Mr. Barnett biting into my sleeve, but I kept pulling. I pulled it tighter and tighter and could see his face turning blue. I could see him losing the oxygen. Still, I pulled tighter until I was knocked off him and kicked at whoever laid their hands on me.

However, another blow didn't come to me. I watched as Navarro slapped handcuffs on Mr. Barnett before he could do anything else. He couldn't fight anyway - he was trying to regain his breath.

I didn't last too long though because I searched the room for Manny and scraped him into my arms. I kissed him on the cheek before I looked around and could see that Navarro was still

                                    AMY KULP

struggling with Mr. Barnett's handcuffs and Carlos was putting the kids who were running around into a crib. When I turned to see that Dr. Dowell was on the floor and was shot, I stepped over him and threw the communication device at Kolleen. Her eyes were open and she was coherent enough to push the button, but I knew she couldn't do anything else.

So, I quickly slipped out of the room with my child in my hands and I ran. I couldn't help them with my side of the mission because I didn't know where Trinity was. I knew that they would take Manny away from me if they found out. Maybe they would ask him where she was. Maybe they would interrogate my son. Either way, I wasn't going to allow it to happen. Manny and I were going to live a good life. We were going to be a happy family. He was my family.

My other family I had helped too. I gave them what they wanted: I gave Navarro the leader, I gave Carlos two locations and the reasons as to why I was doing this, and I gave Kolleen the communication device. They would be able to get out of there, and I knew they would. I helped that family, so now I had to do what was right with my family.

And that meant disappearing.

I'm Emily Washington. While I have a beautiful growing boy, I killed my baby girl. It was finally time for me to put my family first.

------------------------------Chapter17

He was starting to get fussy as I wrapped my arms tighter around him. He felt the chill against his bare skin and nuzzled his face into my coat. I shoved him closer to me as if my body heat would help him against the winds of New York City. I had just given the last of my money to the driver and purposely left my phone in the backseat of the car. I knew what the FBI was capable of. I knew what my organization was capable of. They could track me to New York City, but they would have no way of knowing where I was.

I had to pick an obvious spot, kind of like how they caught serial killers in their homes after years of looking for them. Except I didn't have a permanent home. I didn't have a place that I could remember where I was always welcome back once I was done screwing up, once I was done having fun or getting caught. I didn't have a place that I considered home.

Instead, my home was with my family—maybe not my biological family most of the time. I had Manny, and that was what mattered to me. Any other family or friends who wanted to pop by were no longer welcome. My heart was in my arms, and I felt my face beginning to numb as the cold air persisted.

I had to find someplace for us to stay for the night. Then I could research an obvious place for us to stay. Maybe somewhere that would help Manny and I. After all, I was a fugitive, and I knew if I made myself too known then I would be taken in handcuffs in the back of a police car. They would have the sirens blaring with the lights lighting up the night. I broke my promise to my team, and I didn't deserve to be respected any more.

As soon as I saw the illuminated sign for a motel, I ran as fast as I could toward it. The NO was lit up, but I still knew that there was a chance I could find a room. Or, if anything, I could wait in their lobby until the morning. If I played my cards right, I could manage to trade something in. I could give them my credit card if I really needed to. However, there wasn't any money on it, and they would find that out very fast.

I jingled the door and listened to the bell chime up ahead. As soon as it rung, Manny lifted his face out of my chest and looked around the room. I set him down, and instead of going toward the TV that was playing he sat silently on one of the chairs they had. He laid his head down on the rest and his eyes fluttered shut. He must be exhausted.

"Hi," I said, turning around. An older lady stood at the counter, and I could tell that she was watching Manny. Maybe judging us too.

"We don't have any vacancy," she said. I nodded and set my arms on the counter. My body was just beginning to defrost from the cool winds outside, and looking down I could see my skin becoming blotchy with red spots. I nodded again and she just cocked an eyebrow at me.

"Yes, I saw that."

"And you still decided to come in?" the lady asked. She looked over at Manny sleeping again, and I bit my lip. "Do you want me to call someone for you?" She looked at me, and I answered silently. "We don't have any rooms."

"Do you know of a place I could stay? Or would I be able to trade something?" I asked. I looked at the two doors that were leading out of this room and stared at them. "Can I sleep in a closet?" I wondered. When I looked back at her, she seemed delusional.

"Absolutely not," the lady said to me. "However, I will allow you to stay in here. If someone leaves early, I can give you their room." She shrugged. "It won't be clean but it—"

"Thank you!" I said. I looked back at Manny, who was now snuggling into himself, and I couldn't help but smile broadly at him. "You don't know how much this means to us."

"How old is he?" she wondered. I held my fingers up. "It's not easy being a mother. There's no rule-book or guide to tell you how to do it. I'm sure you're trying your best." She paused and looked at the other door. "There's a bathroom through there if you or your son need it. You can freshen up in there too, but all we have is hand soap."

"Thank you, it's really appreciated."

I sat in the chair next to Manny and just stared at him as his breaths were rapid but steady. This entire time that he was with Mr. Barnett, I assumed he was with Emmanuel. He always told me when he came back how well-behaved Manny was and of his progress growing up. He would tell me all the new words he knew and about any firsts he had witnessed that day. He let me know of the friends he had and any babies he didn't like.

Being in that room, it didn't seem like many of the babies made it to be toddlers. There were about ten cribs with swaddled newborns. When looking at the toddler section, there only seemed to be about four. None of them were girls either. I remember that there used to be. Emmanuel came home and told me that Manny didn't like some girl. I had to wonder what happened to her.

As I massaged Manny's back, I had to wonder what had happened to him. I lifted his shirt a bit and stared at the whipping mark again. They were whipping my boy. Did Emmanuel know about this? I wanted to give him the benefit of the doubt and say he didn't. He would have told me and would have pulled Manny from them. Right? He wouldn't allow our baby to be whipped and tortured and whatever Dr. Dowell was there to do.

Without disturbing his peace, I brought Manny into my arms and knew the tears were escaping my eyes. I held him close, and he snuggled into me as I breathed in his hair. He needed a bath. Were they making sure he was clean? Were they making sure that he knew how to keep himself hygienic?

"Come on, Manny, we need to get you cleaned up."

He snuggled further into me as I carried him to the door that I was told was the bathroom. I walked slowly to it and quickly looked at the clock and knew that he would be cranky if he didn't get to sleep for a little bit. Or at least, that's how he was when he was a bit younger. Maybe he's changed since I have last seen him. He has definitely gotten taller and all of his teeth were finally in. I remember being worried about that for a while. I was always reassured that he was getting the best treatment and that Emmanuel was watching over him. Clearly, that was a lie.

When I opened the door, I was shocked to see that while there was a bathroom here, there was also a bedroom. Looking around, I felt more tears spring in my eyes as the exhaustion hit me. I had to wash Manny first. I had to show him how to take care of himself. He was still so small, but he needed to know these things just in case. He needed to be aware of what the world was like if he smelled.

I undressed him as I got to the shower and ran the warm water over my fingers before I plopped him inside. His sleepiness was gone, and he started splashing away in the water. Okay, I got the temperature correct. I knew that he would be more amused with toys, but I didn't have any. I looked around for what I might be able to use but couldn't find anything. I had to resort to pouring water over his head by making it a game. He giggled when it splashed him, and I couldn't help but laugh as well. I loved him so much, and my heart was so full with him by my side.

It wasn't until all the water drained from the tub and I wrapped him up in a towel that he started to get drowsy again. I looked in drawers to see if there was lotion, but unfortunately I was out of luck. I placed him on the bed and dried him off while playing peek-a-boo. It didn't seem to make him smile like it had the last time I was with him. I tucked the blanket over his body and up to his chin before he grabbed fistfuls of the blanket and curled his body to get a good night's sleep. I watched for a while after he fell asleep.

I continued to watch until I felt drowsy too.

I knew that I probably smelled too, but my feet were sore from walking, and my arms were sore from carrying Manny the entire time. The only task I allowed myself to complete was taking my bra off and throwing it off to the side. Once I was free, I crawled right next to Manny, and once my head hit the pillow I fell asleep.

It was one of the most peaceful days I have had.

****
****

I stretched my body out when I woke up and turned over to the lump that was beside me. I had a restless night and kept waking up for short periods. Were they at all coherent? Absolutely not. Each time, I checked for Manny next to me, and whenever I saw the lump in the comforter I smiled and went back to bed. It felt like I had been watched halfway through the night though. Each time, I told myself to enjoy my rest and just go back to sleep. I could not shake the feeling though. After all, I was the third-most wanted criminal.

Opening my eyes, I could see the blankets nestled over Manny's body and decided that I would wake him when I was done cleaning myself up. I needed a little me time and knew that I probably had blood somewhere in my hair, on my body, or some that seeped into my clothes. The clothes would have to do, but at least I could wash those. I took my shirt and pants off first and threw them in the sink. A little hard work would do this some justice. When I was done with those, I hung them on the rack that was designated for the towels and did the same with my bra and underwear. It wasn't perfect, but it would work for now.

I turned back around to stare at Manny as his body stayed in his warm burrito. Smiling, I turned my shower water on and hopped in. It wasn't more than five minutes before I dried off and wrapped the towel around me. I grabbed the hand dryer and began to dry my clothes before I kicked the power. When I looked over at Manny, he still wasn't moving. I smiled at myself but knew the implications of that.

He probably wasn't allowed to move until he was called.

I put my undergarments on first before grimacing at the feel of the wet clothing. While it wasn't disgusting wet, I knew that I might get a rash from the underwear. However, I continued to slip the shirt and pants on and was relieved that they were a little dryer. I couldn't handle being completely wet.

I took the toothpaste that they had and quickly squirted some along my finger. I brushed vigorously and combed my hair while I was doing so. The quicker we got out of here, the quicker we can be safe. I wanted to go to a state that nobody would suspect me to go—so that ruled out New York, New Jersey, and Pennsylvania. Although maybe those would be so obvious that the police wouldn't think to look there.

Spitting out the gunk in my mouth, I wiped my mouth on the towel before turning around and walking toward Manny. I pushed his body slightly so that I wouldn't startle him but was met with very little resistance. After a second of no movement, I whispered his name and started to undo the blankets that were there. It just seemed to be blankets and blankets and blankets and blankets.

Where was my son?

I quickly threw the blankets off to the side and searched the rest of the bed. Of course, he wasn't there. I looked around the room in case he was playing hide and seek and continued to search. I looked around in all the small places. I whispered his name over and over again telling him that it wasn't funny to hide from Mom, telling him that this wasn't a game and we needed to leave. Tears started pouring down my face at the thought that my dream would be gone. My dream of living with my family. Living with my heart. Where was he?

I grabbed my shoes that I threw somewhere the night before and turned to the door. Maybe he got out of the room somehow. I grabbed my wallet from the nightstand and grabbed the doorknob. However, I didn't move it. Instead, I read the note that was on the back of the door, on my side of the door.

He wouldn't kill our baby, would he? I crumbled up the note and quickly opened the door. I couldn't let them kill Manny. I couldn't. I knew what the options were, and I knew that I was going to be tortured for the rest of my life, but if that meant that I could see Manny from time to time then it was worth it. I wanted to be with my family. I wanted to watch him grow up. I wanted to see him become a teenager and then start his own life. I wanted to argue with him and then make up. I wanted to see him develop his own family, and then my family would become bigger. I guess it didn't matter where we were as long as I could see him.

I wanted to see him live, thrive, and be happy.

It did not matter if I wasn't.

I thanked the lady who was there at the counter with me last night and zoomed out of the room. I had no idea how I was going to get there with no cash, but I was desperate. I would find a way.

I was running until something hit my back, and I landed on the ground. The weight moved on top of me, and I felt my hands being forced behind my back roughly. My face was pressed harder into the cement as I wiggled, and it wasn't until the handcuffs latched together that I was forced up by my arms. I was turned around and was greeted with the grizzly sight of Carlos pointing a gun at me and Navarro holding me down.

"Emily Washington, you are under arrest for the kidnappings of over four hundred girls. You have the right to remain silent. Anything you say can and will be used against you in a court of law. You have the right to have an attorney present now and during any future questioning. If you cannot afford an attorney, one will be appointed for you at no cost..."

I'm Emily Washington and my baby boy was going to be murdered.

National Human Trafficking Hotline

1 (888) 373 - 7888

Read the first chapter of
Innocent

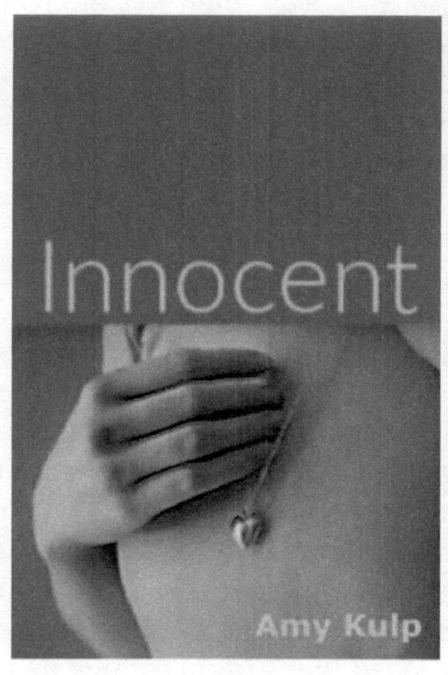

Chapter One

"Don't. Touch. Me." I gritted my teeth and yanked my shoulder away from the hand that was planted on it. I forced myself up and hurriedly opened up the door. Since it was after school, I knew that I wasn't being followed. Everyone who stayed was probably practicing for whatever sport, program, or club they were a part of. When I checked the hallway in case of stragglers and didn't find any, I ran to the nearest bathroom stall and cried.

***

"You need to bring that energy more." I smiled but kept punching the bag as hard as I could. My trainer, Missy, rarely gave out compliments like that. She steadied the bag for me and I hit harder as her compliment radiated throughout my body. "Stance." I was forced to look at my posture and change my position. After all of this training, I still couldn't manage to fix my form without her telling me that I needed to. "Alright, I think that's good for today." She moved from the bag and looked down at the bandages around my knuckles. They were starting to be speckled with light red droplets. I couldn't help but smile at accomplishing this. It meant I worked extra hard. "Let's go practice in the ring."

I nodded and grabbed my water bottle. Nothing like working up a sweat and then tasting that first drink of ice water. It almost always sent a painful tinge down my throat until I could get used to it. I barely got any in my mouth though. I hung it over my face in desperation to cool my body down. When the water overflowed from my mouth and dribbled down my chin and onto my bra, I couldn't help but stare at my abs. Mixed with the water and my sweat, they were glistening under the overhead lights.

"Tanner!"

I blushed red as I realized that I was just caught enticed with my own body. Not wanting to make Missy mad, I ran over to the benches. I prepared myself by removing my shoes and massaging them for a few seconds to help soothe their aches. She did not like shoes in the boxing ring because of the scuffing they made. When my feet were done with their preparation, I took notice of my hands. I had to apply new bandages since blood was visible. Another gym rule. Once my new bandages were on, I took my hair out of the sagging ponytail and repositioned it higher off of my neck. I hated when my hair touched my skin. The last essential tool I needed from my bag was my mouthguard. While it wasn't required to have one in, I was not taking my chances with Missy. She was a powerhouse and could knock my teeth out. I didn't want to have any missing teeth since the school year was starting soon. I needed to make a good first impression.

"You ready?" she asked as I stepped into the practice ring with her. I nodded my head before she glanced over at the headgear that I had forgotten about. If it's not in my bag, I usually forget about it. I growled in response when I placed a spare on and she smiled at me. She put her mitts up and I struck them. Right, left, right-left-left, kick. "I need you madder!" she yelled. I growled at her and hit harder. "You're being predictable! Catch me off guard!" I pounded harder and harder until I felt the blisters begin to reopen. "Come on, Tanner!" I hit again and kicked. Losing my balance, I felt myself fall on my back. When I opened my eyes, Missy was smirking down at me. "I think we're good for today."

I needed to work on my balance. She threw the mitts off and helped me up. She instantly hit my head playfully and I knew she wasn't mad. I did not want to disappoint her by forgetting the simple forms I should be practicing. When I got down near the bench, I took the headgear off and popped my mouth guard out. When I finished placing everything back in my bag, I tried to relax on the bench.

"Is the AC even on?" I yelled.

"It's on high Tanner," she replied. "Quit complaining. You don't hear Aaron moaning."

I hated when she compared me to other people. I was my own person. It pissed me off even more that the comparison was with Aaron. While there was nothing wrong with him, she only compared us because we were similar in age. Everybody else was either a child or an adult. Besides, from what I had gathered about Aaron was that he was only allowed to train here because he worked here. Missy had a scholarship program where people can train discounted or free depending on how much they wanted to work. Rumors I had heard through the grapevine are that she gave Aaron an even bigger discount than most people because he was bullied at school. I have never seen him train, but if he was so great, why couldn't he defend himself?

Realizing that my body was not going to cool down on its own, I grabbed my bag and headed towards the showers. Since boxing was a male-dominated sport, I usually had the locker rooms to myself. I always kept my bag on me, but if I wanted to, I could keep my bag in here without worrying about anything being taken. So when I saw that the coast was clear, I stripped and found myself an empty stall. The cold water felt amazing on my body and I watched as it washed the blood off of my skin. The open blisters were nasty to look at but it was something I thought was satisfying to see as well. No pain, no gain.

Finishing up, I shivered and wrapped a towel tightly around my body. I came back to my bag and dug out the clean clothes. The first thing I noticed about it was the soft scent of fresh linen. I loved that smell but it wouldn't last long if it was near my bag. I needed to throw it in the wash too - it stunk.

Once I tied my sneakers and finger-combed my hair, I threw it up in a sloppy bun and headed towards the gym entrance. I patiently waited in the parking lot as I looked for my mom's car but it didn't arrive for another five minutes. I was surprised since she was usually early. I grinned as I approached the car to let her know that training had gone well but as I approached, it vanished when I saw who the actual driver was.

"Mom's running late from work so she told me to come and get you," my brother, Luke said. He rolled down the window to talk to me but I already had the backseat open to hear him. I placed my bag on the seat and felt like my voice was going to tremble as I spoke.

"I-I think I-I'll walk." I couldn't meet his gaze as I said this and he groaned in response.

"You're crazy." He rolled his window down farther and leaned over. "It looks like it's going to rain and this is a bad part of town."

"S-so?"

"You're only wearing a sports bra." I shrugged my shoulders and looked up at the sky to see if he was telling the truth. "You're my little sister, if anything happens to you it would be my fault." I remained still as he tried talking me out of it. He must've known that I was stubborn and wouldn't change my mind though because he clasped his hand over my wrist. My first reaction was to flinch out of his grip.

"D-don't touch m-me."

"Chloe, are you okay?" I still refused to look at him, but I was able to hear Luke get out of the car. He stood taller than me by one inch, but it felt like he towered over me by one foot. My body shrank and I started shivering even though my body was still sweating.

"D-don't call me C-Chloe!" I managed to yell. "It's T-Tanner."

"*Clo-ee*." He smirked down at me and I felt tears overflowing from my eyes. I hated being called that. I finally met Luke's gaze and the smirk he had on before, had now vanished. I hated crying in front of people so instead, I decided to run.

I heard him yelling after me but I couldn't keep the tears from coming. I hated crying. I felt so vulnerable whenever I let my emotions out. That was one of the reasons I was taking boxing, so I could get all of my tears and anger out. Also so I could protect myself.

I ran down the street as if my life depended on it. I knew that people were staring at me like I was crazy, but it helped to ease my mind. As I continued to run, though, I knew that it would take me a while to get home. It took about ten minutes in the car and since I was not as fast with my running, it would probably take thirty or forty minutes. If anything, this could give me time to think. I heard that running was also a stress reliever. While I have never tried to do it besides cardio warmups, I could try to use it like that.

I had so many worries I could think about: new school, new friends, new teachers, reputation, not knowing the school layout, where I would sit during lunch, what clique I wanted to belong to. I was mostly worried about my reputation and who my new friends would be. I'm used to moving, which I tend to do every year. What if people had heard about me? Or what if they started looking me up online? I've looked myself up before and I haven't found anything juicy but that doesn't mean other people can't. This can deter people from wanting to be my friend. I usually am only able to make a couple of decent friends. Usually, once I move I don't keep in contact with them. Luke is the complete opposite though. He is always part of the popular group and makes friends easily. I'm always jealous of him.

When I got home, I was the first one back. No cars were in the driveway which meant my mom, dad, nor Luke had made it yet. My dad was probably still at work. I haven't figured out his new hours yet to know for certain though. My mom worked around the clock and was constantly having important meetings. It felt like she valued her work more than her family sometimes. I know she tried though. I think that Luke was still looking for me, but I wouldn't be surprised if he stopped for fast food instead.

I knew that we had a spare key under one of our loose stepping stones so I grabbed it out of place. I was still nervous that Luke was going to arrive and see me coming home, so my hands were jittery. I was barely able to put the key in, but once I was able to, I slammed the door shut and bolted to my room.

I could finally try to calm down now.

With my door now locked, I felt free enough to open my window. When I looked out, I noted how dark it was. Was it this dark when I got home? How was I able to see while running? If Luke was still looking for me, he wouldn't be able to tell if someone was me or just some random person running on the sidewalks.

When I grew bored with that, I turned my desk lamp on and pulled out my diary from the drawer. I often forgot to jot down my thoughts in this but I figured when I did remember it was good enough. I felt my nerves starting to calm down but when I thought about what I wanted to write on this page, I began to cry. Today's entry was barely two lines but they were starting to blur from the small teardrops covering them.

When I heard a car door slam shut, I pushed my diary back into my drawer. Even though my door was locked, I didn't want anyone to see me writing in it. It was embarrassing. What if they wanted to read it? When I knew my diary was secure, I flung my body to my bed. I pulled the blankets over me and pretended to be sleeping. If it was my mom, she would try to talk to me for hours. If I was asleep, she would get the hint and stop. If I was awake, she would somehow know. I had to make it look like I was sleeping for them to leave me alone.

"Are you in there, Chl... Tanner?" I heard Luke say. I felt my muscles tense as his voice grew louder at my door. "I don't know why you hate the name, Chloe. It's a beautiful name, that's why mom picked it. Anyway, I hope you're alright and nothing happened. Mom has pizza downstairs if you're wondering and your gym bag is by your door." I listened to some shuffling outside of my door and didn't let my muscles un-tense yet. "I'm sorry about earlier."

I was able to see light shining from underneath my door. I watched as the shadow moved away and the hall lights were then turned off. As I thought about what he said, my stomach growled. I forced myself to ignore it. I didn't want to see my family and while the food was alluring, I didn't want to talk about why I'm acting the way I'm acting. I always explain to them that I'm a teenager and I'm probably going through puberty, but none of them believe me. The fewer interactions I have with them, the better. Even if that meant I had to fake sleep until I actually fell asleep.

Even if that meant that I fell into a series of nightmares that I couldn't shake.

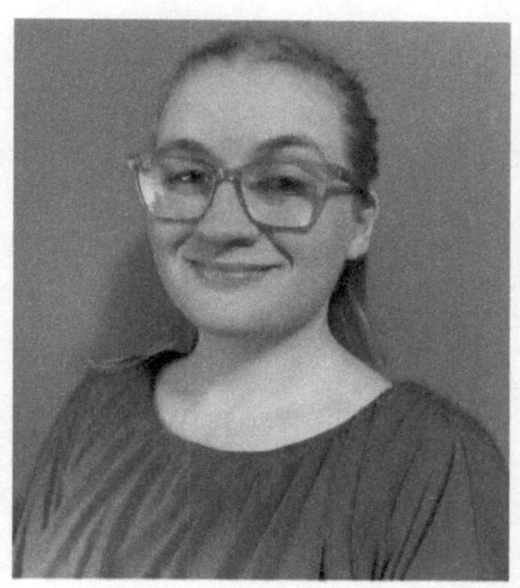

ABOUT THE AUTHOR

Amy Kulp is a middle school STEM teacher and theatre director with a passion for writing novels that break YA genre norms. An avid reader and writer since childhood, Kulp now enjoys creating stories that investigate darker, more challenging topics and help young adult readers feel less alone in their struggles. Wanted is Kulp's first sequel to a book and she immediately knew she wanted to write it when she concluded the end of Missing.

www.ingramcontent.com/pod-product-compliance
Lightning Source LLC
Chambersburg PA
CBHW021144310726
48971CB00002B/481